Over the
HORIZON

Over the HORIZON

PENNY ZELLER

ALSO BY PENNY ZELLER

Maplebrook Publishing

Standalone Books
Love in Disguise
Love in the Headlines
Freedom's Flight

Wyoming Sunrise
Love's New Beginnings
Forgotten Memories
Dreams of the Heart
When Love Comes
Love's Promise

Love Letters from Ellis Creek
Love from Afar
Love Unforeseen
Love Most Certain

Chokecherry Heights
Henry and Evaline (Prequel)
Love Under Construction

Horizon Series
Over the Horizon
Dreams on the Horizon
Beyond the Horizon

Whitaker House Publishing

Montana Skies
McKenzie
Kaydie
Hailee

Barbour Publishing

Love from Afar
*(The Secret Admirer
Romance Collection)*

Freedom's Flight
*(The Underground Railroad
Brides Collection)*

Beacon Hill Press
(Nonfiction)

77 Ways Your Family Can
Make a Difference

Dedicated to all who have loved someone
with dementia or Alzheimer's disease.

Although the fig tree shall not blossom, neither shall fruit be in the vines; the labour of the olive shall fail, and the fields shall yield no meat; the flock shall be cut off from the fold, and there shall be no herd in the stalls: Yet I will rejoice in the Lord, I will joy in the God of my salvation. The Lord God is my strength, and he will make my feet like hinds' feet, and he will make me to walk upon mine high places.

- Habakkuk 3:17-19

CHAPTER ONE

IDAHO TERRITORY, 1872

PAISLEY HURRIED THROUGH THE town of Cornwall, lost in an area she'd never before been. Passersby paid her no mind. But why would they when they didn't know her? Didn't know why she stumbled along the boardwalk in search of somewhere to hide?

Lord, please help me.

Behind her, Ivan called her name. He'd arranged for them to exchange wedding vows at one o'clock, and she feared his demands of her becoming his wife might come to fruition.

She scanned the businesses located along the boardwalk. Where was the sheriff's office? The church? She'd only been to Cornwall a handful of times since her family moved to the Idaho Territory. It was at least five times larger than the town of Pringle where she lived.

Perhaps she could confide in the reverend, a man whom she'd never met, and express to him her reasons for refusing to marry Ivan. Would he help her? Or would Ivan convince the reverend otherwise?

There was no time to ponder what may or may not happen.

Paisley ducked into an alley and pressed herself against a building's wall. Her chest heaved and her breath emerged in gasps.

"There you are."

She startled and spun around to see cold, harsh eyes boring into her. She attempted to run, but Ivan yanked her by the arm and clamped his fingers over her wrists. Pain seared through her as he dug his fingernails into her flesh. "And don't you dare scream. They'll only believe you are of unsound mind just like your father."

"Someone would believe me." But even in her own ears, her voice sounded doubtful.

Ivan chortled, his evil laugh sending shivers down Paisley's spine. "No, my dear, no one will believe you." In an instant he sobered again, a scowl covering his face. A vein throbbed in his jaw, and his warm breath, smelling of stale tobacco, lingered in the air. He bridged the distance between them, his face mere inches from hers. "You will marry me, Paisley. Your pa agreed to it." A spit particle spewed from his mouth.

She recalled that moment when Papa, his voice muffled and incoherent, gave Ivan Marchesi the blessing to marry his only child.

Papa, why did you promise Ivan my hand in marriage? What have you done?

This was a nightmare. It had to be. For in real life, her father never would have promised her hand to a cruel man.

She wouldn't marry Ivan Marchesi. Couldn't marry him. Among other reasons, she knew what he'd done to poor Mr. Leander when he refused to sell Ivan his farm.

Heavenly Father, please help me.

Ivan's gaze traveled the length of Paisley's appearance, lust filling his sinister brown eyes. Bile rose in her throat, and despite the heat, she shivered.

"And don't you cause a fracas when we arrive at the church," he warned.

Even if she did cause a disturbance at the church, would anyone help her?

Tears threatened at the hopelessness of the situation, but she refused to allow them to fall lest Ivan see her weakness. "I won't marry you." The words escaped her mouth before she could give a thought to the consequences.

He released one of her wrists and raised his hand to slap her. She held her breath, preparing for the impact.

A woman and her young child crossed the street at the edge of the alley. The woman looked toward them, then prompted the child to move quickly as they proceeded on their way. Would anyone hear Paisley if she screamed?

Ivan lowered his hand. "You *will* marry me and you *will* give me the deed to the land. Not owning the Abbott farm is one of the only things preventing me from owning most of Pringle." Ivan clenched his teeth, and his already-large nostrils flared. "You *will* do it, Paisley."

The deed. She'd folded and tucked it into her coin purse, then slipped the purse into the pocket in her skirt.

Ivan mustn't find it.

"Why would you want the farm? Most of it was destroyed by the flood."

"Makes no difference to me. The waters will recede, and when they do, I'll have added more fertile farmland to my holdings. You know I aim to own the entire town of Pringle."

Yes, she did know Ivan's goals of obtaining acreage, and she also knew his manipulative and oftentimes dangerous methods of attaining it. Greed was a prevalent part of his nature. While marrying her would make his scheme appear legal to onlookers, Paisley doubted he would hesitate to use whatever means necessary to seize the deed—and then convince the law he'd obtained it legitimately.

Ivan again grabbed her other wrist and shook her hard, giving in to the volatile temper that ruled him. Why he would want to marry her was a question that plagued her ever since Ivan visited Papa and asked for his blessing. While she would never willingly give him the deed or sell the farm to him, he didn't *need* her to procure the land he thought he was entitled to. The vile man had other methods of obtaining what he wanted.

"Now. Are you ready to go to the church?" he hissed, his hands again at his sides.

A man strode by them. "Everything all right here?" he asked.

"All is well, my friend." Ivan pasted on a grin.

"Sir, if you could please..."

But the man had already gone about his way.

Ivan shoved her against the wall. She struggled to maintain her footing as she stumbled backward, her heel catching the hem of her dress.

It was then Paisley noticed the pile of discarded items on the ground beside her. A rusty kettle rested among the heap. She'd needed strength so often in the past few days, and this moment was no exception.

A noisy wagon clamored past, drawing Ivan's attention. She snatched the kettle and swung it toward his head, catching him hard on the shoulder. Stunned and caught unaware, Ivan staggered and gripped the injured area while emitting a stream of profanities.

Paisley dashed from the alley and searched for the main thoroughfare, her sense of direction altered in the unfamiliar area of town. How many precious minutes did she have before Ivan came after her?

Lord, I beseech Thee to help me with this plight.

She passed several buildings before pausing in front of the livery. Standing on tiptoe, she peered about. After a few seconds of obscured vision, she noticed Ivan stumbling down the boardwalk in her direction.

Paisley's heart pounded in her ears, and she staggered forward on weak legs. Should she hide inside one of the businesses?

A horse neighed and she flinched. Paisley hurried down another nearby alley, halting when she noticed an abandoned wagon full of lumber.

The perfect place to hide.

Not caring how unladylike she appeared, Paisley gathered her skirts and climbed into the back of the deserted wagon, sliding into a narrow spot between the lumber and some tools. Then, spying a bedroll, she quickly unrolled the dingy brown sleep sack. Grasping the ends of it with trembling hands, she pulled it over her body and most of her head, leaving just enough space to breathe.

Paisley shifted beneath the bedroll, wishing for a handkerchief to dab at the perspiration collecting at the back of her neck from both the heat and her jumbled nerves. Periodically, she heard the clip-clop of horses' hooves, the sound of wagon wheels, or voices in conversation.

Then came the dreaded sound of Ivan's sharp, raucous voice. "Where is that impertinent woman?"

She fought the rising panic. Would Ivan see the tip of her head in the wagon? Or realize someone hid beneath the bedroll with a few pieces of lumber strewn on top? No. He mustn't find her. His disheartening obsession with her left an uneasy feeling in her stomach.

She moved slightly, but enough to bump her left elbow on something hard in the wagon. Tears filled her eyes, and she barely contained the gasp that threatened to escape from her lips. Ivan would find her for sure if she uttered even the most reticent of sounds.

"Excuse me, sir," Ivan said.

"Yes?" another man answered.

"Have you seen a woman about twenty-two or twenty-three years of age? She's slender with brown hair and hazel eyes and is wearing a blue dress."

"Not that I recollect. What is your reason for wanting to locate her?"

"She's my wife."

Paisley's eyes widened and she gritted her teeth. Ivan was so adept at lying that he likely believed himself.

"I'm sorry, I haven't seen her. Best of luck finding her."

She heard footsteps, followed by what sounded like the tipping over of barrels. After what seemed like an interminable amount of time, all was quiet.

Paisley released the breath she'd been holding. She was safe. For now.

Tyler Shepherdson carried the three wrapped parcels toward his wagon. Albert, Lucy, and Mae would love the small gifts he'd purchased for them at the mercantile while on his trip to Cornwall. Perhaps they'd realize having to live with him wasn't such a bad thing after all.

With barely a glance at the contents of his overloaded wagon, Tyler tucked the three gifts safely in the back before watering the horses and climbing onto the buckboard. If he got a good start now, he'd be on schedule and make it to Ingleville, the halfway mark between Cornwall and Horizon, before nightfall.

He prompted the horses and followed the road out of town. It felt good to leave the city of Cornwall behind. In all his meanderings while looking for adventure and purpose in his life, he'd never much cared for large towns and cities—and he had lived in several. Not that he'd planned to settle in Horizon for the rest of his life, but he much preferred small towns.

Tyler whistled "Oh! Susanna" and settled in for his journey home. Home. He hadn't thought of Horizon being his home in years. Of course, relocating with three orphans would be more difficult, but since when had Tyler not welcomed a challenge?

For now, he would continue trying his hand at farming, and once a month, he'd leave for Cornwall to pick up items for folks in Horizon. The job paid well, and the trip afforded him time to think about Albert, Lucy, and Mae. They filled his mind often.

So much had happened since he'd left Horizon four years ago at the age of nineteen.

CHAPTER TWO

A PARTICULARLY ROUGH BUMP jolted Paisley awake. She blinked, but remained motionless tucked beneath the bedroll. Where was she? For a moment, her mind tumbled through the events of the day, and she struggled to recall how she found herself in this predicament.

Then she remembered.

In bits and pieces, Paisley recalled Ivan demanding she go with him when he'd found her walking along the road to Cornwall. He bragged about forcing her into marriage and said that the law would take his side, should she choose to flee. *"And if anyone should in the slightest be convinced of your dilemma, I'll share with them about your pa and his questionable ailments. Surely a man with such problems of the mind would have a daughter with the same condition."* Ivan's mockery sent her heart spiraling into pain and uncertainty. No one would help a woman whose papa had succumbed to an unexplained illness that had taken over his mind and memory.

Neither she, Mama, nor the doctor from Cornwall knew the reason for Papa's memory lapses, his confusion, and his inability to complete a sentence. He could no longer finish a task such as mucking out the barn or plowing the fields. The most upsetting part of his unusual and concerning behavior was that he only sometimes recognized Mama and never recalled who Paisley was.

The doctor, a snobbish man irritated at having to travel to Pringle to see a patient, rushed through the visit and dismissed most of Mama's concerns. His last words before packing his black leather doctor's bag were, "Perhaps your husband ought to be taken to an asylum."

Then she'd lost both Mama and Papa in a terrible storm. Pain at the loss of her beloved parents and guilt at being the only one who survived consumed her thoughts. She missed them and found it difficult to comprehend why the Lord allowed them to be taken from her. So much had happened in such a short amount of time.

A squelched sob stuck in her throat. Many had perished in the town of fifty people. The flood had taken everyone in Pringle by surprise.

With considerable struggle, Paisley redirected her attention to her predicament. She inhaled the scent of lumber and felt tiny pieces of grain against her hand. She heard whistling and the sound of wagon wheels on the hard earth. Where was Ivan? Had he found her? Fear surged through her, meshing with the expansive range of emotions.

Ivan was much too refined to whistle, so the driver had to be someone else. But if it wasn't Ivan, who was it? Hadn't the wagon been deserted?

Discreetly, so as to avoid being noticed, Paisley pulled the bedroll slightly below her eyes and peered at the sky above. She turned her head slowly from side to side, but

10

could see nothing save the lumber and tools on one side and the interior wall of the wagon on the other.

How long had she been there? Craning her neck, Paisley saw the back of a man's head as he drove the wagon. Over and over again, he whistled "Oh! Susanna", as if it were the only tune he knew.

Paisley drew a deep breath and tugged the bedroll over her once again. Her racing heart caused her chest to hurt. Who was this man? What would he do when he discovered she'd hitched a ride in his wagon? Was he dangerous? Unsettled emotions and anxiety warred in her mind.

She would stay put in the wagon and avoid making any noise. When the man reached the next town, Paisley would climb *out* of the wagon without him so much as noticing her. Just as she had climbed unnoticed *into* the wagon.

The wagon moved along at an agonizingly slow pace, the bumping over the road causing the lumber and other items to periodically shift. *Lord, I beseech Thee for protection and for the peace only You can provide. Please guide me and give me wisdom.*

How often over the past several months had she prayed a similar prayer? And when all seemed hopeless—as it had over the course of her newly-orphaned life—God had provided. He would provide again.

Wouldn't He?

She quietly shifted beneath the bedroll, noting her stiff back from lying in one position far too long. A soft breeze blew, for which she was grateful since she was tucked beneath a warm bedroll. Suddenly, a piece of dust tickled her nose. Paisley pursed her lips together and held her breath. Sneezing would never do if she wished to avoid the driver's detection.

Her eyes watered and her nose twitched. But try as she might, Paisley failed at thwarting the sneeze. The "ah-choo" erupted like a loud snort mixed with a rumbling expulsion of air.

The wagon stopped so abruptly that Paisley's head nearly collided with the stack of lumber.

The whistling ceased and all fell silent. Paisley held her breath and dared not move.

Was there a chance the driver wouldn't notice a sizable lump beneath the bedroll?

Please, Lord...

The wagon shook as the man presumably climbed from the buckboard. "Is someone there?"

If only Paisley could make herself less noticeable.

Would the man reach over the side of the wagon and remove the bedroll? Ought she take precautions now rather than wait?

Lord, please go before me.

Without another thought, Paisley flung off the bedroll and grabbed the first thing she saw—a stick of lumber.

She hoped her choice of weapon would be somewhat beneficial if the stranger had dishonorable intentions.

It made her feel safer at least.

Paisley rose to her knees and gripped the piece of wood tightly in both hands. As she slid it into a comfortable position, several sharp slivers became embedded in her hands, and she winced.

The man stood facing her. "Who are you?" he asked.

"Do not come near me. I will use this!"

The man cocked his head to one side and gave her a quizzical look. A smirk lined his features. "Reckon I'm mighty afraid."

He might not be afraid, but Paisley was. She knew nothing about the man. Was he anything like Ivan? Fear mixed with regret flooded her. She had been utterly foolish to hitch a ride in the back of a stranger's wagon. What if he meant her harm? She glanced first to the right, then to the left, then to the right again. Nothing but open prairie, sagebrush, and desolation. No one would hear her if she screamed. Surely they were hours from Cornwall, or any town for that matter.

While the piece of wood may not be the best choice for a weapon, it could do damage. Just as she surmised the kettle had when she used it to enable her escape from Ivan.

If she were still alive, Mama would applaud Paisley for her quick-thinking tenacity. Both then and now.

CHAPTER THREE

DID THE STOWAWAY BRANDISHING her weapon think she could protect herself with a flimsy board? Even if she was strong for a woman, he could easily overtake her. Not that Tyler would do anything to harm her. For he was a God-fearing man of integrity.

But who was this woman? Why was she in his wagon? Didn't he have enough to think about without further complications?

Tyler studied her. A slender woman with long, disheveled fawn-colored brown hair and suspicious hazel eyes stared back at him. Her jaw was clenched, her mouth formed a straight line, and her determination and fortitude amused him. She might be beautiful had her hair been combed and her frown replaced with a smile.

As if Tyler's life hadn't taken enough unexpected turns in recent days, now he had to contend with this? What was he to do with this woman? Leave her alone on the prairie? No, he couldn't do that. There was nothing for miles, and it would put the woman in danger.

Take her back to Cornwall? No, he couldn't do that. Time didn't permit that option. He'd promised he'd return to Horizon tomorrow to deliver the lumber and retrieve the children.

Should he take her to Ingleville? What if she was a fugitive on the run from someone? Judging from her rumpled appearance, it could be a possibility.

"Ma'am, I'd be much obliged if you'd tell me why you're in the back of my wagon." He kept his eye on her just in case she saw fit to swing the piece of wood at him.

During his time in a mining camp, he'd dealt with bandits, drunks, outlaws, frigid winter weather, bears, a fire, and more. A woman wielding a board was hardly a threat, but he didn't relish the possibility of that board connecting with his head.

She should never have flung herself into the back of the wagon. Now she was alone in the middle of nowhere, had no help for miles, and was entrapped by fear. But Paisley would not let the stranger see that fear. She would keep the man in clear focus and attempt to appear calm, even though anxiety permeated her every heartbeat.

"I need some answers," the man said.

"Yes, I do as well."

"But there's a huge difference. You're in *my* wagon."

Paisley couldn't deny that. "True, but I couldn't possibly have known it was *your* wagon."

"And I couldn't have possibly known there was a stowaway in the back of my wagon when I left Cornwall. If I had noticed, I would have removed you then."

If the man had found her and removed her from his wagon, would she still be running from Ivan? Still in search of safety?

The man removed his hat, revealing thick dark hair. Paisley regarded him for a moment. Blue eyes, a day's worth of whiskers, and somewhat tall. What type of person was he?

"How long have you been in my wagon?" The man returned his hat to his head and pulled the brim low over his forehead.

"Since Cornwall." Panic reared within her. Did the man notice that her voice shook when she spoke? Was her life in jeopardy? The stranger didn't *appear* dangerous.

"I'm headed to Horizon, but I plan on stopping in Ingleville for the night before continuing on my journey. I can give you a ride there."

Ingleville? She'd never heard of Ingleville. Or Horizon, for that matter.

Paisley weighed her options. Should she trust the stranger and allow him to give her a ride to the next town? The day was warm and pleasant, and a gentle breeze blew that provided a welcome respite from the heat of the past few days. Perhaps she could walk to Ingleville. "How far is it to the next town?"

"Not too far in a wagon but much too far on foot if that's what you have in mind." The man shrugged. "Or you could walk if that's what you want. Makes no difference to me other than my ma raised me better than to leave a lady alone in the middle of nowhere."

Paisley quirked an eyebrow but said nothing. The stranger must have some scruples if his ma had raised him to be a gentleman. He could remove her from the wagon and insist she find her own way.

"Perhaps riding on the buckboard might be more comfortable," the man suggested.

"Yes, of course you're right. I accept your offer of a ride."

"You'll have to put down your weapon first."

Paisley studied the piece of wood still in her hands. She lowered it, noticing the ache in her arms from holding it taut.

He lifted her from the wagon, then offered his hand as he assisted her onto the buckboard.

When his calloused hand met with hers, Paisley winced and jerked her hand away, noting multiple splinters lined both hands.

"Are you all right?"

"Yes." The slivers stung, but Paisley again held her hand out to him. He took it, his gaze lingering on her hand.

Her eyes darted to where the imprints of Ivan's fingers had caused bruising. A scab had formed over a deep arc-shaped imprint he'd left behind when he'd dug his nails into her flesh. Had it only been a few hours earlier that she'd nearly been forced to marry him? Another perusal of her hands once again indicated slivers from hastily grabbing the rough-hewn piece of lumber. When she looked up, she noticed the man regarding her.

"I'm Tyler Shepherdson," he finally said, breaking the silence.

"Paisley Abbott."

"Nice to meet you, Miss Abbott."

"You as well, Mr. Shepherdson."

"I've never found a woman in the back of my wagon before and never had one threaten me with a board. Are you running from something or someone?"

Paisley swallowed hard. Running from something? Yes. From someone? Yes. From the pain of grieving a great loss? Yes.

"Well?"

Tyler Shepherdson was persistent. "There's nothing left back there." She pointed toward the direction from which they'd come. No sense in sharing more information until prodded or forced to do so. The fewer words the better. "I'm off to start a new life."

The man shook his head. "How often have I said those same words myself."

"Pardon me?"

"Nothing."

Silence filled the air between them. Finally, the man spoke again. "We should quit the idle chitchat and get back on the road. I plan to reach Ingleville before nightfall."

Seconds stretched into minutes and minutes into an hour or more, although she had no timepiece to know for sure, only the sun's location in the sky. Paisley folded her arms across her middle and kept Tyler Shepherdson in constant view from the corner of her eye. She attempted to think about things other than the predicament in which she found herself.

The scenery passed at a slow rate of speed. Just how far was Ingleville?

Although Paisley had spent a fair amount of time in the back of the wagon before being discovered, exhaustion still remained. Fatigue settled in her neck muscles, and her stomach growled with hunger. The day seemed divided into two portions: first the incident that morning with Ivan, and now the turn of events leading her to travel to an unknown town with a stranger. She waffled back and forth in her assessment of the matters at hand: desperation, fear, weariness, anxiety, and even a bit of anticipation thrown into the mix. When they reached Ingleville, they'd go their separate ways and two things would be certain: she'd never see Mr. Shepherdson or Ivan again.

After some time, he stopped whistling "Oh! Susanna" and asked, "Do you have a family? A husband?"

His unexpected question caught Paisley unawares. "I beg your pardon?"

"Do you have a family? A husband? It's not proper or safe for a woman to be out here all alone."

Paisley had worried about her reputation no less than a dozen times since Mr. Shepherdson found her in the back of the wagon. Her dire need to escape Ivan had certainly led her to this desperate measure. "No to both inquiries." The ache of losing her parents returned. Would it ever get easier living without them? Thankfully the Lord had seen fit to rescue her from marrying Ivan.

"I see."

"Do you have a family? A wife?" The question sounded strange coming from her lips. Would the man think her inquiry too forward?

"Not married, but I do have some family."

Paisley noticed a wistful flicker in the man's eyes as he answered. Turning to face forward again, she clasped her hands together and placed them in her lap.

"I noticed you had a few splinters in your hands."

"Yes."

"If you'd like, I can help you with those once we reach Ingleville."

"Thank you."

The man diverted his eyes from the road ahead to glance at her. "Are you sure you're not running from someone? I don't need any trouble. I've got enough of that as it is."

"No, I'm not running from anyone. No one at all." Except Ivan and a life in which she'd lost everything that ever mattered.

No family. No money. No home. And nowhere to go.

Lord, please show me the way.

Doubt consumed her and she struggled to brush it aside. Surely the Lord would give her the guidance she sought.

CHAPTER FOUR

TYLER WAS BOTH LEERY and curious about the woman riding beside him. During his travels and while working many diverse forms of employment, he had experienced no shortage of unexpectedly meeting dubious individuals. If found assisting a fugitive, it would make his already gloomy circumstances worse. He needn't any further frustrations than what life had recently bestowed on him.

What if Paisley Abbott was a con woman? He'd heard about a notorious con woman in Pennsylvania who duped many a man out of his hard-earned money.

Tyler also found himself intrigued by his passenger. Maybe she needed a new start in life through no fault of her own. If so, he couldn't blame her for that. He had needed a new start many times and sought to take every opportunity that presented itself. He'd never done anything wrong during those times. Well, unless he counted disappointing his parents and likely the entire town of Horizon.

Tyler was just about to ask Miss Abbot a question when he noticed a wagon ahead pulled to the side of the road. Did they need assistance?

So often on the wide-open expanses of the Idaho Territory, one wouldn't see another person for miles. He tugged on the reins and drew up alongside the other wagon. "Hello, there. Do you need any help?"

The second the driver leaned forward, and Tyler immediately recognized him.

"Oren?"

"Tyler?"

Tyler climbed from the wagon the same time Oren did and clapped his friend on the shoulder. "How long has it been?"

"At least three years or so," said Oren. "This is my wife, Lottie." He gestured to a woman on the buckboard who smiled and waved.

"Nice to meet you, Lottie." Tyler jabbed Oren in the shoulder. "Married and all."

"And is that your wife?" Lottie asked.

"My wife?"

"Yes, in the wagon?" Oren chuckled. "You do know there's a woman in your wagon, right?"

If only Oren knew the circumstances behind *finding* Miss Abbott in his wagon. "Ha ha, I can see you haven't lost your wit after all these years. Yes, I do know there's a woman in my wagon."

"And here I thought ol' Tyler would never marry. He decided wandering across God's Creation like a nomad and seeing how many jobs he could pursue before settling down was much more important. Appears you've done changed his mind." Oren touched the brim of his hat. "Nice to meet you, ma'am."

Tyler looked from Oren to Miss Abbott and back to Oren. "She's not my wife. She's just a..." *Woman I just met when she stowed away in my wagon.* But he didn't want to embarrass the woman, so he nodded toward her. "She's a friend. Her name is Miss Abbott."

Lottie's raised eyebrows indicated questions. But how could Tyler explain?

"She's a friend who needed a ride from Cornwall to Ingleville."

"Ingleville?" Oren asked. "You have family there?"

"No," said Miss Abbott, speaking for the first time since meeting Oren and Lottie. "Although I do have some business to tend to there. Mr. Shepherdson was gracious enough to offer me a ride since he was going this way."

Seemed like a good time to change the topic. "Last I knew you were hoping to buy some land in Horizon for a farm," said Tyler.

"Things changed. I went to Cornwall to work with my uncle for a few years and that's where I met Lottie. We married nearly two years ago, and our little one will be born in a couple months." Oren's round face beamed and his eyes sparkled. Lottie blushed and dipped her head.

The couple exchanged an adoring glance, and a fleeting moment of envy struck Tyler. He tossed it aside. Marriage and a family had never been something he yearned for as there was too much of the world calling him away from conventional matters. He leaned against the wagon. "Moving back to Horizon, then?"

"No, we're actually moving to Varner City. Found us a nice spread there at a reasonable price and a cabin already built. With the baby coming and all..."

How could it be that so much time had passed since Tyler left Horizon that one of his closest friends was already married and about to be a pa? "Congratulations."

"Thank you," said Oren. "We're excited. Seems a good place to start a new life with my bride."

Lottie blushed again and fluttered her lashes at Oren.

Tyler cleared his throat. "Well, then. With nightfall in about three hours, we're going to stop in Ingleville."

"We are as well. This load is a bit much for the horses. Mind if we caravan with you into town?"

"Sure. We'll see you there." Tyler noted the overloaded wagon with what was likely all of Oren and Lottie's possessions.

"They seem like a pleasant couple," Miss Abbott said after Tyler beckoned the horses.

Tyler thought again about how much time had passed since he'd last seen Oren. The man had done well for himself. "Oren and I were friends in Horizon."

"I've never been to Horizon."

"It's a town with a lot of good folks. Larger than Ingleville but smaller than Cornwall. I moved there with my parents in '66. Do you live in Cornwall?"

She didn't answer for some time, and he was about to repeat the question figuring she hadn't heard him.

Finally, she answered in a voice so timid Tyler wondered if it was the voice of the same woman who'd so brazenly confronted him when he'd discovered her sleeping in the back of his wagon.

"I don't live in Cornwall, but in a tiny town outside of Cornwall known as Pringle. My parents had a farm there."

"And you would want to run from that?" *Hypocrite.* The accusation hit him in the chest. But it was true. He'd had a good life in Horizon before he decided to run from it.

Miss Abbott peered toward the opposite direction as silence met his question. Had he been too nosy?

When she turned to face forward again, he saw her dampened face. He'd clearly upset her. Miss Abbott remained staring straight ahead, her face wet with tears and her arms folded tightly across her middle. Women. Who could figure them out? Tears at the mere sound of an innocent question. "I'm sorry I asked." And he was.

"It's all right. I...I recently lost my parents."

Tyler didn't know what to say. He knew all too well the pain from a loss such as hers. "I'm sorry, Miss Abbott."

She sniffled and Tyler transferred the reins to one hand and fetched a handkerchief from his trouser pocket. "You're welcome to use this."

"Thank you." She dabbed at her eyes and softly blew her nose.

Tyler waited for her to say more, but when she didn't, he focused on watching Oren's wagon in front of them and thinking about the challenges ahead with the children.

And while he was new to submitting prayer requests, it was a guarantee that the three children left in his care *needed* prayer.

While he figured the Lord would assist him in caring for the orphans, he wasn't as confident that God had truly forgiven him for neglecting his parents and failing to see them as the blessings they were while they were alive.

"This really is the first time I have talked with anyone about it, and it seems so real now."

"Losing your parents is difficult." Tyler himself hadn't fully mourned the grief he'd experienced so recently. Not that he would mourn as a woman did, but Tyler knew the time would come when the awareness of all he'd lost and all he still stood to lose would truly affect him.

The woman clutched his handkerchief, and a tear trailed down her cheek. What was a man to do in such a circumstance? Especially since he didn't even know Miss Abbott?

Perhaps sympathizing would be of benefit. Hadn't Reverend Marshall spoke of how sharing with others about the trials we ourselves have faced was beneficial? "I recently lost my parents as well from the fever. It hit Horizon in a way that no one expected."

"I'm sorry, Mr. Shepherdson. I suppose that means we're both orphans."

"Reckon it does." Although that term was nearly impossible for him to comprehend. In the short weeks since the death of his parents, so many emotions had run through Tyler's mind. Guilt for not being there, regret for the way he'd disappointed his parents, and frustration at not being able to save them. He cleared his throat. "I'm fine if we call each other by our given names if you are."

There. He'd changed the subject that pained him too much to discuss.

"I'm agreeable."

"Good then. Why did you not stay on your parents' farm in Pringle?" There he went, prying into her business again. "If you don't mind talking about it."

"I don't mind. There's nothing left of my parents' farm, and I have no family left. And there are other reasons for not staying in Pringle as well."

"Sorry to hear that." It appeared Tyler wasn't the only one who'd suffered greatly in the recent past. His parents' faces flashed before his mind. If only he had one more chance to make amends.

CHAPTER FIVE

FOR SOME ODD REASON, Tyler Shepherdson was easy to converse with. Perhaps it was the fatigue overtaking her or maybe just the hope of passing time away while they slowly drove toward Ingleville.

The man seemed pleasant enough from the meager time knowing him. However, things could have gone awry. He could have left her on the open prairie, or worse, harmed her. It had been unwise on her part to seek a ride with a stranger, even in desperation. *Lord, forgive me for such foolishness.*

They also shared some sort of comradeship, having both lost their parents. How Paisley had longed for a trusted friend to come alongside her in her time of grief. To be able to share her fear of Ivan and what would happen should she be forced to marry him, or how she would be able to prevent him from taking the farm.

Yet there were no friends to be had. For a while, Paisley considered finding a way to return to Kansas. But years had passed, and besides, she had no funds to secure her trip.

Staying in Pringle wasn't an option. Not with Ivan. Nor was living in Cornwall. He would likely find her there just as easily.

Tyler whistled and Paisley fidgeted with the clasp on her coin purse. "Do you happen to know a man named Ivan Marchesi?" The words tumbled from her mouth before she could continue her contemplation.

"Can't say as I recognize his name. Where is he from?"

Paisley's fear eased. "The Pringle area, but he is known in Cornwall as well." Slithery snake Ivan knew how to put on a façade many would never see through. But Paisley had.

Tyler shook his head. "Can't say as I know him. Since you're not returning to Pringle or Cornwall, have you given thought to what you'll do in Ingleville?"

Paisley had given no thought to what she would do next. There had been no time to plan. "You mentioned Horizon is larger?"

"By about one hundred people or so. Horizon has much more to offer than Ingleville."

Another realization hit Paisley. What was she thinking? That she could easily find employment in a foreign town? Yes, she could sew. Maybe she could be hired as a seamstress. But it was likely there were plenty of women to do that.

She could cook. Well, not really. Maybe a restaurant or boardinghouse would be willing to give her lessons while she worked. Or maybe Paisley could find a larger city where employment would be more plentiful. But how would she get there? Depend on the kindness of Tyler Shepherdson to drive her all over Creation?

Paisley's choices were limited. She could return to Kansas, move to Ingleville, or go elsewhere. She'd heard that parts of the Montana Territory were booming with gold to be found. Maybe she could find a job cooking for miners. But first she'd have to learn how to cook...if such a feat were possible.

And what if no honorable occupations availed themselves?

Paisley shuddered at the thought of what women sometimes had to do in order to make a living, and she prayed she'd never have to succumb to that type of lifestyle.

She chewed on her lip. Perhaps she could be a caretaker. She'd worked diligently alongside Mama caring for Papa during his illness. She'd forsaken all opportunities a woman her age sought. Mama needed her, and she'd loved her parents something fierce. Yes, Paisley could hire on as a caretaker if such a position became available.

But as soon as she resolved that thought, another question popped into her mind. Where would she live? She had no money and no home.

Tyler's inquisitiveness interrupted her thoughts. "Tell me about this Ivan Marchesi. Is he the one you're running from?

"Who says I'm running from someone?"

Tyler shrugged. "It's as clear as a blue sky on a hot Idaho day. I'd be much obliged if you'd share a bit about what led you to hitch a ride in my wagon." He studied her, waiting a few seconds before speaking. "Is one of the other reasons you can't stay in Pringle or Cornwall because of this Ivan fellow?"

"Yes, because of Ivan." Paisley took a deep breath. She'd had no one to help her, no one in whom to fully confide about Ivan. Mama had her hands full with Papa's illness and running the farm. The townsfolk in Pringle had shunned Paisley's family because of Papa's behavior. She had no friends.

Paisley clutched her coin purse. She still owned the deed to the farm, such as it was after being destroyed by the flood. Ivan wanted the deed. Wanted the fertile farmland to enhance his spread. Nearly everyone else had already sold their land to him.

Papa's promise for her hand in marriage and Ivan's near success at manipulating him out of the deed to the farm reminded her of her father's lack of judgment. Had his illness been so profound that he'd not seen the truth about Ivan as Paisley had?

"I am running because I have nowhere to go."

CHAPTER SIX

EVEN AMID ALL OF his wanderings, Tyler always had a place to go. A place to return to. A home where he was loved and welcomed. Forgiveness for the asking.

The regret permeated his thoughts, kept him awake at night, and made him wish for a way to do over all that he'd done wrong.

In contrast, Paisley had nowhere to go. Nowhere to return to and no home. Tyler contemplated their conversation. Although he was desperate, she'd lost even more than he had. Given the fact she was a woman on her own and likely had no money, her situation boded much worse. He, as a man, could secure employment anywhere, and he already had a home. Well, not *his* home exactly, but his parents' home. At least Tyler was settled and would be able to make a life for himself.

If he could stay settled and not allow the notions of the unknown to fill his imagination.

Already, he had wondered on more than one occasion how he would manage to sink his roots into one place. Especially a place that held the memories of profoundly disappointing his parents.

Whoever Ivan Marchesi was, Paisley feared him or else she wouldn't have stowed away in the wagon.

The crooked, dilapidated sign announcing their entrance into Ingleville greeted them on the outskirts of the town. Tyler stopped the wagon, climbed down, and adjusted the sign so it stood upright once again.

If Paisley planned to stay in this town, what would she do to support herself?

She wasn't sure what she was expecting when they entered Ingleville. A sprawling town, perhaps? A thriving community where she could temporarily make a new home until she sought help to sell what was left of Mama and Papa's farm?

Instead, a ramshackle hamlet awaited her. On the right-hand side of the nearly vacant street was a saloon, a mercantile, and a hotel with a barn, their worn buildings appearing much older than they likely were. On the other side, a second saloon and a cabin.

"Welcome to Ingleville. It's mainly a stop between Horizon and Cornwall and nothing more. There are a couple of farms on the outskirts and gold was found a few years back, but once the gold ran out, nearly everyone left." Tyler slowed the wagon and followed Oren and Lottie to the hotel.

Dread and trepidation overwhelmed her. How would she find employment in such a place?

Lord, please guide me.

Paisley bit back the tears so close to the surface. Immediately after Mama and Papa's death, she'd doubted the Lord would provide for her. A bleak future with few choices awaited her.

Yet even though she doubted, in her heart she'd known God was faithful.

A morsel of disbelief again threatened to emerge, and Paisley called upon the verses in the Bible she'd long memorized. A portion of Psalm 32:7 provided comfort. *"Thou art my hiding place; thou shalt preserve me from trouble."*

Paisley reminded herself that the Lord's faithfulness had endured from the time she was a foundling and He'd blessed her with loving parents. He'd protected her when the floodwaters came and took away everyone important to her. And He'd protected her from Ivan. He would continue to preserve her.

She need only to trust.

Tyler stopped the wagon near the hotel. Oren lifted Lottie from their wagon and planted a kiss on her lips before offering his arm. "We'll see if they have any rooms available," he said without removing his loving gaze from his wife. The two proceeded into the hotel, leaving Paisley and Tyler behind.

"Before we go in, I'd be happy to take a look at those slivers."

"The slivers? Oh, yes, the slivers. Surely there's a doctor in town?"

"Not in Ingleville. Too small of town for that."

"In that case, I'd be grateful for your help."

"I have salve and tincture in a box I keep in the wagon." Tyler escorted Paisley to the back of the wagon. He located the rustic wooden box and removed it.

"Have you done any doctoring before?" Surely a man who carried medical supplies knew a thing or two about tending to the sick and injured.

"Not much. However, while panning for gold a few years back, I had to tend to some injured men from time to time. A man I worked with taught me a thing or two about minor medical issues as there always seemed to be some type of injury and no doctor for miles." He opened the wooden box and removed three of the five items.

Paisley held her palms up and allowed Tyler to inspect them. When his hands touched hers, she flinched. He stood so close to her, and with his hands holding hers, the moment seemed uncomfortably intimate.

Tyler stared for a moment at her hands and gently turned them over. "Who did this to you?" he asked.

Paisley presumed he meant the bruises rather than the slivers. "Ivan."

As close as she stood, she could see the vein throb in his jaw. His gaze met hers, and she saw the compassion in the depths of his eyes. "I don't ever cotton to a man hurting a woman." His serious tone indicated his sincerity.

"That's one reason why I couldn't marry him," she whispered.

"You were going to marry him?"

"Not by choice."

Something flickered in his eyes. While Paisley knew nothing about him, he acted genuinely concerned.

"You have a number of splinters. You'll have to be more careful next time you handle a weapon."

Paisley saw a hint of teasing in Tyler's eyes. "Will you be able to remove them?"

"It'll take me a few minutes, but it shouldn't be a problem." Tyler set about dislodging the splinters with the pair of tweezers. A few of the slivers came out almost immediately, while others were more stubborn, and Paisley attempted not to wince from the pain.

"I'm sorry if it hurts a bit. I'm trying to be as gentle as possible." Tyler squinted as he examined a particularly deep sliver embedded in her pinky finger.

Paisley appreciated that he was attempting to be gentle. She thought of Ivan and suppressed a shiver. He wouldn't have been gentle at all.

"There. I think we got them all." Tyler rubbed some salve over her hands where he had extracted the splinters. "Are you all right?"

"Yes, thank you."

"Anytime. I mean, not that I want you to keep getting slivers." He shifted.

"No, of course not. I don't plan to make it a habit." Paisley looked away first. She was thankful the sun had set and the light was dim to prevent Tyler from seeing the blush that likely lined her cheeks. It would have been far better if Tyler had been an old decrepit man, rather than a handsome young man.

"Should we go inside the hotel?"

"Yes, of course." The hour had grown late, and her thoughts had mixed into a jumble. A warm bed and a comfortable pillow couldn't come soon enough.

"I reckon I forgot to ask if you have any belongings in the back of the wagon you'll be needing to have taken into the hotel?"

"No, this is all I have." Paisley held tight to her coin purse. A purse void of any money, it held only a torn piece of paper with Papa's favorite Bible verse scrawled in his handwriting and the deed, both of which she'd found on a top shelf in the house after wading through water following the destructive flood.

What Paisley wouldn't give to have her Bible. But everything and nearly everyone, including the parents she loved so dearly, had been lost when the floodwaters overflowed the sides of the nearby Cornwall River.

Tyler opened the door of the hotel for her, and she followed him inside. A rawboned man with thick, round glasses perched halfway down his nose greeted them at the counter. "How may I assist you?"

"I have a reservation to sleep in the barn tonight, and I'll rent a room for the lady," Tyler answered.

"Breakfast is served at seven a.m. sharp in the foyer. Miss, your room is number three up the stairs and to the right." The man nodded at Paisley.

Tyler plunked down a coin.

"Thank you," she told him, grateful he was willing to pay for her room.

Paisley perused what the man deemed to be the foyer, which was nothing more than a tiny room with no windows and one table.

"Not much of a foyer. I recall the first time I saw it on my way to Cornwall." Tyler said. "We'll meet Lottie and Oren tomorrow for breakfast before we continue on our way."

Moments later, Paisley trudged up the stairs and turned the doorknob to room number three. She released a huge breath of air, listening as it echoed in the near-vacant room.

While she was grateful to have a place to sleep for the night, Paisley had no idea that her room, dingy and drab with a dank odor, would boast only a bed with no blanket and wires poking through the thin, overused mattress. However, because of overwhelming exhaustion, the second she rested her head on the shabby faded pillow, she fell asleep.

Chapter Seven

TYLER MULLED IT OVER so many times he feared he'd scarcely had a minute of sleep. An absurd idea for sure, but it just might work. Especially since they were both desperate. She needed a place to live since she wouldn't be staying in Ingleville, and he needed someone to assist him in caring for three orphans.

He would announce his mutually beneficial plan to her in the morning on their way to Horizon. The worst that could happen would be that she would say "no".

Which, he hoped she wouldn't. For he had no alternative plan.

The next morning, Tyler and Paisley continued toward Horizon. It took until after they'd reached the junction and bid farewell to Oren and Lottie that he worked up the courage to present his plan.

A weathered sign marked two roads. One to Horizon and the other to Varner City. Tyler stopped the wagon, and he and Paisley meandered to where Oren and Lottie stood.

"I wish you and Lottie could settle in Horizon," Tyler told his friend.

"As do we, but we've already secured the loan for the acreage in Varner City. Hopefully after the baby is born, we'll pay a visit to Horizon."

"Or maybe we could visit you in Varner City," Tyler suggested, although he was certain with his new role as a father it might be some time before they were able to venture to the other town. He shook Oren's hand. "It's mighty good to see you again."

"You as well."

Lottie took a step toward Paisley and embraced her in a hug. "It was so nice to meet you," the shorter woman said, clasping both of Paisley's hands. "I'm sure we'll see each other again. Oren says Varner City is only two days' travel from Horizon."

"Yes, I do hope so."

While Tyler didn't know much about Paisley, he'd noticed that Lottie had been drawn to her immediately.

Lottie rested one arm beneath her rounded stomach and a hand on her back. "It will be delightful to be settled. Our hope was to have the house ready before the baby comes. A new baby, a new town, and a new home. It's all so thrilling."

Oren placed an arm around his wife and pulled her close. "It will be an adventure."

Tyler considered both Oren's and Lottie's words and wished he could be as thrilled about the fresh start that awaited him—a potential new wife, new children, and a new occupation.

They continued in pleasant camaraderie before Oren reminded them that if they wanted to reach their next destinations before nightfall, they best be on their way.

A few miles from Horizon, Tyler transferred the reins to one hand, shifted his hat higher on his head, and wiped the perspiration from his brow. He was accustomed to making decisions without giving them much thought, but even this idea sounded preposterous the moment Tyler uttered it.

Perhaps he should have prayed about it first before presenting his idea to Paisley. But he *had* mulled it over multiple times last night when he should have been sleeping.

"We could get married," he heard himself say. "A partnership of sorts. You need a place to live, and I need someone to care for my sisters and brother."

He didn't know which made him chuckle more: the thought of himself—Tyler Shepherdson—settling down to marry, or the look on her face when he voiced his suggestion.

"It would suit us both, and it would be only for convenience's sake. It wouldn't be for love as is the case for most folks, but then I don't see any way around it. I haven't been able to find someone to care for the children, and you'll find that jobs are scarce in Horizon."

Paisley's mouth was in the shape of a large "o" and her eyes grew wide. Perhaps she felt the same way about marriage as he did, especially given what she'd already told him about that Ivan character.

Should he proceed with his newly-devised plan? Or should he give her a chance to voice her thoughts once she recovered from her shock? He really did need someone to care for the children, especially since he knew nothing about being a father.

Being a husband was likely much easier.

"We could wait and marry a few days after reaching Horizon. That would give us a chance to get better acquainted with each other." Tyler cleared his throat. He'd worked dangerous jobs in his life, had once outrun Indians on horseback in the Wyoming Territory, and had survived more frightening situations than he cared to remember.

So why were his nerves on edge at the thought of marriage? Especially when it was a necessity?

"I'm sure we'd have to see when Reverend Marshall would be available to perform the ceremony. He's a busy man." The sooner Tyler had someone to care for the children the better. Surely a few days would be sufficient time to get things in order before their wedding vows.

Paisley uttered no words, only a wheezing sound that caused Tyler to ponder if he should stop the wagon and ask if she was going to live.

Maybe he could use poetry or flowery words to persuade her. Didn't women revel in the expression of such romantic notions? But he had no experience with women or poetry. He was never one for flowery words, and he'd certainly never had time to court a woman and pursue a relationship.

He'd been too busy pursuing his own selfish ambitions.

Paisley's countenance hadn't changed. She remained staring at him with raised eyebrows and a slack jaw.

Tyler could do worse. Much worse. Paisley was easy on the eyes, seemed somewhat intelligent, and she likely knew how to sew and cook if she thought she could pursue a job in Horizon or wherever she planned on going. She seemed to be a religious woman, which he'd have to verify before fully committing to his idea.

And he was an upstanding man. He worked hard, always had. Pa had commended Tyler many times on his work ethic. He had an easygoing personality and tried to laugh a lot. That was better than being crotchety. In addition, he'd never partaken in any bad habits that would have disappointed his ma.

He continued his attempt to persuade her and himself that his idea was worthwhile. "Folks marry for convenience all the time. When I worked for a short time at a blacksmith shop in Virginia City in the Montana Territory, I knew two couples who did that very thing. Their spouses died and they needed help raising the young'uns. Love was the furthest thing from their minds."

Why did his words sound more like he was attempting to convince himself than convince her?

Chapter Eight

Paisley listened in astonishment, struggling to comprehend Tyler's plan. They'd only just met, and surely a man of his appearance would have many prospects. He wouldn't have to settle for a woman who had hitched a ride in his wagon—a woman he didn't even know.

"A marriage of convenience?" she squeaked, noting her voice sounded incredulous, dubious, and hollow in her own ears.

Tyler sat up straight as though presenting a speech. "Yes. You no longer have a home, which leaves you with an uncertain future. Your willingness to ride a considerable distance with a stranger tells of your desperation. As for me, I recently inherited three children and need someone to care for them when the older two aren't in school and I'm working in the fields. I know nothing about children and even less about being a father to them."

"These three children—they are your sisters and brother?"

"Yes. It's a lengthy story."

"It appears we have a lengthy ride ahead of us." Hadn't Mama always mentioned Paisley's penchant for speaking her mind? And she needed answers, especially if she were to consider joining in matrimony with him.

Tyler sighed. "All right. My parents adopted three young'uns from the orphan train when it came to Cornwall. They've always wanted more children since I was their only one. When my parents passed, the logical choice was to leave the children to me. Seeing as how I've never raised children before, it presented some challenges."

Paisley knew the pain of losing parents. She also knew about adoption since her own parents adopted her. She'd thanked the Lord many times for loving parents who were willing to adopt a foundling and raise her as their own.

Thinking of others who needed someone to care for them caused her to entertain his suggestion. "Where are the children now?"

"They're staying with the reverend and his wife, but Reverend Marshall and Maribel are getting on in years and they made it clear that it's a temporary situation only for when I travel to Cornwall for my once-a-month deliveries. The rest of the time, the children are with me."

"How sad your parents passed away before being able to raise the children to adulthood." Paisley swallowed hard. She'd at least had her parents until adulthood, unlike the children Tyler referenced.

"A bad situation all the way around."

Paisley waited for Tyler to elaborate, but he didn't. A shadow of sorrow cloaked his expression, and she resisted the urge to press him for further details. He was a man attempting to carve a life for himself while raising three children. But weren't there any other women who would take the task of being his wife and the children's new mother? She needed to know.

"What about the women in town? Surely there is another you could marry. Perhaps one you fancy?"

"There aren't many unmarried women in Horizon. Sure, there are some widows, but they're much older. Most of the unmarried women are too young or too old."

She needed to pray. Spending time with the Lord always comforted her, and she sought His will in all areas of her life, especially for something that would make a permanent impact on her life.

But it hadn't always been that way. At one time in the not-too-distant past, Paisley doubted the Lord's faithfulness. She doubted the Lord would provide because He hadn't answered her prayer to heal Papa. And when she'd prayed for her parents to survive the flood last week, He hadn't answered that prayer either.

After their deaths, and with nothing and no one else, Paisley had once again turned to Him and was reminded His love was constant. That He never left nor forsook her, as was written in His Word. That His ways were not her ways and that He had a different plan for her life than she would have desired, even if His plans allowed unfathomable grief.

"Like I mentioned before," Tyler was saying, "It'll be a partnership of sorts—a marriage for convenience's sake only."

It was a partnership all right, but not what Paisley had in mind when she thought of someday marrying. What happened to romantic love or an abiding love like what her parents experienced after a couple of decades of marriage?

Wasn't that what love was all about? Not a partnership where she had somewhere to live and he had someone to care for his orphaned siblings.

"I'm sure Reverend Marshall would be happy to make it official and all. He's been rightly concerned about the children."

Why was it that she couldn't marry a man because she loved him and he loved her? First Ivan's attempts to force her hand in marriage and now Tyler's idea of a marriage of convenience. "I'm not sure. We hardly know each other."

"Exactly. That's why you could stay on with someone in town—maybe at Miss Greta's boardinghouse—for a few days until we could marry."

"A few days is hardly enough time to get to know someone." Did Tyler genuinely think such an arrangement was suitable?

"We'll have our entire lives to get to know each other." His response was more of a muttering, not at all persuasive. "Besides, the children need a mother...and you need a home."

What of a partner for life? Someone on whom you could depend and love for all of your days? Someone who would love you? Just like Mama and Papa. What of that? "May I think about this for some time? I'm skeptical after Ivan and such."

"Sure. Take your time. We have several hours ahead of us before we reach Horizon."

"Several hours is hardly enough time to think and pray about such a life-changing decision. Especially if..." What if Tyler was like Ivan? Hateful, manipulative, abusive, and tyrannical? "Isn't there a woman who is willing to take

47

care of the children—even one you wouldn't have to marry? Perhaps a nanny or governess? Or what about the reverend's wife? You mentioned she was getting on in years, but what if she only cared for the children during the day while you're in the fields? I presume you plan to work on a farm? Or perhaps the children could care for themselves if they are old enough or the elder child could care for the younger ones."

Her words emerged in an endless rush of concern. Surely there was another way for these precious children who had already lost so much.

"You're full of possibilities, Paisley, but I've given thought to them all. I've asked around and people are willing to help on a temporary basis, but not on a permanent one. It's not because they don't want to, but most already have families they're caring for and enough work to keep them busy. I can't think of anyone who'd want to be a nanny or governess for Albert, Lucy, and Mae, because well, they're…" His voice trailed.

"Is there something wrong with the children?"

"Wrong with the children? Why would there—why would there be anything wrong with the children?"

Tyler's stuttering, combined with his rapid blinking and the fact he'd transferred the reins to one hand while he tugged at his collar gave Paisley pause. Why was he flustered? "Well besides all of that, I must know a few more things about you before I am able to make an informed decision." Was she plumb crazy to marry a man she'd just met even if she was homeless? Even if she was attempting to escape from Ivan? Was Tyler truly an upstanding man of character? What was wrong with the children? The questions crowded her mind.

"Feel free to ask," Tyler said, interrupting her thoughts.

"I beg your pardon?"

"You said you needed to know a few more things about me before you could make a decision. What would you like to know?"

"Oh, yes." Years ago before Papa became ill, Paisley made a list of attributes she hoped to find in a future husband. She based much of it on godly principles, a lot from what she gleaned from her own parents' marriage, and some was personal preference. When her family moved to Pringle from Kansas three years ago, Papa subsequently fell ill and all thoughts and plans for marriage evaporated.

Paisley recalled most of the items on her "list"—crucial things. Yet she'd written the list when she'd planned to court someone in a conventional way, which was now unlikely to happen. She shoved aside the disappointment. "Are you a God-fearing man?"

"Yes, although I am new to following God's plan for my life."

"And do you partake in the drinking of whiskey?"

"No, I never have and don't plan to."

Paisley closed her eyes and mentally viewed the list once so elegantly written on a sheet of stationery from the mercantile in Kansas. She wouldn't know after just meeting Tyler whether he was gentle, kind, compassionate, and selfless. Although assisting her with the slivers would count as being gentle and kind. And paying for her room at the hotel constituted generosity.

She wouldn't at first know several of the other items on her list—whether he possessed a sense of humor and was honest, patient, and law-abiding. Those were character traits she'd discover only after spending more time with him. But according to Tyler, there wouldn't be much time before they said their vows.

Paisley cast a glance his way. Some of the lesser-important items on her list consisted of a man's outer appearance. She was relieved to note that he was not toothless and he seemed to have good hygiene.

"Do you work hard to provide for your family?" The last thing she wanted was to marry a sluggish dawdler who dillydallied the time away. "And are you, or have you ever, been in trouble with the law?"

"Whoa—one question at a time. I do work hard. I'm fixin' to continue farming as my pa did. I also have this job for deliveries, and I've worked other jobs as well. I've never been in trouble with the law, and I intend to keep it that way."

Lest she think he might be a near-perfect candidate for her list of things she could know without really *knowing* him, she reminded herself about Ivan. Papa was convinced he was a suitable candidate for Paisley's hand in marriage, even though Ivan failed to meet any of the requirements on Paisley's list.

Oh, Papa, how could you have ever thought Ivan would be a fitting husband? You were always such a good judge of character.

Paisley swallowed the lump in her throat. Even Mama hadn't understood Papa's decline in ascertaining someone's integrity. Papa had also been a man of his word and wouldn't rescind his blessing for Ivan to marry her, despite Mama and Paisley pleading with him otherwise.

She inhaled a sharp breath and asked another important question she recalled from her list.

"Are you a man of your word?"

Chapter Nine

Tyler avoided her gaze. All of the other questions had been easy. This one, not so much. He hadn't always kept his word. Hadn't done so when he'd promised to return home after a stint of working his first job in the northern part of the territory. Hadn't kept his word about regularly writing Ma, despite knowing how much that would have meant to her. Further, Tyler hadn't been a man of his word when he'd promised to help Pa run the farm—a farm Pa had spent years of his life tending to and working the soil. A farm built from nothing into something when they'd first moved to the Idaho Territory from Missouri. A farm Pa planned to pass on to his only son. The grief of disappointing his parents smothered him.

No, Tyler Shepherdson wasn't a man of his word. So how could he answer her question with honesty?

"I know I have a lot of questions, but your answers are imperative to my decision."

Tyler sighed. "I try to be a man of my word, Paisley, but I'm not perfect." That was certainly true.

"Will you be a man of your word in our marriage? I've heard of men leaving their wives and children and never returning."

If Paisley knew how he'd left his parents with no thought of returning, she would dismiss his idea in a matter of seconds. But Jesus had changed him. Changed his priorities. Changed his focus from himself to things that *really* mattered. Things like the Lord and the children and settling down in one place. The prior restlessness and selfishness evaporated, and now Tyler hungered for the life the Lord wanted for him, even though such yearnings were new to him. He took a deep breath. "When you speak of me being a man of my word, I promise you I would never leave my wife and children and that's the truth." A niggling voice jabbed at his heart with accusations that God hadn't *really* changed him, and with effort, Tyler shoved those accusations aside. "Besides, my ma taught me better than that." But was it the truth? Ma may have taught him better, but the sorrowful look in her eyes when he told her he had no plans to remain in Horizon would haunt him forever.

But those days were in the past. If only he could leave them there.

"I suppose those are all the questions I have at this moment. Do you have any questions for me?"

Tyler hadn't thought of questions to ask her. Perhaps he was too trusting or maybe his brain just didn't function that way—thinking of questions and answers and recording them all in a mental book. He'd not given a whole lot of thought to marriage, but knew that when he did someday find the woman he planned to marry, he would want someone like Ma. A caring and kind woman who laughed easily and was a good mother to their children. And of course, a woman who loved the Lord was paramount. But men didn't ponder all those things like women did. Yet now that he faced impending nuptials, he ought to ask Paisley some pertinent questions.

He had to think quickly as only three more miles separated them from Horizon. "I do have a couple questions."

"All right."

The children need a godly ma who will love them and care for them, and forever is a long time to be married to someone if she's an untrustworthy woman. Best you ask her some questions. Besides, you know you can't raise these children on your own.

He wanted to ask those important questions. He really did. But the words that came from his mouth resembled nothing like what he *should* ask. "Can you sew?"

"Yes, I'm quite adept at sewing."

"Good. The children's clothes always need mending." How did he know about children's clothes needing mending all the time? Of course, he *supposed* children like Albert, Lucy, and Mae would need mended clothes on a regular basis. "Speaking of children, are you good with young'uns?" From what the reverend insinuated, the children had already lived difficult lives. They needed a loving mother.

"When I was twelve, I assisted a widow with her seven children. We lived in Kansas then." She paused, as if contemplating her next words. "I came to learn quite a bit about caring for and nurturing children."

"Are you a God-fearing woman?" That would have been something really important to Ma. She wouldn't want the children raised by just any woman, but one who took her faith seriously.

"Yes, I've known the Lord since giving my life to Him at fourteen."

"Do you have any brothers or sisters?" All of these things he would have learned about her if he had the chance to court her. But there was no time for courtship. Albert, Lucy, and Mae needed a mother and someone to correct their wayward behavior.

Besides, Tyler didn't have time for the foolishness of courtship.

"No, I have no brothers or sisters."

A far-off look crossed her face before she continued. "My parents adopted me as an infant from the orphanage. They were older and never could have children of their own."

Did Paisley wish she'd had a sibling? Tyler had wished that a time or two while a young'un. Having been adopted herself might be helpful in her understanding of the challenges the children faced. Albert's, Lucy's, and Mae's faces flashed in his mind.

The wagon creaked and groaned, and the sun bore down on them. Thankfully they would reach Horizon soon, and already, the far outskirts of the town came into view. He thought of another question for Paisley. "Have you ever been married? Surely someone of your age and...uh... would have been married at one time." He had almost said someone of her age and beauty. Thankfully he'd caught himself before embarrassing himself further. She didn't need to know what he thought of her appearance.

"Someone of my age?"

Tyler detected annoyance in her voice. He recalled Ma and her friend, Wilhelmina, speaking of the sensitivity of women when called spinsters. Perhaps Tyler should have phrased it a different way. But it wasn't as though it was an everyday occurrence to ask a woman about herself, especially a woman he planned to marry. "What I mean to say is, most women are married by your age."

She glared at him, and he knew immediately that his choice of words was lacking. "And what age do you presume me to be, Tyler Shepherdson?"

Tyler scrutinized her. There was no right answer he could give her. If he said too young, Paisley would think he thought her immature. If Tyler said too old, she'd likely never speak to him again. What a dilemma he found himself in! "I'm not sure. I just know most women of your maturity are married by now." Tyler prided himself on his word usage. All that time spent reading all the books he could get his hands on as a youngster had been beneficial.

When Paisley scowled at him, her eyes narrowed and her jaw taut, all of his boastful pride slipped away. Tyler's hope that his answer didn't sound offensive backfired worse than a defective revolver.

"I'll have you know I'm likely younger than you are."

"You're likely right."

"Besides, not everyone is married at age sixteen."

"No, not everyone is," Tyler agreed.

"And I'll have you know I am not a spinster. And no, I've never been married before, although I've been given ample opportunity." She paused. "But sometimes life doesn't go as planned. Besides, discussing a woman's matrimonial status is far beyond the boundaries of etiquette."

"Reckon I don't read etiquette books often." Nor would he want to. He'd rather eat liver, his least favorite food, every day of his life than read a book about etiquette. Tyler shook his head as he recalled a book at the mercantile in

Horizon he'd seen titled *Manners and Proper Etiquette for the Modern Woman*. Who would read such a thing?

Time to ask a more critical question—one of the most important. "One last question. Can you cook?"

CHAPTER TEN

COULD SHE COOK? *GOOD question.* And a much better question than his insinuations about her spinsterhood. That question had stung Paisley's heart in places she'd not bared to anyone. It wasn't Tyler's business, even if she was to wed him, why she wasn't yet married. She'd not share that her devotion to her family had outweighed matrimonial prospects, or at least she had to remind herself of that many times during the course of Papa's illness. And while an option for courtship had presented itself in Kansas, the gentleman moved before seeking Pa's blessing.

Paisley desired above all else to marry a godly man and raise a godly brood of children. But that hadn't been the Lord's plan. He had needed her elsewhere.

Paisley thought of the irony that now, when all she desired was to find somewhere safe to live and to make a new start with her life, she was being given the opportunity to wed. But was that the Lord's plan or a quick way out of the predicament in which she found herself?

Only time and much prayer would tell.

Knowing Tyler awaited her answer on the last question and attempting to forget that someone her age wasn't yet married, Paisley again pondered Tyler's cooking inquiry.

How could she be discreet with this answer? She didn't want to lie. If she told the truth about the fact that she had once burned water, he would certainly rescind his proposal. Yet, wouldn't that be better since she didn't even know him?

"I am a student of cooking," Paisley finally answered. Feeling quite smug at her intelligent answer, she peered across the fields that had begun to dot the landscape. *A student of cooking indeed!*

"You'll be doing your fair share of cooking," Tyler said.

"Yes, to be sure with three children and a husband." How much could Tyler and the children possibly eat? Besides, maybe one of the women in town would assist her in her furtherance of learning. Not that it had done any good when Mama had tried to teach her. Paisley had much preferred to spend time outside in the fresh air assisting Papa on the farm and tending to Mama's garden to being inside learning how to cook. And after Papa's illness, she spent a considerable amount of time attempting to maintain the farm in addition to assisting Mama with Papa's care. Of course all of those hours of hard work hadn't prevented the devastating ruin that stole two lives and destroyed their home.

"The children are always hungry," Tyler said, interrupting her thoughts.

Paisley cringed to think that cooking had never been something she'd been overly eager to embrace. "I'm a competent housekeeper." Would that compensate for her lack of cooking ability?

"Good. The house can get messy at times with three children."

Paisley could only imagine. Was she ready for this new chapter in her life? What else could she do? Ask Tyler to wait for a year or so while she came to know him better? He seemed overly anxious to get married to a stranger. Should that concern her?

Should Paisley try to seek a job in Horizon? Save some money until she could move somewhere that held the promise of safe employment for a single woman? Was there even such a place? Or should she take a chance on Tyler's plan?

Tyler's continued chatter drew her mind away from her decision.

"Are you one of those women who likes to chitchat all the time? I'm asking so I can be prepared. I remember as a young'un it took us forever to return home after church because Ma liked to chat the day away with the women-folk."

What a peculiar question. Tyler worried that she might like to chitchat the day away? Paisley couldn't recall the last time she'd had a friend—a true friend outside of family—to prattle with. All of her close childhood friends were in Kansas, and as small and spread out as Pringle was, Paisley hadn't the opportunity to build close friendships. That and the stigma that came with a father who wasn't of sound mind. In addition, caring for Papa and trying to manage a farm left no time for idle chitchat. She and Mama only had each other in those times when life proved unmanageable.

How could Paisley tell Tyler she longed for a friend with whom she *could* chitchat the day away? She recalled the looks and the whispers from the townsfolk when Papa's illness overtook his mind and body. One particular time remained embedded in her memory.

Paisley had welcomed a reprieve from the farm due to an exceptionally grueling day. Papa had been easily agitated, with turbulent outbursts becoming more frequent. Prior to his illness, he'd been a calm and mild-mannered person. Mama insisted Paisley be the one to retrieve a few items from the mercantile, even though Paisley didn't want to leave Mama behind to manage Papa on her own, even for a short time.

The trip to town hadn't been the reprieve she expected. The mercantile owners and fellow patrons cared little if their disparaging remarks reached Paisley's ears. Rumors about Papa succumbing to paranoia, mania, or even drunkenness stabbed Paisley's heart as though they were physical knives.

And despite Paisley standing there, she was ignored. No one wanted to speak to a woman whose papa sometimes didn't even remember he had a wife and daughter. They only wanted to gossip.

Paisley hadn't told Mama of the incident when she returned home. It was difficult enough for her sweet mother to lose any semblance of the husband she'd always loved and treasured. Her mother needn't hear of the spiteful talk in Pringle, a town with a population of fifty residents, but with not one who cared to come alongside the Abbott family in their time of need.

"Paisley?"

Tyler's voice drew her from her memory. "You needn't worry about such things," she said.

"That's good to know. Not that I mind as I know a woman needs her time with other womenfolk, I just wanted to be warned that's all."

Paisley waited for more conversation from Tyler, but he said nothing more. She contemplated her circumstances and Tyler's questions and answers. If he spoke the truth about who he was, their marriage might have a chance.

She could do worse. Much worse. She could be marrying Ivan. And if she married Tyler, she would never have to worry again about Ivan marrying her if he found her. She thought of the deed tucked in her coin purse. Someday she would need to return home and see if she could salvage all that the flood destroyed. And she would need to visit the bank in Cornwall for a balance on what was owed on the farm.

Paisley snuck a sideways peek at Tyler. He had rolled his sleeves up to expose muscular forearms. The man who would soon be her husband was strong and capable. Paisley mentally added those things to her list of good qualities of the man she'd met only hours before.

But while there were some positive aspects to the marital arrangement, how could Paisley possibly marry him without getting to know more about him? Her hands grew cold and clammy, and panic filled her at the decision she must make. Could Tyler be masquerading himself as Ivan had to Papa, pretending to be someone he wasn't? What then?

Never again would Paisley subject herself to someone like Ivan Marchesi.

That much she knew.

Just when Tyler thought he might have persuaded Paisley to agree to his proposal, she began to speak again, the sound of emotion etched in her voice.

"Tyler, you couldn't possibly understand, but Ivan demanded the same thing of me—an unconventional marriage." The look in her eyes bore truth to how much this Ivan had hurt her. Tyler knew something about hurt. He'd hurt his parents in a way that he wasn't sure was ever forgiven.

"Paisley, I don't know Ivan, but I assure you that my motive is not to force you into something you oppose."

"But—but—how am I to know that?" Paisley paused and Tyler waited for her to continue. He noticed the wind had kicked up, blowing the prairie grasses with its hot breeze. He shifted in his seat, perhaps from the heat, but more so because of the discomfort in what she had suggested.

Should he prompt her to continue? "Paisley..." Tyler watched as she took a deep breath before speaking.

"When I first met Ivan, I thought that he was—different. He was cultured and smart. His parents had emigrated from Italy and over the years had accumulated wealth and a lot of prime farmland in the Idaho Territory. When his parents died, Ivan inherited it. I think that was a turning point for him, and he couldn't overcome his desire to own as much land as possible. I soon saw Ivan's sinister side. He coerced two of our neighbors into selling him their land. Said he wanted to own all of Pringle. No one could do anything because of Ivan's shady influence both in Pringle and in Cornwall."

"You don't have to tell me the rest if you don't want." When was the last time a woman had shared her feelings with him? He couldn't recollect. Tyler cleared his throat. He'd never been good with dealing with emotions.

"No, it's all right."

Tyler sensed that while she seemed a bit hesitant, she needed to share with him. Something about being needed warmed him on the inside, but he wouldn't let on.

Tyler gave his full attention to Paisley as she continued. "You see, Papa had fallen for Ivan's persuasive façade. He appeared to be the perfect gentleman in every way. But after some time, I saw through his schemes. I can't go through that again, Tyler."

"I understand. Take a few days to think about it. And to put your mind at ease, folks in Horizon can vouch that I'm nothing like Ivan." *But they could vouch that I left my parents when they needed me the most.*

Paisley said nothing then, leaving Tyler to be skeptical of his forwardness. He glanced at her, then the open road ahead, then at her again. And he realized that in those extremely desperate moments, one does foolish things.

And Tyler was desperate.

The war of emotions overtook Paisley, and she chastised herself. Why had she opened her heart and shared so much with Tyler? And why had she even considered for one second the thought of marrying him? He could be like Ivan, and she would be fooled once again.

Forever was a long time to spend with someone of bad character.

But the truth of the matter was, she was desperate. And sometimes, in those extremely desperate moments, one does foolish things.

Paisley took a deep breath and straightened her posture. "I will."

"You will?"

"I will marry you."

"You'll marry me?"

Had Tyler expected her to say "no"?

His eyes widened and a smile tugged at his lips. "I never thought proposing would be such an easy task. Not that I ever really gave it much thought, but…

"And never did I think I would be accepting of such an unusual proposal." Only those in such a dire situation would ever dream of saying "yes" to a marriage-of-convenience offer when they'd only known the person for less than a day.

CHAPTER ELEVEN

THE SUN HAD NEARLY set when Paisley and Tyler reached the outskirts of Horizon. Tall, majestic mountains rose above timbered hills. Green meadows grew adjacent to freshly-tilled fields. The site nearly stole her breath. As a child in Kansas, she'd not seen mountains, and Cornwall and Pringle were relatively flat with sagebrush.

Their words had been few the remaining miles to town. Paisley had spent most of the time praying for guidance and direction, and Tyler had spent most of his time whistling "Oh! Susanna".

Paisley craned her neck to see the buildings they passed. True to what Tyler said, the town appeared bigger than Ingleville, but smaller than Cornwall. A few people meandered along the boardwalk, several of whom waved as they passed.

"I'll take you to Miss Greta's boardinghouse first thing and get you settled. Then we'll stop by Reverend Marshall's so you can meet the children."

Meet the children. The children for whom she would soon be responsible. The children she'd promised Tyler she would mother. What if they didn't like her? Was she ready to be a ma? Would she make a suitable mother? Was it too late to change her mind?

Paisley then remembered she had no money to her name, not even one shiny copper penny. "I'm sorry, Tyler, but I don't have the funds to pay for my stay at Miss Greta's." She fiddled with the clasp of her coin purse, reminding herself it was void of money.

What had she gotten herself into?

Paisley's shoulders slumped as if she bore a heavy burden. She truly had nothing. And while he didn't have much, he did have more to his name than two crumpled pieces of paper in a coin purse. Gratitude mixed with shame filled his heart. His parents had left him a home and a farm.

But he'd done nothing but disappoint them.

"I have a plan for your stay at Miss Greta's," Tyler said. *Now if only Miss Greta will agree to it.*

Known as a cantankerous woman around town, Miss Greta didn't often agree to much. But Paisley's stay would be temporary—only a few days or so—therefore, it was Tyler's hope Miss Greta would be amenable to his suggestion.

"There it is—just up ahead on the right."

Tyler stopped the wagon in front of a house with a large wooden sign supported by two posts that read *Miss Greta's*. The clean two-story home boasted a yard full of flowers and an expansive front porch.

Tyler opened the door for Paisley and followed her inside. A rotund woman wearing a dark purple dress approached them. Flaming red hair escaped from a bun, frizzing at the ends in static disarray.

"Do you have my delivery for me?"

Tyler smirked. No "hello, how are you this fine evening?" Or "who is the woman at your side?" Or "did you have a safe trip?" No, nothing but a direct question about her lumber. Miss Greta had been candid, straightforward, and tactless since Tyler had known her and it was unlikely she'd ever change.

"Yes, Miss Greta. The lumber for your new outhouse is in my wagon. I can unload it around back."

"That would be fine." Miss Greta turned, and with an exaggerated swish of her skirts caused by her ample behind, headed in the opposite direction.

"Uh, Miss Greta?"

"What is it, Tyler? Can't you see I'm busy? I can't be standin' around visitin' when there's work to be done."

"Yes, I realize you're busy." Tyler took a gander around the room. "The place looks nice."

Miss Greta softened then, just slightly. She turned again to face them. "Thank you. Now what is it?"

"I wanted to introduce you to my betrothed."

"Your betrothed?" Miss Greta planted a plump hand to her chest. "Didn't know you was even courtin'."

He wanted to say he *wasn't* courting because the words and the thought both sounded so foreign to his ears, but instead, Tyler put his arm around Paisley and pulled her next to him. "This here is my soon-to-be-bride, Paisley Abbott." He felt her flinch and pondered removing his arm, but then decided against it. Tyler might as well convince Miss Greta and maybe himself in the process.

"Well, I'll be." Miss Greta appeared to be struggling to hide a smile. "Welcome to Horizon."

"Thank you." Paisley's voice sounded so small and timid that Tyler barely heard her. Miss Greta was intimidating all right. But she had a kind heart beneath her petulant exterior.

"Miss Greta, I was wondering if we might strike a deal of sorts."

"A deal?" Miss Greta's grumpy demeanor returned. "Don't have no time for deal-makin', Tyler."

He brushed her words aside and continued. "Paisley will need a place to stay for the next couple of days while we make plans for the wedding. I was thinking she might stay here."

Miss Greta eyeballed Paisley and narrowed her eyes, appearing to not be sure if she wanted another customer or not.

"And I will make a deal with you. I will build the new outhouse for you and won't charge you a cent in exchange for Paisley's room and board. It's a good deal, Miss Greta, and then you wouldn't have to hire someone else to do it. I have experience in building from helping my pa and from assisting in the construction of the assay office in Boise City. In my travels once, I even saw a two-story outhouse. Could build you one of those if you'd like."

Miss Greta scowled. "A one-story is sufficient. Just be sure you do it all proper-like."

"Yes, ma'am."

"Before I make any deals, how much does she eat?"

"Not much at all," Tyler said, realizing that his arm was still around Paisley's shoulders and that she had stiffened against him.

Why did he suddenly have the urge to plant a kiss on her cheek the way he'd seen Oren do with Lottie? Maybe to make the façade seem more real?

"And for how long?"

"Only until our wedding. We just arrived in town, and I'm not sure when Reverend Marshall will be available to make things official. But it won't be for long. You have my word on that."

"Didn't figure you to be hitched, Tyler. The way you done up and left all those years ago. But I suppose I can agree to your deal. Know this, though, that if she's here more than a week, I start to charge you. I can't go around givin' people free room and board. I won't stay in business long if I do that."

"I understand, Miss Greta, and that's more than generous." Tyler averted his attention to Paisley and grinned. Her weak smile in return did nothing to reassure him that his plans would succeed. "I'm taking Paisley to meet the children now at Reverend Marshall and Maribel's house. We'll be back shortly for Paisley's first night here."

"I'll have the Desert Rose room all ready," said Miss Greta, her alto voice almost monotone.

"Thank you, Miss Greta. I'll set to work on your outhouse right away."

"See that you do."

Tyler's plan was coming together.

CHAPTER TWELVE

BACK IN THE WAGON once again, Paisley mulled over the happenings of the past fifteen minutes. Miss Greta didn't seem any too friendly. Hopefully, Paisley would only have to stay with her for a few days. And then Tyler's arm around her. She hadn't known what to think about the warmth of his hand clasped on her shoulder or the nearness of him. Or how an odd flutter had taken up residency in her stomach. *I suppose for appearance's sake, such a show of affection was necessary, and I should become accustomed to his arm around my shoulders if I shall become his wife, however...*

"Don't give much thought to Miss Greta. She's a different sort, but you'll be fine staying at her boardinghouse," Tyler said, interrupting Paisley's thoughts.

"I'll try not to eat too much."

Tyler chuckled and Paisley realized she was beginning to enjoy the low rumble of his amusement. "Miss Greta is a bit, shall we say, frugal."

"I appreciate you building an entire outhouse just so I can stay there for a few days."

"It seemed a good idea and one that would be fair to everyone."

71

Had he seen her lack of funds in her coin purse? Paisley caught a glance at her future husband. He just confirmed once again his generosity.

Paisley gripped the side of the wagon as Tyler rounded the corner to the home where Reverend Marshall and Maribel lived. A modest whitewashed house in the center of town next to the church, it boasted a humble porch with two rocking chairs. Tyler parked in front of the house and assisted Paisley from the wagon. She moistened her lips and attempted to ignore the trepidation of meeting someone new.

Tyler knocked on the door. A petite woman with an abundance of blonde hair rolled into a bountiful chignon answered.

"Good evening, Maribel. We're here for the children."

"Please come in," Maribel invited.

Tyler gestured for Paisley to enter the house, then he followed.

So many people to meet in this place I'll be calling home.

"We were just reading to the children from the Bible before they went to bed. We weren't sure if you would arrive in time to take them home or if they should stay another night," commented Reverend Marshall. His voice held no malice, only a matter-of-fact tone.

"Thank you for caring for them in my absence," Tyler said. "It was a long trip, longer than I remembered." Tyler paused and glanced at Paisley. "I'd like to introduce you to my betrothed, Paisley Abbott."

Heat rushed up her face. Was it just her imagination or did Tyler seem to be beaming? Would it be this way whenever he introduced her?

Maribel rested her hand on Paisley's arm. "Congratulations, dear, and it's so nice to meet you. I had no idea Tyler was even courting someone."

"Welcome to Horizon," said Reverend Marshall, his demeanor much more subdued than that of his wife.

"Thank you. I'm looking forward to meeting all of the townsfolk."

A glint touched Maribel's eyes. "And when might we be expecting a wedding?"

"As soon as we can ask the fine reverend here to make it official," Tyler said, grinning at Reverend Marshall. His arm went around Paisley again as if it was the most natural thing. But to Paisley it didn't feel natural, although part of her could easily grow accustomed to his show of affection.

"How about next Tuesday?" Reverend Marshall asked.

Tyler moved his lips as if counting the days. "Yes, Reverend, that'll work."

Paisley inhaled a sharp breath. In just six days, she would be married.

Maribel waved a hand toward the table. "Would you care for some coffee?"

"No, thank you," said Paisley. Tyler's arm remained fastened around her shoulders, and Reverend Marshall's and Maribel's eyes remained fixed on her.

"I think we'll gather the children. It's been a long day. Paisley will be staying at Miss Greta's for a few days, and I'll be in touch with you, Reverend, about the wedding."

"The children are in the parlor. I'll retrieve them." Maribel brushed past Paisley on her way to the parlor.

"Hiya, Tyler," said a short, scrawny, brown-haired boy a moment later.

Tyler removed his arm from Paisley's shoulders and reached over and ruffled Albert's hair. "Hello, Albert. Did you miss your big brother?"

"No," said Albert, taking a step backward.

Unaffected by Albert's rejection, Tyler instead moved toward two little girls standing side by side. "And how are my little sisters?"

"We're fine," said the eldest one. The youngest said nothing, only stared blankly ahead.

"Paisley, I'd like you to meet my brother and sisters. This is Albert. He's nine and this is Lucy. She's seven." Tyler reached down and scooped up the youngest girl. But she showed him no emotion and made no effort to clasp her arms around his neck. "And this here is little Mae. She's four."

"Hello, Albert, Lucy, and Mae. It's a pleasure to meet you." Paisley offered a smile, which wasn't reciprocated.

Lucy wrinkled her nose. "Are you going to live with us?"

"Yes, I am."

"Oh." Lucy shrugged and walked over to stand by Maribel.

Mae climbed down from Tyler's arms and skulked near the doorway. Paisley's heart broke for her. What was wrong with Mae? Why was she so distant? Why had she rebuffed Tyler when he'd scooped her up in his arms?

Tyler shifted. "Well, shall we go?"

As they bid farewell to Reverend Marshall and Maribel and proceeded to the wagon, Paisley determined the children soon to be in her care would need more than just love. They would need her prayers.

CHAPTER THIRTEEN

PAISLEY HEARD THE DOOR close as Tyler left the house. She stood still for a moment, taking in her surroundings. The aroma of fresh biscuits permeated the air, and Paisley's stomach growled in response. When was the last time she had eaten?

Then Paisley remembered that Miss Greta had asked about her appetite. She best not ask for anything to eat. Especially not at this late hour.

But there was something she did want to ask. Something that had flitted through her mind on the way from Reverend and Maribel's house. Perhaps if she had more time to court Tyler, she wouldn't feel so uncomfortable about marrying him. After all, six days was hardly enough time to acquaint herself with the man she would pledge to spend the rest of her life with.

If she had a job, she could stay at Miss Greta's while they partook in a lengthier courtship. They could wed in a few months, rather than a few days. She could also ensure ample time to help with the children in the meantime.

If she had a job at Miss Greta's, she could earn her room and board.

Paisley caught a glimpse of the owner in the kitchen scrubbing the dishes from supper. "Miss Greta?"

Miss Greta, a pained look on her face at having been interrupted, turned to face Paisley. "What is it?"

Intimidated and not sure if she should proceed, Paisley glanced at the floor at her worn boots.

"I said, 'what is it', child?' I don't have all day for your lollygaggin' around. Speak up."

"I was wondering if—if you had any employment available." There. She'd said it. Her question would serve two purposes: her ability to stay longer at Miss Greta's while she extended the courtship and an alternative plan in case Tyler decided he didn't want to marry her. After all, hadn't he hesitated when Paisley had asked if he was a man of his word?

Miss Greta assumed a combative pose, her hands positioned firmly on her wide hips and her lips pressed in a thin, straight line, making them nearly disappear altogether. "Now, do I look like I need help runnin' this place?"

"No, ma'am, not at all. I was just inquiring." Was Miss Greta always this disagreeable? If so, what a blessing the woman didn't have any employment available.

"So why would you be seeking employment here? From what I've heard, Tyler has a nice farm. Besides, if he's to be your man, you won't be needin' any other employment. Your hands will be more than full with those rambunctious young'uns."

Her man? There was more to the story than what Miss Greta knew. "I was just inquiring."

Miss Greta scrutinized Paisley, and her eyes narrowed into slits. "You're not thinkin' of goin' back on your word about the weddin' now, are you? I don't agree none with what that boy did when he ran off and left his parents here with no help to run that farm, but I don't want to see you do something that'll cause him grief."

"I was just asking. That's all." Paisley wished she could sink beneath the floorboards of the quaint home in an attempt to disappear from Miss Greta's probing gaze. Was the woman always this impudent?

"My advice? You gotta hang on to true love when you have it, not that I'm about to give you no free advice." Miss Greta paused and shook her head. "You know, I was in love once. Matter of fact, he was the love of my life. Ran off and got hisself killed in the war. Just was so sure his callin' was to go and fight. Well, that was the end of him. Now look at me. I'm fifty-five-and-a-half years old and running a boarding-house." Miss Greta appeared wistful for a moment, and Paisley wondered if she should hug her and offer condolences. But Miss Greta's countenance abruptly changed. "If you got yourself a good one, don't let him get away," she snapped. "And like I said, I don't agree none with what Tyler done, but he's a good man." She cleared her throat. "Now I have work to do, work that I'm quite capable of doing all by my lonesome. Your room is right around the corner on the right. Now, if you'll excuse me."

"Yes, of course." Feeling uncomfortable, Paisley walked toward the direction of her room. When she found it, she stood gazing at the ornate surroundings. The room boasted a bed covered with a log cabin quilt, a rocking chair in the corner, and a bureau with a mirror.

Paisley stood with her back to the bed and allowed herself to fall backward onto the warm quilt. She feared she might like to stay here forever.

Gazing up at the ceiling, she thought of her old room at home. It wasn't half as fancy, but it had contained her bed, a quilt made by Grandmama, and a trunk that held Paisley's meager wardrobe.

Paisley's heart ached as the homesickness settled in and the "if-onlys" consumed her mind. Would she recover from losing so much?

She thought of Mae. What had she lost in her life that had caused her to be so unresponsive? She thought of Papa's aloofness and how she and Mama struggled to comprehend the pronounced and unexpected change in his personality.

Paisley recalled one particular time when she situated a blanket around Papa's shoulders. He'd lost some weight due to his lack of interest in food and was cold, even in the warmer spring temperatures. His gaunt cheekbones were more pronounced, and he stared vacantly past her somewhere into the distance as she attempted to talk with him.

After saying nothing for some time, Papa finally spoke. Not in response to her question, but an inquiry of his own. "Can you tell Lyndon it's time for supper?" he asked.

The first few times Papa mentioned his brother, Lyndon, Mama had gently reminded him that Lyndon had passed away over ten years ago. But Mama and Paisley both soon realized that such an explanation was futile.

A tear slid down Paisley's cheek and onto the quilt. She and Mama had tried to understand Papa's illness. They'd prayed and prayed and then prayed some more for healing and for answers. But neither came. Why hadn't God answered their prayers?

More than once, Paisley witnessed Mama holding Papa's hand and sobbing and begging him to come back to her. Watching her mother's pain at losing the man she loved was almost more than Paisley could bear. She and Mama had clung to each other, mourning the loss of a man they once knew.

Paisley slid beneath the quilt and tugged it to her chin. A constant flow of tears slid down her face. She trembled as the sobs came.

Mama, I miss you so much. You were so sweet and kind and always so giving of yourself. It was one thing to lose Papa, but to lose you too? Lord, how could You have allowed this?

It was a question she asked the Lord often in the days since Papa's illness and her parents' subsequent deaths in the unforeseen flood that destroyed a significant area of Pringle. The heavy rains. The overflowing river on their property just beyond the barn. The loss of the lives of several townsfolk and livestock. The destruction of homes. How was it that she had survived when so many others had perished?

If Mama had survived, life would be manageable. Paisley wouldn't have to travel this road of life all alone.

Paisley dabbed at her nose with a handkerchief she found on the bureau beside the bed and attempted to conceal her choked sobs. It wouldn't do for Miss Greta or the other guests to hear her.

She didn't have so much as a tintype of her parents. Only a memory she knew would fade with time. That frightened her. Paisley always wanted to remember the smiles on her parents' faces. The joy of being blessed by God having chosen them as her parents. Mama's gray hair that curled at the ends when she let it down from her bun and her contagious laughter. Papa's peppered whiskers and eyes that once lit with excitement. They'd been in their late forties when they adopted Paisley. Mama always said each and every baby the Lord created was a miracle, but Paisley was a double miracle because the Lord had chosen her to be theirs after they'd lost three of their babies before they'd had a chance to be born.

Lord, please comfort me. Give me peace as I endeavor to go on without the ones who meant so much to me.

While she didn't understand the Lord's ways, she did know He was faithful. She reached for her coin purse and removed Papa's handwritten scripture verse from Habakkuk 3:17-19. Through blurred vision, Paisley read the words she had long ago memorized and allowed them to provide balm to her soul.

"Although the fig tree shall not blossom, neither shall fruit be in the vines; the labour of the olive shall fail, and the fields shall yield no meat; the flock shall be cut off from the fold, and there shall be no herd in the stalls: Yet I will rejoice in the Lord, I will joy in the God of my salvation. The Lord God is my strength, and he will make my feet like hinds' feet, and he will make me to walk upon mine high places."

After a few minutes, peace enveloped her. The Lord *was* faithful, even though she doubted it several times after the loss of her family. He *would* see her through the pain.

Paisley knew without hesitation what she must do. She would marry Tyler Shepherdson if only for little Mae. Mae needed a mother just as Paisley had needed her ma. While Lucy and Albert tugged at her heart too, it was Mae who cemented Paisley's decision to take a chance and marry a man she'd just met.

CHAPTER FOURTEEN

TYLER CLASPED HIS HANDS behind his head and stared into the darkness. He hadn't been sure how the reverend and Maribel would take the news of his pending marriage. They hadn't even known he was courting, not that he was. But then, the people of Horizon—including the reverend and his wife—knew very little about him since he'd returned from his four-year hiatus.

In the short time since he'd been back in Horizon after his parents' deaths, Tyler hadn't taken much time to reacquaint himself with the townsfolk. He figured that would come later. When he'd overheard some folks talking about the delivery job, he'd offered to take it without a second thought. It had done his mind good to get away and mull things over, even if only for a short time.

He hadn't banked on finding a wife in those days away from Horizon. It had all happened so fast. But Tyler felt confident that his choice would work for the best.

When Tyler carried Mae into the house from the wagon, he had watched her for a moment while she slept. More at peace than she'd ever been while awake, Tyler prayed that Mae would someday know that peace during waking hours.

No wonder Ma and Pa had fallen in love with her the second they saw her off the orphan train in Cornwall. Delicate in features, fragile in strength, and wordless when it came to conversation, Mae needed someone to care for her. Tyler could imagine Ma allowing her gaze to settle upon Mae. If only Ma had been able to raise the girl to adulthood.

If Ma and Pa couldn't raise them, it would have been far better for someone like the reverend and his wife to raise the children. Or even someone else in Horizon. But there was no one else and Tyler had made a promise to Ma, a promise he intended to keep, no matter how difficult the challenge.

The memory of Ma on her deathbed would be forever embedded in his mind. Her hand limp in his. How many times had she held his hand during the night when he was little and had nightmares about snakes falling from trees? Many a night for sure. And the times Ma had held his hand while he'd been sick and the time he broke his arm when he was four and fell from the loft in the barn. He'd begged Ma not to leave his side. She had remained there for as long as he'd needed her.

And how she begged for him not to leave her side. And Ma begged for something more.

"Tyler, promise me you'll raise Albert, Lucy, and Mae." Her *weak voice was barely audible, and Tyler had to lean forward just to hear her. "Promise me."*

He'd promised. Really promised. Not an empty pledge, but a true promise.

Emotion welled in his heart. He'd cried that day over the loss of both of his parents. Over regrets. Over guilt. Over disappointing them and disappointing the Lord.

He vowed to keep his promise to Ma, no matter what it took. He would raise Albert, Lucy, and Mae the best he could. While he was ill-equipped at being a father and the burdens of caring for his new family seemed all too much, he would succeed by the grace of God.

His thoughts then turned to Paisley. Would she fulfill her agreement to proceed with the marriage? Would she be a suitable mother for the children? Would she love and care for them the way Ma had?

He took a deep breath. Turning over to the Lord small things, big things, and everything in between was still so new. *Lord, I've learned so much about You in the past weeks. I know You hear every prayer, least that's what Reverend Marshall says. So I pray for Your hand in raising these young'uns. And, Lord, I pray I'm doing the right thing in asking Paisley to marry me.*

Chapter Fifteen

PAISLEY AWOKE THE NEXT morning to the sound of birds chirping outside her window and the aroma of bacon wafting through the air. When was the last time she'd felt as content as she did this very moment? She couldn't recall.

Her contentment was short-lived, however, when she heard the clanging of a loud bell and Miss Greta's irritable voice. "Breakfast!"

Paisley flung herself from the bed, nearly tripping over the twisted quilt around her ankles. Fortunately, she owned only one dress and she was wearing it, so no change was necessary. However, she would have much preferred a bath before beginning her day, especially after the long trip yesterday.

"I said, 'breakfast!'" Miss Greta yelled again.

Paisley ran the brush she'd grabbed from the top of the bureau through her matted hair. Yes, a bath was certainly in order. But it would have to wait if she planned on eating any breakfast today.

Unlocking the door, Paisley stepped out into the hall. She heard the voices of the other boarders, and the smell of bacon grew stronger. Her stomach rumbled in response.

"It's about time you joined us for breakfast," snarled Miss Greta. "Let it be known that if you don't make it to the table on time, the breakfast'll be gone."

"Yes, ma'am." Paisley pulled out a chair and sat down. The other boarders didn't acknowledge her but instead focused on the food before them. Paisley reached for a slice of bacon and a clump of scrambled eggs from the platter. Her mouth watered. She said grace then took a bite of her food, savoring every bite.

A knock at the door interrupted the meal. Miss Greta excused herself and returned a moment later. "Paisley, your betrothed is here to see you."

Paisley glanced up to see Tyler and his three siblings. "Good morning, Paisley."

"Good morning."

"When you gonna start buildin' that outhouse, Tyler?" Miss Greta asked, her mouth full of scrambled eggs.

"Soon, Miss Greta, soon."

"How 'bout you fix on doin' it today? After all, your betrothed here has already stayed a night and she's already showin' me her healthy appetite."

"Yes, Miss Greta, I aim to start as soon as possible." Tyler had removed his hat and stood facing Miss Greta. A tuft of dark wavy hair stood on end as if he, too, had had little time to groom himself before beginning his day. "I came today to see if Paisley would care to join us for a tour of the farm."

The other three boarders and Miss Greta followed the conversation with a turn of their heads from Tyler to Paisley. Heat crept up her cheeks.

"Can't see as how you're gonna build me no outhouse if you're off gallivanting around the farm. She'll see it soon enough since she's gonna be livin' there." Miss Greta dabbed at her face with a cloth napkin.

"Would it be all right if I took Paisley to the farm first and then commenced to building your outhouse? I'd be much obliged."

The boarders looked from Tyler to Miss Greta as if in anticipation for her answer.

"Don't care none if you're obliged or not, Tyler. A promise is a promise, and you done promised to build me a new outhouse. Ain't no way, no how, I'm waitin' until you're done traipsin' all over God's Creation."

"Yes, ma'am. I'll get to building the outhouse right away."

Paisley attempted to hide her disappointment. How nice it would have been to take a tour of the farm—her new home—with the man she was to marry. She avoided the temptation to show her frustration with the arduous Miss Greta.

Would she and Tyler be able to spend any time together before they said their wedding vows?

Tyler led the children outside. The last thing he wanted was to start construction on Miss Greta's new outhouse. Not because he minded the work, because he didn't. However, if he'd wanted to work, he would have stayed on the farm today and tended to the fields. And what was he to do with the children? Pass them off to Paisley? Miss Greta was feistier than a squawking chicken. But what could he do?

"Why do we have to stay here?" Albert moaned. He shoved his hands in his trouser pockets. "It ain't fair."

"It's not fair," Tyler corrected.

"No, it ain't. Not one bit," added Lucy.

Tyler gave up on correcting Lucy. He just didn't have the patience to continually correct Albert and Lucy on their improper grammar. Perhaps Paisley would have more luck. If only he'd been able to show her the farm and spend time with her today. How was Tyler supposed to know if he'd made the right decision in asking for her hand in marriage if their time together was severely limited?

"Now, I have work to do. I want you children to behave, and Albert and Lucy, you both are to take care of Mae."

"We *always* have to take care of Mae," Lucy muttered.

"That's right. Big brothers and sisters are supposed to take care of younger brothers and sisters," said Tyler. "Albert, I will be needing your help on the outhouse once I get everything situated." He examined the pieces of lumber he'd unloaded yesterday. It would be beneficial to teach Albert about construction, just as Pa had taught him.

About ten minutes later, Tyler looked up to catch sight of Paisley walking toward him. She'd pulled her hair into a long braid. She was prettier than he'd remembered from yesterday. *It's not nice to stare, Tyler*, he reprimanded himself.

"Sorry about Miss Greta," Tyler said as Paisley approached. Was she disappointed as well that he couldn't show her their home?

"She certainly has a mind of her own."

"That she does. But I guess a promise is a promise. Say, would you mind taking care of the children while I start working on this project? It should go fairly quickly once I get started."

Paisley's smile appeared forced. "Yes, of course."

"Much obliged." Tyler picked up his hammer. "Did you sleep well?"

"I did. It was nice to be in a comfortable room after..."

"After the room in Ingleville?"

"Exactly." This time her smile was genuine, and Tyler returned it. If things continued as they were today, being a married man would be effortless.

"Glad you found your accommodations satisfactory."

Paisley nodded at him, and he found himself nodding back. They stared at each other in silence.

"Uh, well, I reckon I should get to work here." What else could he say? This might possibly be the first time in his life that he'd been rendered wordless.

"Yes, yes, of course."

Paisley turned toward the children. "Shall we walk into town?"

Lucy scrunched up her nose. "Do we have to?"

Tyler shook his head. Marrying him might not be a hardship, but mothering those children just might make Paisley run away and never look back.

When Paisley left Tyler, he was whistling "Oh! Susanna" and digging a hole. With the moping Mae and the constant moaning and bickering between Albert and Lucy, Paisley would have much preferred to be building the outhouse herself rather than assuming motherhood duty.

Paisley reached for Mae's hand, but the little girl yanked it away and slid her hand behind her back. "Lucy, will you please hold Mae's hand?" Paisley asked. The last thing she needed was to lose one of the children on her first outing with them. That would never do.

Lucy shook her head and stuck her chin in the air. "She don't like nobody holding her hand."

Paisley resisted the urge to correct Lucy's grammar. Something told her it would be futile. "I just don't want her to get lost."

"Stay with us, Mae," Albert ordered, kicking up a cloud of dust with the tip of his worn boot.

Mae said nothing, not even a nod of her head gave proof that she'd heard a word. Paisley offered a quick prayer heavenward for the little girl who was the main reason for Paisley's acceptance of Tyler's marriage proposal.

CHAPTER SIXTEEN

THE POUNDING OF HOOVES sounded like a rush of thunder. Townsfolk in the street hastily jumped to safety on the boardwalk.

Paisley averted her attention from the children who shuffled along behind her and instead fixed her gaze in the direction of the commotion.

A bright red wagon with yellow wheels slowed to a stop beside her. A well-dressed gentleman hopped from the seat. "Hello, ladies and gents!" The man removed his black top hat to expose white-blond hair. He flashed a charming smile. "It is my delight to enter the town of..." the man paused as if to recall where he was, then continued. "The town of Horizon, Idaho!"

A crowd had gathered and several people cheered. Voices clamored in response.

"Did you hear how he said the name of our town?"

"What a privilege he chose to visit Horizon!"

"We've never hosted the likes of a famous person in our town."

Paisley's eyes drifted from the exuberant man to his wagon. Printed in bold, fancy writing on the side were the words "Lamar Labelle's Fine Novelties." To the left of the words toward the top of the wagon was a small glass window with a tasteful yellow curtain.

She'd never seen such a thing in all her life.

The crowd hushed, and all eyes fixated on the gentleman from the wagon. "I am Lamar Labelle. I'm sure many of you have heard of me."

Paisley's heart pounded. She'd never before been in the presence of someone famous.

She scanned the crowd. Many people nodded as if they'd heard of Mr. Labelle.

"Children, come closer and listen to this," she whispered to Albert, Lucy, and Mae. Paisley put her arm around Mae, who ducked away.

"I have traveled far and wide across this great country and nearly all of her territories with my first-rate wares. It is your lucky day because you fine folks of Horizon have the opportunity of a lifetime to purchase some of these wares at astonishing prices." Lamar smiled a grin wider than the expanse of the sky, revealing white, shiny, and perfectly straight teeth.

He was a handsome man, really, and Paisley could see that already he had intrigued the crowd. Many had lined up in front of Lamar's wagon to purchase items.

"What type of items do you have?" someone asked.

"You'll never believe the variety of novelties I carry in my wagon of wares. I have fine soaps, which until now have only been used by the wealthy in New York City. I have buttons all the way from Europe, beads made by the Indians, and fabric not available anywhere in the Idaho Territory or surrounding states and territories. Men, why not purchase your wife a lovely hat that she will desire to wear to more than just church on Sundays?"

At Lamar's invitation, three men stepped forward with coins in their hands.

"And lest you think my goods are pricey, let me reassure you that you won't find a better deal anywhere else for the quality of items I sell." Lamar's eyes traveled from person to person, and he personally handed a handsome smile to each one.

Paisley stood in line. Even if she couldn't buy anything, she had to see what wares Lamar Labelle hid behind the walls of his wagon. People pushed and shoved and a fight nearly broke out, all in anticipation of responding to Lamar's invitation.

Lamar opened a door on the side of the wagon, and the townsfolk jostled their way to the front for a gander inside. "Now, now, friends," announced Lamar. "Let's not be hasty. I'll be here until tomorrow, so there's no rush. Kindly allow your fellow citizen a glance inside the wagon. There's enough time for everyone to have a peek. And don't forget, this is the opportune time to purchase something special for your sweetheart or pick out a Christmas gift for a loved one. While it's only June, Christmas comes quickly and I dare say you'll want to be prepared."

Sometime later, the crowd had settled somewhat. "Would you children care to see what's inside the wagon?" Paisley asked.

"Reckon we would," said Albert, his eyes the size of the big round platter on Miss Greta's breakfast table.

"Let's step closer then," Paisley suggested. The pushing and shoving of the crowd had alleviated, and only a few people remained to catch their first glance inside Lamar Labelle's fabulous wagon.

Paisley took her turn at the wagon door. "What lovely lady do we have here?" Lamar greeted her, ignoring the children behind her.

"I'm Paisley Abbott."

"Paisley, what a resplendent name!" Lamar took her hand in his. "I saw you from afar when I first entered the town of Horizon. Did you notice I stopped right by where you stood?"

The warmth crept up her face. She *had* noticed.

"How could I not stop my wagon of wares next to the most exquisite woman my eyes have ever gazed upon? It is a pleasure to make your acquaintance."

Paisley nodded. The young and dapper Lamar Labelle was even more charming up close than he had been from the boardwalk.

The children inspected the outside of Lamar's wagon.

"Would you like to see some of the fine wares I have inside the wagon?"

"Yes, please." She noticed him staring at her. With wide-set pale brown eyes, he was tall, thin, and wearing impeccable clothing, despite what must have been a dusty ride.

"Very well." Lamar waved a hand toward the inside of the wagon. "I have anything a heart could desire from notions to fabric; from beeswax to leather goods. You name it, I likely have it."

"You made mention that you've traveled all over the country."

"I have. I've been to most territories as well. I'm a well-traveled man. But none of those trips could compare to the voyage I made with my parents as a young child from the French countryside to the United States."

"You're from France?" Paisley had never known anyone from France.

"Yes. My parents were, bless their souls, both French. They couldn't wait to step foot on the shores of this great country. It was my father who taught me the respectable art of selling, and I carry on his legacy to this day."

"It's nice to meet you, Mr. Labelle."

"Please, do call me Lamar."

"Lamar."

"Good. Now, what would you like to purchase today?"

Paisley's gaze rested on his expensive black leather shoes. "I'm just perusing at the present time."

"Ah, my fine lady. No shame in that. Many folks survey the wares two or three times before determining just how much they need that particular item. What about this?" Lamar retrieved a jeweled brooch from one of the shelves in the wagon. "This is the only thing that can even begin to compare with your beauty." Lamar rolled it across his fingers. "It's real gold, you know."

"Really?"

"Yes. I purchased it from a dealer in Boston. It didn't come cheaply." Lamar sighed. "But alas, I knew I would save it for just the right person. That person is you." Lamar offered the brooch to Paisley.

"Thank you, but I can't purchase it at this time."

"No need to make a purchase. I'm giving it to you."

Paisley's mouth dropped open. "But how can you afford to just give expensive items away?"

"My dear lady, be assured I don't just give items away. You are the only one I have chosen to give a special gift to. It's your beauty—the way your eyes shimmer in the sunlight—that has persuaded me to request the honor of gifting this brooch to you."

Paisley knew her face bore the color of a bright red tomato. "Thank you, Lamar, but I couldn't. I wouldn't feel right taking it from you."

"All right then." Lamar returned the trinket to its place on the shelf. "Then say you'll join me for supper tonight at that restaurant I saw when I entered town."

Paisley covered her mouth with her hand. "Lamar, I am honored, but I am a betrothed woman."

Lamar closed his eyes and shook his head. "Sadness shall follow me all the way to the next town upon hearing your declaration that your heart belongs to another." He took her hand and held it in his. He then opened his eyes and again fixed his gaze on her. He turned her hand over and pressed his lips to it. "Your soon-to-be-husband is a lucky man."

His kiss and gaze made her uncomfortable. She averted her glance from him and attempted to pull her hand from his, but Lamar held firm. His charming façade reminded her of the first time she'd met Ivan.

"Paisley?"

Paisley turned to see Tyler walking toward them. "Hello, Tyler." Paisley yanked her hand from Lamar's grasp.

"Well, well. You must be this lovely woman's soon-to-be-husband." Lamar offered his hand to shake Tyler's.

"Tyler Shepherdson."

"Lamar Labelle."

"I was desiring to present your betrothed with a small gift."

"We won't be able to pay you for your kindness," Tyler said. Paisley figured he attempted to sound polite, but she could hear the agitation in Tyler's voice.

"No worries at all. It's not every day I glance upon such a lovely woman as your betrothed. A lucky man you are, my friend. Had Miss Abbott not already been spoken for, I might have expressed my desire to court her myself."

The warmth in Paisley's face and neck grew hotter. Lamar didn't even know her. Why would he express desire to court her, and boldly in front of her betrothed no less? *But you barely know Tyler and you've agreed to marry him.*

Yes, but that's different. Tyler seems more ordinary. Lamar likely says that line to every woman he meets in each town he visits.

Yes, but wouldn't you have preferred to marry someone like Lamar and travel the world? Instead you'll be stuck in Horizon for the rest of your life with three disagreeable children and with a man you barely know. Don't you wonder what life with someone like Lamar would be like?

Paisley's inner debate was interrupted by Tyler's words to Lamar. "Well, she is spoken for and we'll have to decline your gift, but thank you for your generosity."

Tyler cupped her elbow and turned Paisley away from the gawking Lamar. "Come, children."

Paisley walked with Tyler in silence back to Miss Greta's house. At one time, she might have been interested in someone like Lamar Labelle and his charming ways. While she'd been intrigued by the goods inside the fancy wagon and Lamar's willingness to give her an expensive gift, Paisley would choose Tyler any day of the week.

Tyler had needed some more supplies from the mercantile when he'd stumbled across Paisley and the children taking a gander at Lamar's wagon. And then he'd seen Lamar take Paisley's hand and kiss it. That's when an emotion Tyler had never known existed within himself before had taken over.

An emotion called jealousy.

As he led Paisley back to Miss Greta's, he thought of how little he had to offer her. Yes, he had a farm and by the Lord's grace would hopefully be able to make just enough to pay the bills and support a family, but he couldn't offer her a life of adventure like Lamar Labelle could. And he wasn't suave and sophisticated like Lamar. He was a country boy with dirty trousers, a stained button-up shirt, worn cowboy hat, and calloused hands. Why did he think he could offer her much at all? His parents' humble home and three troubled and disobedient children could hardly compare with the chance to travel the countryside hawking wares and meeting new people at every corner.

But Tyler's jealousy of Lamar's brazen affection for Paisley was rivaled by his jealousy of something else. Lamar led a life of excitement—the kind of life Tyler had led before returning to Horizon. He visited places most people only dreamed of, rather than waking up to the same hard work on the farm that Tyler now faced. In short, Lamar lived the kind of life Tyler had imagined himself living—the kind of life Tyler had lived—before he realized what was really important in life.

CHAPTER SEVENTEEN

THAT EVENING, PAISLEY AND Tyler met at Reverend Marshall and Maribel's house for supper. Tyler hadn't spoken much on their return from town to Miss Greta's except to mention the invitation. Paisley wondered if he was given to moodiness.

Maribel greeted them at the door. "It's so nice to see you again. Do come in and find a place at the table. Supper is nearly ready."

Paisley entered the home, followed by the three children, and finally, Tyler.

Tyler removed his hat and placed it on the hook by the door, then took a seat directly across from her. For the first time as she sat across from him, Paisley saw the man she was about to marry—really saw him. Noticed his handsome, clean-shaven, and rugged appearance, his strong shoulders, and the small scar below his left eye. His gaze caught hers, and she hastily looked away and fiddled with a button on her dress.

"Do tell how you two met," said Maribel, after Reverend Marshall said grace.

"Perhaps Paisley should tell the story," suggested Tyler, a glint in his eyes.

Paisley attempted to gather herself from the embarrassing moment just seconds before and now Tyler suggested she share how they met? Her mouth opened, but she uttered no words. What could she say? That she and Tyler met because she had hitched a ride in his wagon? That they had known each other only a few days? She glanced from Maribel, to the reverend, then to Tyler.

"We met in a surprising way," Paisley heard herself say.

Reverend Marshall passed the plate of potatoes. "Sounds intriguing."

Did the reverend expect Paisley to elaborate? "We met near Cornwall. In a—in a—surprising way." Was her stuttering and repetition obvious?

"My, but you have quite a knack for keeping us in suspense. Do tell!" Maribel leaned forward to catch every word. "I have always loved to hear how other couples met. The reverend and I met in such a common way at a barn dance. So, please, Paisley, do go on."

Tyler smirked and his eyes crinkled at the corners. Apparently his moodiness from earlier had been replaced by a more cheerful disposition.

"Well, we…" Paisley looked from Albert, to Lucy, and then to Mae. This would be an opportune time for one of them to begin making a menace of themselves. But instead, they sat quietly consuming the delicious meal Maribel had prepared. "Tyler really should be the one to tell you."

Tyler shifted in his chair. "Really, Paisley, I couldn't take such a grand opportunity from you, my dear. You go ahead and tell the reverend and Maribel how we met."

My dear? Paisley resisted the urge to purse her lips at his response.

Maribel made a hand motion for Paisley to continue. Was her floundering, what she was sure was a reddened face, and her lack of words causing Maribel and the reverend to be suspicious? "You see, Tyler is such a kind gentleman. I had a situation I'd found myself in, and he quickly came to my aid. Taken so was I by his benevolence that he and I..." Paisley held a hand to her heart for dramatic flair. What was it she'd read that time in a book by that famous woman author who penned romance novels? "So taken was I by his benevolence that I knew at once he would be the man I would marry."

"Oh! How romantic!" Maribel exclaimed, closing her eyes as if to envision the scenario Paisley described. "I love the way the Lord brings people together. And yes, Tyler does have a benevolent heart."

Maribel was almost off the edge of her seat in anticipation. "And how long have you courted?"

Paisley gasped. She refused to lie, although the temptation did arise. "We..."

"Maribel, my darling, allow the girl to eat some supper before you interrogate her," chuckled Reverend Marshall. "There'll be plenty of time for questions later."

"Oh, gracious, yes. I'm so sorry, Paisley. Do eat before your food gets cold." Maribel stared at Paisley, as if willing with her eyes for Paisley to elaborate.

Everyone continued to eat their meal and for the moment, Paisley figured the secret she shared with Tyler was safe.

After the supper dishes had been cleared, Maribel invited the adults to the parlor while the children played on the floor with some marbles Maribel found packed away from when her children were youngsters. "I'll make all attempts not to inquire again as to the fascinating way you both met, but I would like to hear more."

Paisley smiled a weak smile in response to Maribel's statement. "Tyler is the better storyteller."

Tyler arched an eyebrow at her. Good. Now it was his time to squirm.

Tyler ignored Paisley's cursory glance in his direction. If she thought she could make him answer what could easily be deemed an unanswerable question, she was mistaken. Not that the question was completely unanswerable—but Tyler had his pride and he was sure Paisley did too. Besides, he respected Maribel and Reverend Marshall far too much to fabricate some type of story to appease Maribel's curiosity.

"Thank you, sir, for agreeing to perform the ceremony on Tuesday as we'd like to be married as soon as possible. Do you have a time in mind?"

Reverend Marshall stroked his short brownish-gray beard. "How about two o'clock in the afternoon?"

Maribel covered her mouth with a delicate, wrinkled hand. "My, but isn't this all so romantic? Remember how you wanted to get married so soon after we started courting, Marshall? Of course, Pa encouraged us to extend our courtship, but in the end, we married only four months to the day from the day we met. A short courtship for sure, but after thirty years of marriage, I would say it's worked out well. And I am quite fond of you, Marshall."

Reverend Marshall grinned at Maribel. "And I am quite fond of you as well." He and Maribel held each other's gaze for several seconds.

Tyler gulped. If only Maribel knew just how short a courtship could be—or a lack of a courtship altogether—she'd be aghast.

Maribel emitted a dainty laugh. "I just love weddings. When Marshall decided to be in the ministry and shepherd God's flock, I knew right away I would have two favorite parts— when someone comes to Christ is my very favorite—followed by weddings."

Tyler hadn't been sure how the reverend and Maribel would take the news of his recent engagement, but from all appearances, they, especially Maribel, were taking it quite well. Especially since neither had known he had even entered into a courtship just a few days ago. Given the fact that the people of Horizon knew very little about him since he'd returned, he'd half expected more questions.

He heaved an inward sigh that they hadn't inquired as to more about Paisley and her background. Clearly Maribel exhibited a fondness for things of the romantic variety, things Tyler cared to know nothing about. Thankfully the inquisition into their courtship ceased.

"Two o'clock next Tuesday works fine, but this is quite soon, Tyler. Perhaps you'd like to wait a week or so."

"Tuesday at two o'clock suits me. Does that work for you, Paisley?"

Tyler couldn't decipher her expression, but he did notice she paused before speaking. Was she already having second thoughts about their agreement? He hoped not.

For more than one reason.

Or was she thinking about Lamar and how she'd rather court him?

Paisley finally answered with a meek "Next Tuesday at two o'clock is fine."

Reverend Marshall nodded. "Very well then. Next Tuesday at two o'clock it is."

Maribel's smile—the smile that drew everyone she met to her—broadened. "Have you already been to the mercantile to retrieve a wedding ring?"

Tyler felt a case of indigestion welling in his stomach. A wedding ring? No, he hadn't given any thought to that. For an occasion that lasted mere minutes, there seemed to be so much to remember. Tyler wasn't much of a planner and preferred the spontaneity of things. What if he forgot something—something important? His nerves felt a bit rattled. "Uh, I plan on doing that soon."

Paisley caught his eye. Were her nerves rattled as well?

Maribel smiled. "I know Tabitha carries a meager variety. If you had more time, you could look through the catalog for just the perfect ring."

"I reckon so."

"Just remember, when you marry, it's a vow forever—through the good, through the bad, and through the times in the middle."

"Yes, ma'am." What was he supposed to say? Tyler hoped his marriage to Paisley would be forever, just as his own parents' marriage had been until their deaths. But the way they were starting off caused him some apprehension.

Maribel's words took Paisley aback. She supposed she and Tyler appeared as any other couple planning a wedding, but they were anything but typical. In three days, they would both say "I do" to a person they knew little about. And as for a marriage vow being forever? Paisley knew that remained to be seen. Was Tyler who he said he was? Would he honor those vows? Self- doubt filled Paisley's mind. Would she be able to honor those vows as well? Should she even marry him after knowing him only a matter of days?

In many ways, she wished they didn't have to rush the wedding but instead take time for courtship. That's what wisdom would dictate. But she knew he needed a mother for the children. Mae's face flashed in her mind. How the tiny girl needed a mother!

Besides, Paisley couldn't very well stay at Miss Greta's forever, especially knowing that the price to board there wouldn't be cheap.

So yes, Tyler was correct. Necessity deemed expediency.

Maribel reached for Paisley's hands. "It's all settled then. In a few short days, you'll be Mrs. Paisley Shepherdson."

Mrs. Paisley Shepherdson.

Just what kind of life would the new name bring?

Chapter Eighteen

Paisley appreciated Tyler's invitation to tour the farm. She'd wondered when he would ask her once again to peruse the place she would call home in less than a week.

On the way to the Shepherdson farm, Tyler spoke with pride in his voice as he told her about the farm and the crops he tended that his pa recently planted. He told of his new horse, a lovely black quarter horse mare Lucy named Shadow.

Seeing his passion for the home she would soon share with him helped her to temporarily disregard the constant squabbling between Lucy and Albert and Mae's melancholy expression as she crouched in the back of the wagon.

Acres and acres of farmland and the view of the snow-capped mountains provided a scene like none she'd ever seen.

"I think you'll like the house. Ma had a way of decorating that many women in town praised her for. It's not a big house, but it's fine all the same, and you're welcome to change what you'd like and do as you see fit."

For the first time since Paisley had accepted Tyler's proposal, hope filled her heart. She could decorate the home as she saw fit? Make it their own? The thought brought back memories of adorning Mama and Papa's home with the meager belongings they owned. Each week, Paisley would rearrange the few knickknacks and personal belongings along the mantle and rearrange the family Bible and other important possessions on the rustic corner of the triangular-shaped table near the fireplace. Such minor changes brought about major results.

The only thing that truly alarmed her was the fact that she could not cook. Once she and Tyler were married, he would expect a warm meal on the table each night for supper, not to mention two other daily meals. Paisley swallowed hard. She had to learn how to prepare meals before she became a wife. But how? She'd attempted to watch Miss Greta prepare food in the kitchen, only to be rebuked and sent on her way. And Paisley didn't yet feel comfortable asking for Maribel's assistance.

"Well, here we are," Tyler said, interrupting Paisley's concern over cooking meals.

The long dirt road meandered through expansive green fields toward a humble two-story home with a porch in need of repair. A large oak tree stood nearby with branches that seemed to embrace the house in a refuge-like fold. A garden overgrown with weeds had been planted not far from the house, and a barn stood nearby.

"What do you think?" Tyler asked as he assisted Paisley from the wagon.

"It's nice."

"After my parents became ill, things deteriorated, and I've been slowly making repairs, but it's taken longer than I'd like."

They stood, both facing the house, and for a moment, Paisley pretended theirs was a courtship of normalcy. A courtship like the ones she'd read about in the books and had desired to someday have.

On such a day, what could possibly go wrong?

For the first time since he could remember, Tyler had appreciation for all the toil his parents had done to provide this home for him. Ashamed that he had taken it for granted before, he longed only for Ma and Pa to be here with him now. He also wished for a marriage that would make them proud. Last night, Tyler prayed that Paisley would be able to assist him in raising the children in a proper and godly way. He had no ability to do so on his own and didn't even know where to start.

Paisley seemed to like the farm, and Tyler's confidence had taken a turn for the better because of it. He'd seen the way her pretty face lit up when he mentioned she could decorate the inside of the house as she saw fit. "I noticed there was a new stove down at the mercantile. I'll start saving to purchase it. I hear it's much easier to cook on than the one we have now." He grinned. What wife wouldn't want a new stove?

What had been a smile on her face quickly became a frown. Did she not want the new stove in the mercantile? Had Paisley seen better stoves in Cornwall? She'd insinuated she hadn't come from a wealthy family, so surely she hadn't grown accustomed to cooking on a fancy piece of equipment. "I mean, seeing as how women love to cook and all and having a good stove makes it easier for bread and such."

Her sullen expression remained, although it appeared she attempted to smile. "Thank you."

"Ma has had that old stove since I was a young'un. We hauled it all the way here from Missouri. If we get a good crop this year, that new stove will be the first thing I'll purchase."

"I—I appreciate that, Tyler."

"Ma loved to cook. What I wouldn't give for a slice of her bread right now, lathered with freshly churned butter." He continued to grin at her. But why wasn't Paisley returning his smile?

"So, this is the garden?" she asked, pointing to the bleak area just beyond the house.

Taken aback by her change in subject, Tyler looked in the direction of the garden. He'd meant to clean that area up, but he hadn't yet had the time. Ma would be disappointed if she saw the present state of it.

Before he could answer, Lucy interrupted. "There's someone coming down the road."

Sure enough, a man on a horse rode toward the house. Who could be visiting this time of day? As the rider drew closer, Tyler received his answer. His friend, Ike Hulsey—whom Tyler hadn't seen in almost a year—was paying him a visit.

Thankful for the reprieve from the discussion regarding the new stove, Paisley turned to watch as a man dismounted and strutted toward Tyler. "It's good to see you, Shepherdson." The man gave Tyler a playful slug on the shoulder.

"Can't remember the time I last saw you, Ike. How have you been?"

"Been good. Got word that you had returned to Horizon."

"Yes. I haven't been here long yet. Ike, this is my betrothed, Paisley Abbott. Paisley, this is my good friend, Ike Hulsey."

Ike took a step toward Paisley and removed his hat. "Ma'am."

Paisley politely smiled at the thin, wiry man. "Nice to meet you, Ike." Something about his gaze seemed condescending, but Paisley pushed it aside. Surely it was only her imagination.

Tyler nodded toward the children. "And those are my siblings, Albert, Lucy, and Mae. Come on, I'll show you my new mare. She's a real beauty."

Paisley watched as Ike followed Tyler to the barn, her presence all but forgotten. The men took turns nodding and laughing about memories they shared. She inhaled a deep breath of the fresh air, realizing she couldn't wait to explore what would soon be her new home.

Paisley decided to wait on touring the house until Tyler finished his visit with Ike. She didn't feel comfortable about encroaching on his home without him there. Instead, she examined the garden first, keeping within earshot of the children playing nearby.

Then she strolled toward the barn with the intent of heading toward the fields. Such a tour would certainly bring back memories. But she stopped short when she heard the conversation between Tyler and Ike. A conversation pertaining to her.

Paisley tiptoed toward the barn. The door was open, and she could see the backs of Tyler and Ike as they stood facing the new mare. Paisley took a step back and flattened herself against the wall of the barn as she listened.

"So that woman out there is the one you're going to marry?" Ike asked.

"Paisley? Yes."

"I'll admit she's not too hard on the eyes, but a mistake for sure, Tyler."

"Ike..."

"I heard all about it from the townsfolk that you were getting married. That's the first thing I heard when I went to the livery this morning. I don't think you want to do this."

"Do what?"

Ike spit to the side. "Get married, that's what. Why would you want to do that?"

"I need someone to care for the children."

"The children?" Ike's arrogant voice thundered through the barn. "Where did they come from anyway? You told me you were your parents' only child."

Paisley held her breath. It would do no good if Tyler discovered her eavesdropping on his conversation with Ike. Part of her wanted to walk away and not hear what was being said. But an even bigger part convinced her to stay.

"My parents adopted the children, and I promised to care for them after my parents passed."

"Nonsense! You know you won't be happy doing this."

"I have three young'uns to look after, and I need Paisley's help to do that, so we plan to get married."

"So you just leave the life you knew, return to Horizon, find some woman, and decide to get married? Now what kind of life is that?"

"One I hope works out," said Tyler.

"You can't make a man of adventure like yourself settle down. It just doesn't happen. You deserve more than just living here on this farm with a bunch of urchins and a wife. You said you'd never get married. Remember that?"

"I didn't plan on settling down, Ike. It just happened."

"Well, it ain't what your life is about, Tyler. I'm telling you, get out while you can. Take those young'uns back to the orphanage where they belong. They aren't yours anyhow. Secondly, leave the woman behind. If you do someday decide to settle down, there are other women to choose from. Why settle for her? And why settle down with one woman anyhow?"

Paisley awaited Tyler's response, but he said nothing. Was he pondering Ike's suggestion?

Silence ensued and Paisley peered around the corner and watched as Tyler scratched the new mare, Shadow, behind the ears.

"I was gonna wait to tell you, but this seems as good a time as any," Ike continued. "I just heard of a work venture driving cattle. Talk about an adventure and a chance to see some country, especially the southern portion of the United States! I already applied for both of us to get the job. I put our names in and they chose us to start working next week. So, what do you say?"

Paisley's eyes stung. Hadn't she been so thrilled to visit the farm this morning? Hadn't she been so sure nothing could go wrong today? And now Ike had ruined it all with his plans for Tyler's life. Where would that leave Paisley? Where would that leave the children? Could anyone truly be that selfish?

Tyler again said nothing, just continued to pat Shadow, this time on the flank. So long-winded Ike continued. "It's not in your best interests to marry, Tyler. Never has been. And why settle down so soon? You're young. You have plenty of years. Remember all the freedom we had while traveling and working a variety of jobs? We weren't accountable to nobody. You can continue to have that kind of freedom, but only as an unhitched man. The second you say those crazy vows, your freedom slips out the barn door. Is that what you want? Hmm?" Ike jabbed at Tyler's shoulder.

Finally, Tyler spoke. "I did enjoy those times."

"Then come with me and work driving cattle. The young'uns will be fine in the orphanage. That's where they belong anyhow. The woman—she'll recover from you leaving and she'll move on. No harm done. It's something to consider, ain't it?"

Was it her imagination or did Tyler nod in agreement?

Unable to listen to the conversation any longer, Paisley bolted from her hiding place near the door. Would Tyler still go through with the marriage plans after all?

Or did the life Ike proposed seemed like a better option?

CHAPTER NINETEEN

PAISLEY MADE HERSELF SCARCE until after Ike mounted his horse and rode away. She hadn't known what other words were spoken and she didn't care. Or rather, she told herself she didn't care.

Instead, Paisley had first attempted to chat with the children. When that didn't work, she ambled through the fields with a heart heavier than the heaviest wagon wheel.

Tyler remained in the barn, his back to the door when she found him later. "Please take me to Miss Greta's." Tears stung her eyes. The boardinghouse was the closest thing she had to a home right now. But if Tyler didn't want to marry her and instead decided to leave with Ike, she would need an alternative plan for her and the children.

"I was just fixin' to show you around the house and farm."

"Please, Tyler. Just take me to Miss Greta's."

Paisley turned on her heel and began walking toward the road that led to Horizon. If Tyler wouldn't take her to Miss Greta's, she'd walk to town. No matter how long it took.

The tears fell then as questions swarmed her mind.

The rattling of the wagon interrupted her thoughts, and Tyler pulled alongside her.

"Why is Paisley walkin' down the road?" Albert asked.

Tyler put the brake on and climbed from the wagon. He faced her, his eyes searching hers. She wanted to ask him why he hadn't insisted on staying in Horizon and making good on his promise. Why he hadn't disagreed with Ike's assessment of what type of life Tyler should have. But the words wouldn't come.

Finally, Tyler spoke. "Paisley, I'll take you to Miss Greta's."

The only sounds on the way to town were the creaking wagon wheels and the incessant quarreling between Lucy and Albert in the back of the wagon. Paisley chewed on her bottom lip. She would do what it took to make a living for herself in Horizon. Perhaps Maribel or someone else in town would know of some work that could be had. And if Tyler turned his back on the children, she would, somehow, someway, with the help of the Lord, raise them on her own.

"Here we are," Tyler announced as he stopped in front of the now-familiar boardinghouse. "Wait here, children," he said, his voice sounding sterner than he'd intended.

But Paisley neither needed nor wanted his help. She'd already climbed from the wagon herself and was stomping toward Miss Greta's. *What is wrong with her?* Tyler couldn't figure her out. One minute, on the way to the farm earlier today, Paisley had seemed eager to see the place she would soon call home. Her enthusiasm emboldened him and reassured him that he'd made the right choice. Now she stormed toward Miss Greta's. Had those been tears in her eyes?

Lucy stood up in the wagon. "Where's Paisley going?"

"Inside I reckon," Tyler answered, watching as Paisley disappeared through the door of the boardinghouse. She didn't look back once, not at the children, and not at him. What had he done? What had he said? Why had Paisley's mood changed as suddenly as the weather?

He wanted to ask her. He needed to know. "Wait here, children." Without glancing at Albert, Lucy, and Mae, Tyler walked up to the front door of Miss Greta's and knocked.

Miss Greta appeared a moment later, a scowl on her face. "What do you want, Tyler?"

"I was wondering if I could pay Paisley a visit."

"Didn't you just give her a ride here?" Miss Greta narrowed her eyes as though she suspected Tyler wasn't being truthful.

"Yes, ma'am." Why did Miss Greta have to have such a sour disposition?

Miss Greta placed her hands on her wide hips. "And wasn't she just at your farm?"

"Yes, ma'am."

"Then why do you need to spend any more time talking with her? She's probably exhausted from being there the short time she was, with those ill-mannered young'uns and all."

"She might be." What else could he say?

"Come in and I'll see if she wants to speak with you. But just to let you know, I don't plan on being a butler,

Tyler. That's not my job. As the proprietress of this fine establishment, I'm not gonna be doin' anything I don't aim to want to do. 'Sides, I have enough work to do without doin' your biddin'. And are you done with the outhouse yet?"

"Just about." He'd worked diligently for the past couple of days on the project. Pa would be proud of his progress.

"Hmmph," she snorted, "well, see to it that you don't dawdle." Miss Greta left and marched down the hall, calling Paisley's name.

Tyler tapped his boot on the floor, picked at a hangnail on his left thumb, and whistled "Oh! Susanna". Then he heard Paisley's voice.

"I'm sorry, Miss Greta, but please tell Tyler I can't visit with him right now."

Paisley couldn't visit with him right now?

"Did you hear what Paisley said?" Miss Greta asked a second later.

"I did."

"I don't know what's goin' on between the two of you and I don't rightly care, but you need to leave, Tyler. It's clear she needs some time alone."

"Will you try one more time?" Tyler's voice sounded of desperation in his own ears.

"No, I will not try one more time. You heard the lady. Now out with you." Miss Greta swatted him on the shoulder.

Tyler left the house and trudged slowly toward the wagon, glancing back every few seconds with the hope that Paisley would change her mind.

Then he had an idea. Save for the fact that he was a bit intimidated by the overbearing Miss Greta, it might just work.

Tyler sauntered toward the window he believed to be the window of Paisley's room and tapped quietly on it. "Paisley?"

A hand brushed the curtain aside, and Tyler was feeling smug when he realized the hand was not Paisley's. Instead an older woman with thick spectacles and missing teeth glared at him. "Go away!" she mouthed.

"Sorry." Peering about to be sure Miss Greta wasn't watching, Tyler knocked on the next window. No answer. He tried again and still no answer. He knew for certain this had to be Paisley's window since there were only a couple of rooms on the main floor. However, she had chosen to ignore him.

Women, who could figure them out? He kicked at a pebble in the dirt and ambled back to the wagon. That's when he noticed that the children had clearly not obeyed him. Having found a mud puddle from last night's rain, Lucy and Albert had taken it upon themselves to have a mud fight. Mae sat against a nearby tree, face buried in her arms.

For a brief moment, Tyler contemplated Ike's suggestion to go to work with him driving cattle. That had to be preferable to dealing with a frustrating fiancée and three disobedient children.

Much more preferable.

Paisley watched as Tyler and the children left. How had she ever gotten into such a predicament?

She needed to discuss the situation with Tyler. Needed to rectify things. Needed to ascertain whether or not he truly did want to recant their plans. Had she been rash in assuming Tyler's choice for his future? *Their* future?

One thing was certain, she couldn't stay here. Miss Greta hovered about like a mother hen, although not in a kind and compassionate way.

But where could she go? Maribel's house? No. Paisley needed to keep this matter to herself. No sense in confiding in a woman she'd just met, even if that woman was the reverend's wife.

Paisley hadn't been to the mercantile yet. She could go there and look around. Maybe check out the fabric in case she could someday afford some calico for a new dress.

She walked to the bureau and stared at herself in the mirror. Tear streaks, mixed with dirt from the dusty road, lined her cheeks. A swift brushing of the tassel of her braid and her hair would at least make her presentable.

Paisley splashed her face with water from the washbasin. Yes, she would head to the mercantile and take her mind off this afternoon. More importantly, she needed to do one other thing.

Kneeling beside the bed, Paisley prayed everything would all work out according to the Lord's plans.

CHAPTER TWENTY

PAISLEY SCANNED THE ROWS of goods lining the walls of the mercantile. Kerosene lamps, food items, and bolts of fabric gave evidence to the well-stocked mercantile. A pot-bellied stove stood in the corner to warm the store on cold winter days.

"I'm Tabitha," a tall, blonde woman announced, as she walked toward Paisley. "My husband and I own the mercantile." She paused and gave Paisley a quick once-over. "You must be Tyler Shepherdson's betrothed."

"Yes, I'm Paisley. It's nice to meet you, Tabitha." *Am I still Tyler's betrothed?*

"Welcome to Horizon." Tabitha smiled. "It's about time you came in. I know several folks are planning to meet you this Sunday at church.."

"Oh. Yes." Paisley stumbled on her words. The thought of meeting an entire town intimidated her. What would they think of her? She brushed aside the memories of the townsfolk in Pringle when they'd discovered Papa's illness. "Thank you, Tabitha. I look forward to making some friends here in Horizon."

"You are more than welcome. Is there something I can help you find?"

"I'll just take a gander around if you don't mind," Paisley said. She liked Tabitha immediately. Perhaps there was a position open at the mercantile for a hard worker such as herself if the need arose.

A red-haired woman entered the store soon afterward, and Tabitha introduced them. "Wilhelmina, I'd like for you to meet Paisley. She's the one who will be marrying Tyler. Paisley, this is Wilhelmina. She and her husband, Hubert, own the restaurant."

Wilhelmina's round face lit up as she smiled, her jolly countenance contagious. "It is so nice to meet you. I'm sure we'll become the best of friends."

A jolt of joy sprung through Paisley's heart. Having a good friend would be an answer to prayer.

Tyler hadn't known what to do about the way the day's events had transpired. First Ike coming for a visit and trying to dissuade him from marrying Paisley and caring for the children. The lingering thoughts of driving cattle filled his mind. Only a short time ago, there would have been no apprehension on Tyler's part to partake in a new adventure. But things were different now.

Much different.

And then there was Paisley's obvious frustration with him. What had happened between the time they discussed the new stove and the time Ike showed up and he and Tyler spoke in the barn?

One thing was for certain. He had to speak with Paisley about what he had done to upset her. He already felt guilty for deserting her when Ike arrived. What had ruffled her feathers?

Tyler hadn't meant to desert her. Talk about not being a gentleman. Ma would have his hide for sure if she were still alive. He could kick himself for not speaking up when Ike made his crazy suggestions. Put the children in an orphanage? While Tyler had no idea how to raise them properly and the children were far from angels, they in no way deserved to be placed again in an orphanage. Besides, he'd promised Ma, and Tyler would never go back on that promise.

Never.

As for Ike attempting to talk him out of marrying Paisley and settling down, that too wasn't something Tyler would consider. While he didn't know Paisley and they weren't marrying for ideal reasons, he'd also made her a promise. Unless he discovered something about her, for instance that she was a con woman or a fugitive on the run from justice, Tyler's promise remained. Yet, why hadn't Tyler voiced his opinions to Ike?

Why hadn't Tyler told Ike that he was a different man now than he'd been a month ago? Desiring to live for Jesus had changed Tyler, albeit the changes were slower than Tyler would have liked, but he was changing and for the better. He lived for Someone bigger than himself. No more did he intend to go his own way and do whatever he pleased at the risk of hurting others. Even if the cattle drive did sound appealing.

And it had.

However, the entire time Ike spoke, Tyler had remained silent. He hadn't shared his newfound faith or his convictions, hadn't shared the importance of his promise to Ma or to Paisley. Hadn't shared that he'd intended to do what was right, no matter what kind of life awaited him.

All Tyler had said to Ike was that he aimed to go through with his plans and thanked him for getting him hired on the cattle drive, but that Tyler would have to decline. Ike hadn't been happy and had left shortly thereafter. It hadn't been pleasant to part with Ike on those terms, but Tyler had at least done the right thing.

Tyler turned the wagon back around once they reached the farm. He had to talk to Paisley tonight. Had to mend things.

"Why are we turning around?" whined Albert.

"We have to go back into town."

Lucy gave an exaggerated whimper. "Weren't we just there?"

"We were and now we have to go back."

"But why?" argued Albert.

Tyler shook his head. Someday his prayers would be answered and God would show him how to father the unruly children.

When they reached town, Tyler spied Paisley walking from the mercantile to Miss Greta's. "Care for a ride?" he asked, pulling alongside her.

"Thank you for the offer, but I'm nearly to Miss Greta's."

"Paisley, we need to talk."

"I agree."

Lucy climbed forward and leaned her head toward the buckboard, almost even with Tyler's. "Why do you and Paisley need to talk, huh?"

"We just do." Tyler stopped the wagon a few steps from Miss Greta's. "Paisley, can we talk over there?" He pointed toward a lone tree on the edge of Miss Greta's property which he hoped provided sufficient privacy.

Albert folded his arms and grumbled. "What'll we do while you talk?"

"You'll behave and stay out of the mud this time," Tyler remanded. Caked mud covered Albert and Lucy from head to toe and was beginning to flake off into the wagon.

A few minutes later, Tyler braced his arm against the tree. Paisley bit her lip and frowned, a line etched between her brows.

Although he figured he knew the answer, he asked it anyway. "Paisley, are you mad at me?"

Silence.

"Paisley?"

"I overheard the conversation between you and Ike."

Realization hit him. "What did you hear?"

"I heard Ike telling you about the cattle drive job and about him telling you to rid yourself of the children and me."

"You heard correctly."

Her eyes glistened. He ought to say more. "But..."

"And I heard you say nothing in our defense."

Her words stung him. He'd been a dolt. "You're right, Paisley, I didn't say anything, and I regret it."

Paisley's chin trembled, and Tyler had a sudden urge to pull her to him and reassure her he'd been wrong in his failure to defend her and the children. He took a step toward her, and she took a step back.

"What will your choice be, Tyler? I need to know so I can make appropriate plans. Will you leave the children in an orphanage and leave me behind while you stake out an adventure on the plains of Texas?"

"Paisley..." Tyler reached for her, but she shook her head.

"Are you still planning to marry me?"

"I can explain." But could he explain his lack of words in his conversation with Ike?

Paisley's voice quivered. "I'm not here for long-winded explanations, Tyler. Either you are or you aren't. Which will it be? Because I'm not willing to allow the children to go back to the orphanage. I will take them and raise them on my own."

Tyler swallowed the lump in his throat. "I—" He looked over his shoulder at the children in the wagon. Lucy stood, hands on her hips, likely refuting something Albert was saying. Only the top of Mae's head could be seen, and Tyler wagered she'd covered her face to avoid the ongoings around her.

"Paisley, I have every intention of marrying you and of raising the children."

"But Ike..."

"About him..." Her bowed shoulders, her tearstained face, and the hurt in her eyes did something to his insides he couldn't explain. Paisley was a tender and sensitive woman. What advice would Pa give in this circumstance? What would he say would be the best way to make amends? If only Tyler had listened better to Pa's wise words of advice instead of brushing them aside as useless prattle.

"I realize your bonnet is in a knot, Paisley, but please let me explain."

"My bonnet is *not* in a knot."

Tyler regretted his words. Pa would never have said that. He offered a prayer heavenward for guidance. "What I mean to say is that…"

Albert sauntered toward them then. "Are you and Paisley bickerin'? I 'member once I got in a fight with this mean kid at the orphanage 'cause he stole my dessert."

"Albert, I'll talk with you in a minute. Please go keep an eye on Lucy and Mae."

Albert shook his head and scuffed his feet in the dirt. "Do I have to?"

"Yes, you do."

"Oh, all right."

When Albert was out of earshot, Tyler tried to put his thoughts into words once again. "I should have said something when Ike was discussing the cattle drives. I should have told him I wasn't interested. That I wanted to stay here and marry you, raise the children, and farm the land."

Hearing the words roll off his tongue made Tyler realize what a good life that would be. A home. A family.

"The children can be a challenge, you don't appear to be too keen on farming, and you wouldn't have to settle for me, someone who, as Ike says, 'is not *too* hard on the eyes.'"

"The children *are* a challenge. Makes me respect my folks all the more for the times when I misbehaved. But I love them and will do what it takes to raise them as my own. As *our* own. As for farming, I always enjoyed it as a young'un working alongside my pa. When I got older, I figured I was missing out on the world. I'm glad to be back and I want to work the land. As for you not being hard on the eyes, I don't think that at all."

"Meaning?"

"Meaning I think you're uh..."

"Yes?"

Tyler took a deep breath. "Meaning you're like Shadow."

Paisley's mouth fell open and her eyes widened. "So, now I'm like a horse."

"That's not what I meant. I mean, you're like Shadow in that you're..." *Say the right word this time, Tyler. Your future, and perhaps your life, may depend on it.* "You're—you're really pretty."

"I beg your pardon?"

This time her eyes held a different expression, one Tyler couldn't quite decipher. Had she liked his compliment? "When I said you're like Shadow, I meant she's a pretty horse and you're a pretty...woman."

He was thankful he had a day's growth of whiskers to hide the emotion creeping up his cheeks. It was as if he saw her for the first time. Her expressive eyes, the dotting of a couple of freckles on her nose, her full lips. "You're pretty. Real pretty. And while I hadn't given marriage much thought before my parents passed, if I have to marry someone, I would marry you."

"Oh. Well, thank you then."

Tyler reached for her hand and was thankful when she didn't resist. He stared at her small hand in his own large calloused one.

"What about the freedom you once experienced that you'll be missing out on once you marry me and decide to father the children?"

"About that...you see, Ike, he's, well..." Tyler cleared his throat. "He's like I used to be. Living for himself, doing what he wants, not thinking of others. Being selfish. When I left the farm, that's what I did. I sought to find adventure wherever it could be found. I hurt my parents something awful when I turned my back on them. I don't aim to do that again. Since—since desiring to live for the Lord, I've learned there's more to living than the next adventure."

Would she believe him? That it was starting a new life with the woman standing in front of him, even if he didn't know her? That it was keeping a promise to his ma?

"I need to apologize for eavesdropping. If I hadn't done that, none of this would have happened."

"Did you hear the entire conversation?"

"All but the last portion before Ike left."

"You should have stayed for the last of it. While I didn't elaborate, I did tell Ike I intended to go through with my plans." Ike hadn't been happy about Tyler's choice.

Paisley pressed her opposite hand to her heart. "I'm so relieved. I couldn't imagine poor little Mae back in an orphanage. Lucy or Albert either.

"I can tell you're taken with Mae. I am too. I keep praying God will guide me on being a father to the children. I have no idea where to start."

"I have no idea where to start as a mother." A hint of a smile touched her lips.

Tyler was beginning to like her smile. A lot. "Guess we'll pray and learn together then."

He tenderly tucked a wisp of hair that had escaped her braid behind her ear. "I'm sorry also for not showing you the house and giving you the rest of the tour of the barn."

"There'll be another time."

He nodded. There *would* be another time, but there wasn't much time left to court her.

Miss Greta's bell interrupted their conversation, and Paisley turned to see the woman standing on the porch looking in her direction. "And then there's Miss Greta."

"Ah, yes, Miss Greta. She's got a good heart in there somewhere. I better go. I'll retrieve you for church tomorrow then?"

"That would be fine."

Tyler shoved aside a sudden urge to take both of her hands in his and promise he'd do whatever it took for them to succeed at this crazy plan.

Chapter Twenty-One

IN EXCHANGE FOR CLEANING the bedrooms of the other guests, Paisley convinced Miss Greta to allow her to have the several yards of vivid green fabric Paisley had found in the bureau drawer in her room. It hadn't been an easy task persuading Miss Greta to allow her to help, nor convincing Miss Greta to give her the material, but Paisley's request had not ended in futility.

"Here's my portion. I best go prepare supper." Miss Greta handed her the section of the dress she had sewn. "Looks like you might have it finished just in time for church tomorrow."

"Thank you, Miss Greta. I couldn't have done without your help." Paisley took a step forward and gave the woman a quick hug.

Miss Greta stiffened and shifted her glance around the room. "Well, I best prepare supper," she repeated. The owner of the boardinghouse may present herself as being a terse and cantankerous woman, but Paisley ventured that she truly did have a kind and generous heart.

"I'll be along shortly to assist you."

The following morning, Paisley slipped the dress over her head. When was the last time she'd had a new dress?

She couldn't remember. The ornate lace on the sleeves and around the collar had been a charming touch. Miss Greta suggested it when she'd found the lace in a drawer in the parlor.

Inhaling the scent of the unworn fabric, Paisley closed her eyes and envisioned herself in her own wedding dress. But that wouldn't be the case. Although a gifted and efficient seamstress, Paisley doubted she'd find any other unused fabric tucked in any corners in the bureau drawer at Miss Greta's boardinghouse.

A knock at the door interrupted her thoughts, and she finished fixing her hair into a chignon. If Tyler had already arrived to retrieve her for church, she had only a matter of minutes to finish preparing.

"Paisley!" Miss Greta's demanding voice boomed from somewhere down the hall.

Paisley flung open her bedroom door. "Yes, Miss Greta?"

"Tyler is here!"

Paisley wondered if Miss Greta's voice woke not only the guests at her boardinghouse but also the entire town of late-sleepers in Horizon. "Thank you," she answered, closing the door behind her.

This would be the first day Paisley would meet more of the townsfolk, and her stomach gave testimony just to how nerve-wracked she was just thinking about it.

He attempted not to stare when he met Paisley near the front door. She wore a bright green dress that accentuated her eyes. A lovely smile brightened her face.

He found her to be beautiful. And she would soon be his wife.

"Hello, Paisley."

"Tyler."

"Are you ready for church?"

"I am."

Was that a blush he saw on her face?

He gestured toward the wagon. "The uh—the children—are waiting for us in the wagon." Tyler offered his arm. She took it and he led her to the wagon. Would she like the people she'd meet today before and after church? Would Paisley be glad that she'd agreed to marry him and make Horizon her home?

Tyler thanked the Lord again that they'd been able to make amends after their misunderstanding.

He stood, hands at her waist, awaiting to lift her into the wagon. Her gaze met his. "You look beautiful today," he said. "And every day, not just today, it's just that today..."

Paisley slightly dipped her head. "Thank you."

"Are we gonna go to church or just stand here?" Albert asked. "I don't want to miss the opening hymn."

Tyler lifted Paisley into the wagon, then took his place beside her and beckoned the horses the short distance toward church.

Paisley turned around to face the children. "Lucy, your hair looks lovely."

"Have to say I'm the one who braided it all pretty like that." In a whisper meant only for Paisley's ears, Tyler continued, "I'm surprised she allowed me to braid her hair."

"I didn't realize you knew how to fix hair. You did a fine job, Tyler."

"Thank you."

"Tyler, Albert pulled the ribbon from my hair!" Lucy wailed, her exaggerated shriek loud enough for the entire town of Horizon to hear.

"Now, Albert, why would you do a fool thing like that?" Tyler asked, disappointed that his moment with Paisley had been interrupted.

Albert only shrugged and did his best to hide a smirk. Tyler prayed and prayed about what to do about the children. He'd even spent time in the past few days speaking to Reverend Marshall about it. Would there ever be a time when the children would be respectful and kind?

Inside the church a few moments later, several parishioners introduced themselves to meet Paisley. Tyler knew he swelled with pride at each introduction. Perhaps this idea to marry for convenience wasn't such a bad idea after all.

After the singing and passing of the offering plate, Reverend Marshall stood behind his podium for the sermon.

"Today we start a new series I've titled, 'Raising Children in the Lord'. As we parents and grandparents no doubt know, raising children today is no easy task. And it wasn't easy in Bible times either, as we'll see from exploring various passages in the Bible." He paused and perused the congregation. "I want to start by saying that there are many things in our life that are temporary. Our farms, our homes, our crops, our wagons, our horses. All of these things and any other possessions are transient in nature and will someday no longer be here. But eternal life found in Jesus alone is everlasting and eternal. What could be more important than seeing our children in heaven some-day?"

Several "amens" filled the church. Paisley sat next to Tyler and could see from the corner of her eye that he had straightened his posture and gave Reverend Marshall his full attention. While she didn't yet know him well, Paisley did know that properly raising the children weighed heavily on Tyler's heart. Soon she would be a part of assisting him in that pursuit.

Thank You, Lord, that we were able to resolve our disagreement yesterday. I pray for your continued guidance both as Tyler's wife and as the children's mother. I am in desperate need of Your wisdom.

Paisley listened as Reverend Marshall continued his sermon and referenced numerous scripture verses. At one point, Tyler turned to glance at Paisley as if to connect them in the goal of parenting the children. Sitting so close to him, Paisley half expected him to intertwine his fingers with hers to cement that goal. If he did so, she wouldn't object.

She recalled his gentleness in assisting her from the wagon and pulling the slivers from her hands in Ingleville. His willingness to build an outhouse in exchange for her to live at Miss Greta's showed his generosity and selflessness. He was compassionate toward the children. And from what she'd seen, he loved the Lord.

Would she someday grow to love this man God had placed in her life?

The following day, Tyler stopped by Miss Greta's early in the morning to finish the outhouse. Paisley tended to the children, and in the afternoon, Tyler returned from the mercantile. "I purchased a wedding ring." Tyler reached into his trouser pocket and pulled out a thin gold band. "I need to see if it fits."

She gingerly stuck out her right hand toward him.

"Uh, other hand."

"I beg your pardon?"

"It's the other hand I need to place it on. You know, your left ring finger?"

There wasn't even a hint of sarcasm or correction in his voice, but rather a mere suggestion.

"Yes, yes, of course." Paisley instead extended her left hand toward him and allowed him to place the ring on her finger.

Tyler slid the ring over her knuckles. The moment itself leant a peculiar air to the already awkward situation.

"Good. It fits. I thought it would seeing as how your fingers are long and slim and this ring was one of the smallest." Tyler puffed out his chest. "Guess I'm not too bad at this marrying thing after all."

His crooked grin endeared him to her. He *was* dapper. Self-assured and impulsive. Slightly arrogant, but not in a bad way. Her eyes dropped to the ring on her hand. It fit well, and she flexed her wrist and held her hand at a distance. The gold shimmered in the sun. In less than twenty-four hours, she would be a married woman.

The realization hit her with a force she wasn't prepared for, although she'd known the day would soon arrive.

"The townsfolk always love a wedding, so we'll have a sizable attendance tomorrow."

"I never would have anticipated..."

Tyler chuckled. "You never would have anticipated marrying someone so soon after meeting?"

"Exactly."

"Me either. Reckon women give it more thought than men do."

"Yes, we think about flowers for our hair, a dress, and most importantly..." She sighed. "I wish my parents could have been in attendance."

Tyler scratched his chin. "I can't help you with those things," he said. "Especially where your parents are concerned, although I wish mine were here too."

"I didn't really mean to share all of that." She bit her lip and fiddled with the ring.

"I guess to a woman a wedding is more about fancy things than to a man."

"Likely so."

"I'm not a man of means, but I do have some money saved. Would it do to buy some fabric in the next few days and you could sew a new dress or two? It wouldn't be a wedding dress. But Maribel mentioned that the two of you spoke of borrowing her wedding dress."

"Yes, I'm thrilled to borrow Maribel's dress, and I didn't mean to imply that I wasn't grateful for all you've done."

"I didn't take it as such." He grinned at her again.

And for some reason, her knees grew wobbly. Maybe she should have eaten more at the noonday meal, but she just hadn't been all that hungry.

"Paisley? Are you all right?"

"Yes, I'm fine. I think it's just a case of the nerves."

"Well, it's not every day one gets married."

His gaze hadn't left hers.

"No, not every day."

"Now that I've finished the outhouse, I better get back to the farm. The children are in the wagon and likely to start causing trouble if I leave them there for too long. Maribel mentioned she'd be retrieving you tomorrow and taking you to the church, so I'll see you there around noon."

"Yes, around noon." Why was she repeating everything he said?

"Until tomorrow then."

"Until tomorrow."

But neither of them moved. They both stood, hands at their sides, awkwardly staring at each other.

Tyler finally shifted to one foot and took a step toward her.

Paisley held her breath. Was he going to kiss her? Did she want him to? Why was she so nervous around him?

"I—uh, I need the ring. Until tomorrow, I mean."

"Oh, yes, the ring." *And no, not a kiss.* Paisley pulled the gold band from her finger and placed it in his waiting palm.

"I'll walk you back to the house."

"Thank you." She placed her hand through the crook of his elbow, his nearness causing her heart to beat a little faster than usual.

"This will be your last night here," Tyler said, stopping just short of the door.

"Yes."

"I should have shown you the rest of the farm and such before the wedding, but I reckon you'll be seeing it tomorrow and all the days after that."

Was it just her imagination or did his eyes look hopeful? Did Tyler want their marriage to succeed as badly as she did despite its unorthodox beginnings? And why was there a tiny nagging inside her hinting that maybe, just maybe, she didn't want to marry Tyler just for the children after all?

CHAPTER TWENTY-TWO

PAISLEY AWOKE EARLY AND took advantage of the time before breakfast to draw a bath. Soon, Maribel and Wilhelmina would arrive to help her prepare, and Paisley found herself cherishing the thought. It somehow offered comfort and made the loneliness more bearable. *If only Mama were still alive. What a grand day this would be.*

How she missed her parents! They had been taken from this world too soon, and the pain of grief never left. As an only child, she'd been particularly close to both Mama and Papa and always knew they only wanted the best for her. But why then had Papa given his blessing for her to marry Ivan, even when Paisley had told him about Ivan's dishonesty? It didn't make sense. And it would likely be something to which she'd never know the answer.

Only by God's grace was she marrying Tyler instead of Ivan.

Assuming it was for guest's use, Paisley reached for the ornate glass bottle labeled *Maudie Pearl's Fine Lavender Toilet Water* atop the bureau. She removed the lid from the bottle and dabbed some on her wrists and behind her ears. It smelled just like the perfume Papa had purchased for

Mama so many years ago, perfume that Mama had allowed Paisley to use on special occasions.

Her thoughts returned to her upcoming wedding. Would she and Tyler someday grow to love each other?

Best I not get my hopes up. As Tyler mentioned before, this is a marriage of convenience. Not one of love, but a marriage only so the children would have a mother and Tyler would have assistance raising them.

The thought disappointed her.

A tap on the door interrupted her musings, and she opened it to see Maribel and Wilhelmina.

"Paisley, dear, are you ready for your big day?" Maribel asked, carrying a white wedding dress into the room and situating it on the bed.

Wilhelmina placed a headpiece on the bureau. "Tyler mentioned you wished you had fresh flowers. Maribel and I picked a bouquet of phlox, meadowsweet, and bellflower. I've twisted and woven them together to make a lovely hairpiece."

Paisley's eyes misted. While she wouldn't have Mama and Papa at the wedding or a gown to call her own, Tyler had seen to it that she would have the fresh flowers. "Thank you, Wilhelmina." She held them to her nose and inhaled. "They're breathtaking."

"You're more than welcome. Now let's see, I also have this to give you." Wilhelmina removed a pearl necklace from around her neck. "Tabitha said she'd be honored if you would consider borrowing her necklace. A lady needs some fancy jewelry for her special day."

Her new friends were already making her feel loved. "What a gracious gesture. And, Maribel, thank you so much for allowing me to borrow your dress."

"It would have been a bit short on you, so we put on a temporary lace fitting around the bottom hem that can be removed afterward. Now, we don't have much time before the ceremony. Wilhelmina and I will take you to the church within the hour. Remember, it's improper for the groom to see his bride before she walks down the aisle. We'll let you get dressed, and we'll be back to help you with the final preparations."

Paisley slipped the wedding dress over her head, thankful it fit as well as it did considering Maribel was smaller and finer boned. She stood for a minute staring at herself in the bureau mirror.

Tears burned her eyes.

Tears at the realization she would be marrying soon.

Tears at the realization that Mama and Papa wouldn't be there, yet she longed more than anything for their presence.

And finally, tears at the unknown life that lay ahead of her.

She unfolded Papa's handwritten Bible verse and read his precise handwriting. The verse gave her comfort. Whatever happened, the Lord would be her strength.

When Paisley finished dressing, Maribel and Wilhelmina returned to fix her hair and pin the hairpiece in place. "You make a beautiful bride," said Maribel.

"Thank you both. For everything. You don't even know me and yet you've come forward to assist me in so many ways. How can I ever repay you?"

"It's what friends do, and we are honored to assist you in any way we can. Goodness, but it's almost time! Let's make our way to the church." Wilhelmina scooted Paisley from the room and down the hall.

Paisley's feet didn't want to move. And her heart—it wasn't ready either.

Reverend Marshall stood at the front of the modest church with the Bible in his hand. In front of him, Tyler stood facing the door. Albert, Lucy, Mae, Maribel, Wilhelmina, Miss Greta, and Tabitha sat in several of the pews with whom Paisley presumed to be Wilhelmina's and Tabitha's families. Other members of the town filed into the remaining pews, some of whom Paisley had never met.

Nerves assailed her, and she prayed for peace.

Wilhelmina's husband, Hubert, agreed to walk her down the aisle, and Paisley clutched his arm, perhaps a bit too tightly. She chewed on her lip and pondered how many people had chosen to attend the ceremony.

When Paisley and Hubert reached the front of the church, Hubert took a seat next to Wilhelmina. Paisley stood facing Tyler.

Their eyes met, the seriousness in his blue eyes giving no indication as to his thoughts. Goodness, but he was a handsome man! Today he wore what had to be his Sunday best—a black coat over his shirt that stretched across his broad shoulders. He'd also shaved and combed his dark, wavy hair.

Would he someday grow fond of her?

"Dearly beloved, we are gathered here today in the presence..." Reverend Marshall began. Paisley listened as he listed off the vows that both she and Tyler would agree to. "And do you, Tyler Shepherdson, take Paisley Abbott to be your wife..."

"I do." His answer came quickly, then it was Paisley's turn.

"And do you, Paisley Abbott, take Tyler Shepherdson..."

"I do," she croaked. Her voice sounded more like a frog begging to be released from the clutches of a young child, rather than the voice of a woman on what was to be her happiest day. She saw Reverend Marshall squint his eyes at her as if he couldn't quite hear what she said, so she repeated herself in a louder croaky voice. "I do."

"Very well. "Reverend Marshall smiled and nodded toward Tyler. "You may place the ring on her finger."

Her hand trembled as Paisley extended it toward Tyler. He fumbled while attempting to slide the thin gold band onto her finger. It stalled on her knuckle. Undeterred, Tyler placed his left hand under hers and continued to push the ring gently onto her finger. A peculiar flutter filled her belly at his touch.

Reverend Marshall spoke again. "I now pronounce you man and wife. I present to you Mr. and Mrs. Tyler Shepherdson. Tyler, you may kiss your bride."

The color drained from Paisley's face, and her cheeks turned as white as a blanket of freshly-fallen snow. She shrank from him, so slightly that likely only he noticed. Did she not want him to kiss her? What should he do? Tyler didn't want to make her uncomfortable. While they were now legally married, he wanted their first moments as man and wife to be memorable and pleasant.

His eyes traveled to her lips. They seemed to tremble. Was she frightened? Did she find him repulsive? Should he wait before kissing her so as not to embarrass her in front of those in attendance, most of whom she didn't know? Before he could stop the words, he muttered to Reverend Marshall, "Do I have to? I mean, seeing as how she's…"

"Pardon me?"

"Do I—do I—have to kiss her?"

Reverend Marshall's jaw went slack. Paisley looked as though she might cry. Tyler wanted to run from the church and never look back.

The reverend's silence was the only answer Tyler needed. He didn't even dare take a quick peek at the facial expressions of his audience. He would pretend he was only joking. After all, most of the townsfolk knew he had a somewhat witty sense of humor.

Yes, of course he must kiss her. What kind of man asked that he not kiss his bride on their wedding day?

And he wanted to kiss her.

Very much so.

But Reverend Marshall didn't know the full details, nor did Maribel, Wilhelmina, or the rest of the townsfolk. "I mean, of course I want to kiss my beautiful bride," he murmured. And she was beautiful with her long hair pulled back in an intricate plait and the fresh wildflower wreath sitting on her head. He'd always thought she was pretty from the moment he found her in the back of the wagon. But at this moment, she was even prettier.

Taking a step toward her, Tyler reached behind her and placed his left hand on the small of her back. *Maybe that would keep her from falling over should she faint.* He gently met her lips with his. Hopefully she would interpret his kiss as an apology for being such a cad only seconds before.

Reverend Marshall let out a relieved sigh.

Maribel and Wilhelmina clapped.

The rest of the townsfolk cheered.

Tyler stepped back from her and reached for Paisley's hands. He wanted to reassure her that they'd made the right decision, even though theirs might be the most spontaneous wedding proposal in history.

Tyler lifted Paisley into the wagon amidst the well-wishes of the onlookers. Her heart hadn't stopped racing since she'd entered the church for the ceremony. And in less than thirty minutes, she had declared her love to Tyler in a wedding vow to honor and cherish him through sickness and through health. She'd barely lived through the shock of him asking if he had to kiss her, then was taken by surprise when he did.

One thing was for certain—she would never forget this day.

Chapter Twenty-Three

THEY RODE IN SILENCE the short distance to the farm, but Tyler's mind was reeling from the commitment he'd just made. Marriage hadn't been something on his mind until the desperate situation with the children arose.

Tyler had always loved adventure, so maybe he could look at this new chapter in his life as an adventure. And since giving his life to Jesus, Tyler planned to do all he could to live in God's will. Not to say that was going to be easy.

This was the most bizarre plan he'd ever concocted, but he'd never shied away from unorthodox methods of obtaining something he needed. Hadn't that been how he'd managed to slither through the first year of leaving home with only the clothes on his back?

Even Lucy and Albert remained quiet for what might possibly be the first time in their young lives. Tyler didn't even feel like whistling, as he usually did when deep in thought. Instead, a multitude of thoughts entered his mind. He thought of Paisley when she'd walked down the aisle—her slender form in the borrowed dress and the way her hair looked beneath the crown of wildflowers. Her beauty wasn't wasted on him.

He took a glance at her. Although now there wasn't even a hint of a smile on her face.

Did she already regret her decision to marry him?

The jostling of the wagon added to Paisley's uncertainty and anxiety about her new role as Tyler's wife and the mother of three children. Would they like her? Would she like them? Was she fit for the job? What if she failed?

The embarrassing situation with the kiss lingered in her mind. She replayed the scene over and over again. Why would Tyler not want to kiss her? Did he find her distasteful?

Would they live in comfortable camaraderie, leaving any semblance of a romantic relationship at friendship's door as she supposed some husbands and wives did in a marriage of convenience?

Not that she held romantic notions since she was marrying Tyler only to be a mother to three orphans and to avoid being homeless. A man holding her lovingly in his strong embrace, declaring his undying love, and kissing her with a kiss that made her knees tremble and her heart race was only for those who fell in love during a traditional courtship and subsequent marriage.

Tyler stopped in front of the house and assisted Paisley from the wagon. "Here we are," he announced. Paisley looked away as he attempted to hold her gaze.

And Lucy and Albert started to bicker.

"Next time I'm sitting on that side of the wagon," Lucy declared.

"No, I'm sitting there. You can sit next to Mae. My place is on the right-hand side."

"That's not fair. You shouldn't have a side."

"Children, please stop your quarreling," admonished Tyler.

The beginnings of a headache began to form, and Paisley massaged her temples. She finally looked at Tyler, who remained standing directly in front of her.

"You haven't said a word since we left the church. I know this is an odd situation we both find ourselves in..."

"An odd situation indeed when a man argues about kissing his wife during their wedding ceremony." The mumbled words came out in a stream of nearly incoherent babbling before she could stop them.

"Is that what's wrong? This is because I didn't want to kiss you?"

"So you admit that you didn't want to kiss me?"

"What'cha doin'?" Albert yelled from the back of the wagon.

Tyler clasped her hand in his and led her toward the chicken coop. "We'll be back over in a minute. Albert, take care of your sisters for me, please."

"Do I gotta? Can't they take care of themselves?"

Their first squabble since becoming husband and wife and all because his choice of words were lacking. Tyler had no idea how to handle this situation. What did a husband do when his wife was angry with him?

Paisley jutted her chin toward him and firmed her mouth in a thin line. He removed his hat. "Look, Paisley, this isn't easy for either of us."

"I've never heard of a man asking the reverend if he absolutely must kiss his bride. You could have just pretended and got it over and done with."

"I did get it over and done with."

When she gasped, Tyler knew he'd said the wrong thing...again. "That isn't what I meant. Besides, didn't you hear me when I recanted?"

"Oh, yes, that was convincing. And in front of Reverend Marshall and the entire town of Horizon? Most embarrassing, indeed!"

"At least it was only a small crowd and they've likely forgotten about it by now."

"Are you making light of my concern?"

Was he making light of her concern? Well, to be honest, yes he was. But Tyler hadn't seen it as a major issue. Yet, Paisley apparently found this a big enough problem to cause a quarrel. Had he picked a contentious and brawling wife like the one mentioned in Proverbs? Tyler hoped not. He recalled something about it being better to dwell in the corner of a housetop or the wilderness than with such a wife.

"Look, Paisley. I'm sorry about the kiss. I looked over at you during the ceremony and you looked more frightened than a deer being chased by a wolf. The last thing I wanted was to scare you more." *And I thought you might find me repulsive with the way you shrank from me and looked as though you might cry.*

But Tyler didn't say those words. How could he? He had his pride.

"I wasn't scared of you."

"If I'd known not kissing you would bother you so much, I would have kissed you more than once without an ounce of arguing." At his words, Paisley's face turned the color of a strawberry as she stared past him and into the distance.

Tyler lifted her chin toward him. "Do you want me to give you a kiss right now and make amends?"

"I declare, Tyler Shepherdson!"

Tyler chuckled. "All right, then." Married life with Paisley would be anything but boring.

Their first fight had just attested to that.

"I'll show you inside the house."

Paisley followed him toward the house. They'd been married less than an hour, and already they'd had their first disagreement.

They stopped just short of the doorway. In the novels, the husband always carried his new bride over the threshold into the new home they would now share. But this wasn't the books. This was real life.

He gestured toward the doorway and followed her inside.

She scanned the interior. Her first thoughts were that the house was homey and comfortable. A few tintypes and a Bible lined the mantle atop the generous fireplace. An old cookstove stood in the corner, and a large, seemingly-new wood table held its rightful place in the center of the kitchen.

Tears welled in her eyes. She'd once had a home like this with Mama and Papa.

"I hope you'll find the place satisfactory."

"Yes, yes, it's fine. A nice home, really."

"There are three rooms, counting the room upstairs. That's where Albert sleeps. I'll sleep up there too until..."

His voice trailed, and Paisley held her breath at his unspoken words.

Tyler cleared his throat. "Lucy and Mae share the little room on the right, and you'll sleep in my parents' old room over there." He pointed to a larger room on the left with a window facing the front of the house. "Paisley, about the kiss."

"It's all right, Tyler. I shouldn't have made such an issue of it."

"I'm sorry."

"Sorry for kissing me?"

"No." An indiscernible expression crossed his face, as if he wanted to say more but didn't.

"Can we play in the hayloft?" Lucy asked, running through the front door.

"For a few minutes until chore time," Tyler answered.

Before he'd even finished his sentence, Lucy was gone, heading toward the barn. Mae shuffled slowly behind her.

"Reckon it'll take some time to get to know each other since we didn't have a proper courtship."

"Yes, it will take some time."

"It's a change for sure." Tyler paused, his eyes searching hers. "I am sorry about the kiss earlier. I shouldn't have said what I did. And no, I don't regret kissing you. Maribel prepared a meal for us for tonight. I'll fetch it from the wagon. Take some time to look around."

With that, Tyler left the house and headed out to the wagon leaving Paisley to take in the new surroundings...and her new life.

Later that evening after a whirlwind of farmwork, chores, and partaking in Maribel's meal, Tyler prepared to settle in for the night. He walked out to the barn to find Mae sleeping on a pile of hay. He knelt and stared at her for a moment. Was he really a father now? And a husband as well? Somewhere in the house, Paisley likely wondered the same thing about being a mother and a wife.

Tyler carried Mae into the house and placed her on her bed before taking a step backward. Delicate in features, fragile in strength, and wordless when it came to conversation, Mae needed someone to care for her. Tyler imagined Ma's gaze settling upon Mae and deciding she would be that person.

If only Ma were still here.

After ensuring Lucy and Albert were tucked into their beds, Tyler took a seat at the kitchen table and placed his head in his palms. It would have been better for his parents to leave the children with the reverend and Maribel. Tyler was ill-equipped at being a father. *Lord, I've learned so much about You in these past weeks. I know You hear every prayer we pray, so I ask for Your aid in raising these children and in being a husband to Paisley.*

Paisley took a seat across from Tyler, and he lifted his head to meet her gaze. "This is all so new," he said.

"I agree."

"How long have you cared for the children?"

"Less than two weeks total now, and some of that time, I left them at Reverend Marshall's so I could travel to Cornwall and back to Horizon. I reckon neither of us would have expected our lives to take the turn it did."

"No, but I have faith the Lord will see us through whatever life tosses our way."

How could she be so sure? "I reckon you're right. While I grew up going to church and listening to Pa read from the Bible, I never had a relationship with the Lord until recently. I'm still learning about what it means to have a relationship with Him and to trust Him in all things."

"I have known the Lord for quite some time, but I've struggled..."

"Yes?" he prodded.

"It's nothing."

"You've already shared a lot with me, Paisley, about your family and Ivan and your life in Pringle. Remember our trip to Horizon and the time we spent talking?" Tyler remembered it quite well.

"You're right. It's just that I'm ashamed to say that I've struggled a time or two in believing the Lord could handle difficult matters. Mama and I prayed for Papa, but no answer came. Then after they died, I couldn't understand why God would allow such an awful atrocity to occur."

She paused. "Papa's mood and personality changed in such a peculiar way. His judgment was no longer sound, and he even had problems speaking sometimes. No one knew what was wrong with him. People suspected and made hateful presumptions. The doctor suggested we commit him to an asylum."

"I'm sorry, Paisley."

"Thank you. Between that and losing my parents to a devastating flood...well, I just couldn't understand why God wouldn't step in and change things. After all, He had made mountains and oceans and trees and people from nothing but a spoken word, yet He couldn't heal Papa and couldn't prevent my parents' horrific death. I stopped trusting in His plan for a brief time. I'm not proud of that."

Tyler didn't know what to say. She'd shared so much with him, and he had the urge to take her in his arms and comfort and protect her from anything else that might ever happen.

"Sorry I shared so much."

"Never be sorry about that—that's what husbands do for their wives. A husband is here for his wife when she needs him."

He recalled Pa saying those very words to Ma once after they'd lost the baby that was to be Tyler's little brother or sister. Tyler watched as Pa comforted Ma, took her in his arms, and promised to love her and be there for her forever.

That was the kind of husband Tyler wanted to be.

Chapter Twenty-Four

PAISLEY AWOKE TO THE sound of clamorous voices and loud footsteps. She swung her legs over the side of the bed. It was strange having a room all to herself when everyone else had to share.

Paisley rose and ambled toward the bedroom door. She opened it slowly and peered into a world of chaos.

Albert and Lucy ran around the house with untamed energy. "Give me back my dolly, Albert Shepherdson!"

Mae crouched in the corner, covering her ears with her hands.

"You have to catch me first," retorted Albert.

"I mean it, Albert, give me back my dolly!" Lucy caught ahold of Albert's suspender and snapped it hard against his back and attempted to reach for her doll.

"Stop it, Lucy. You're going to break my suspenders." Albert scowled, then took off at a higher rate of speed, slamming into the corner of the table.

Paisley rubbed her temples. Where was Tyler? And what time was it? Surely she hadn't overslept. Or had she? "Children!"

No response. Only the ongoing yelling and shouting as Lucy and Albert continued to run without restraint through the crowded home.

What should she do? And where was Tyler? "Children!" she demanded again.

Lucy glanced her way, then continued on her mission to rescue her doll. Albert ignored her altogether. Mae squeezed her eyes shut and buried her head in her arms.

Paisley nearly collided with Albert as she reached for a pan. With a spoon, she clanged on it until she had the full attention of the wayward children. "Lucy and Albert!" she raised her voice to a higher octave.

Mae left her place in the corner and ran toward her room. Lucy gaped wide-eyed at Paisley, and Albert slunk into a chair at the table.

Paisley took a deep breath. "This is no way to behave, and I'll not allow it in this house. It's disrespectful to say the least." Surprising herself with her staunch position on the children's behavior, she paused. "Now, where is Tyler?"

"He's in town," muttered Albert.

"In town?"

"Yes, he had to go to town for some supplies," said Lucy, as if everyone in the nearby vicinity knew of Tyler's plans for the day.

"Did he mention when he would return?"

"No," said Albert. He placed Lucy's doll under the chair.

"I haven't even made breakfast yet. What time is it?" Paisley asked.

Lucy pointed to the clock on the mantle. "See for yourself. It's seven o'clock."

Paisley gasped. Seven o'clock? She hadn't meant to sleep so long. Exhaustion had clearly overtaken her, much to her dismay. But first things first—she had to resolve the issue between Lucy and Albert. "Albert, please return Lucy's doll."

"Aw, do I have to?"

"Yes, you do. It's ungentlemanly to take someone's doll." Paisley heard her words and thought she sounded like Mama. Just a little.

Albert grumbled, then retrieved the doll and threw her at Lucy.

"How dare you throw my dolly, Albert. She could get hurt," rebuked Lucy.

"It's only a doll," growled Albert.

"Albert, you can be sure Tyler will hear of this when he returns."

"Lucy has taken my things before too. Will Tyler hear about that?"

Oh, my. What had she gotten herself into? Rambunctious children with no direction. A husband who left for town without so much as a note. Breakfast that needed to be prepared and soon. And a missing child. Where was Mae?

Paisley found her answer when she saw Mae hiding in the corner of the room she shared with Lucy. When Paisley's eyes connected with Mae's, Mae hurriedly glanced away and again buried her face in her hands. *Poor child. Lord, direct me on how to console her.*

But first, Paisley marched toward the cupboard and noticed it was empty. "Where do you keep the food?" she asked.

"Food?" asked Lucy.

"Yes, is there any food?"

"Albert and I ate the last of the bread this morning. We don't have any food in the house, not even leftovers from Maribel's fine meal last night."

Paisley panicked. No food in the house? It was stressful enough knowing that she couldn't cook, but there was *nothing* to cook? How had she not given this considerable thought? Oh, how she wished she'd paid closer attention to Mama's cooking instructions!

She handed Albert a bowl. "Albert, would you please gather the eggs?"

"Actually, that's Mae's chore," argued Albert.

"And I am asking you to do it."

"But Mae always gets out of doing chores. All she has to do is go hide and pout."

"Albert, please go gather the eggs." Albert tested her patience like no other child ever had. But then, she hadn't had much experience with children with the exception of assisting the widow with seven children when she was twelve.

"All right." Albert dragged his feet as if Paisley had asked him to walk from the Idaho Territory to New York without so much as a supper break between. She would have to discuss Albert's lack of obedience with Tyler. Maybe he would know how to handle the wayward child.

Paisley turned to Lucy. "Lucy, do we have any food in the cellar?"

"I'm not sure."

"Would you please go to the cellar and see what we have?"

"May I wait until Albert returns from the chicken coop? The cellar is so dark and scary. I don't want to go there all by myself. After all, I'm only seven." Lucy's brown eyes widened, and she clasped her hands together in begging fashion.

"All right. You may wait until Albert returns." Paisley shook her head. Had these children never been made to mind? "I must go check on Mae. When Albert returns, please tell him I said for the both of you to go to the cellar."

"Don't bother talking to Mae. She doesn't speak."

"Ever?"

"Not since I've known her. Somethin' about growing up with a mean pa." Lucy shrugged her narrow shoulders. "I only met her on the train a'fore we came here."

Paisley gasped. Mae never spoke? She had a mean father? "How did you know about her pa?"

"Just do. That's all."

"That is heartbreaking," said Paisley. She stared at Lucy. The girl had mousy-brown, shoulder-length hair and a gaping space where she was missing her two front teeth. A sprinkling of freckles dotted her nose.

"Most of us kids never done known a real family. It's just the way it is."

"And what about you, Lucy? Did you have a family before you came here?"

Lucy shrugged again and placed her hands behind her back. "Yep. I had me a family once. But they all died. All 'cept me. Then I went to live in the orphanage. I was glad to be 'dopted, but then Ma and Pa up and died." Lucy pursed her lips together. "Everyone leaves."

"Oh, Lucy, I'm so sorry." Paisley reached for the young girl, but Lucy took a step back.

"I'm gonna go outside and wait for Albert."

"Yes, that's fine. I'll go see about Mae."

Paisley watched as Lucy opened the door and left the house. She could see her through the window as Lucy waited by the chicken coop for Albert to finish his chore. Paisley knew what it was like to be an orphan. Knew what it was like to be alone. But she'd never had to face that as a child.

Mae remained in the corner of her room huddled in a ball when Paisley entered. Paisley knelt beside her and touched her arm. Mae flinched but didn't lift her head to meet Paisley's eyes.

"Mae, honey, it's me, Paisley. Are you all right?"

No response.

"Would you like to come back to the kitchen?"

Again, no response.

Should Paisley wrap her arms around the tiny child and comfort her? What would Mae do? Would she fight Paisley's affection? Run from her? Ignore her? *Lord, I feel I must try to reach out to this child. Please show me what I ought to do.*

Paisley sat on the floor and wrapped her arms around Mae's thin shoulders, then pulled the child close. Mae resisted and attempted to pull away. Paisley tried harder to pull her closer. Mae lifted her arms, pounded on Paisley's shoulders, and shook her head.

No words, just the look of anguish in Mae's dark blue eyes.

Not wanting to do so, but knowing she must, Paisley released Mae. In an instant, Mae jumped to her feet and ran out the door.

Leaning her head against the bedroom's wall, Paisley lifted her eyes heavenward. How would she ever succeed in what was expected of her in this new life? Three contrary children who had lived lives of such sadness. A husband whom she didn't know. A grieving process from losing her own parents that she hadn't fully faced. An inability to cook for her family and no ingredients to even make a meal.

Heavenly Father, I need You.

CHAPTER TWENTY-FIVE

TYLER PARKED THE WAGON in front of the barn. The short trip to town had done him good. He found that whenever he needed to clear his mind, a few moments to himself did wonders. Besides, the purchase of flour, sugar, and other provisions would solve the problem of the empty cupboards at home. He craned his neck to look at the contents of the wagon. The dishes of food from the townsfolk would make a nice addition to the food situation as well. Friends from Horizon had been more than happy to make a meal for the new couple.

The first thing Tyler saw after he unhitched the wagon was the look on Paisley's face. Happiness would not describe it.

"Hello, Tyler."

"Good morning, Paisley. I have some flour, sugar, and other provisions in the back of the wagon as well as some meals from the townsfolk." He grinned. Didn't grinning always help a bad situation?

She didn't seem to care that he had grinned or that he had brought provisions and meals. Her countenance remained the same. Perhaps he could lift her into his arms and swing her around, declaring his love for her. That's what Pa had done once when he'd accidentally forgotten to do an important errand for Ma while in town. It had assuaged the situation and Ma had forgiven him.

But Tyler couldn't very well lift Paisley into his arms and declare his love for her. He didn't know her well enough to love her. And no matter how charming he could be in his mannerisms, one thing remained. Her annoyance. But why? Hadn't he done what any good husband would do?

"How are the young'uns?" Tyler asked. He grinned again.

She narrowed her eyes at him in response.

The children must have caused trouble again. He didn't know Albert, Lucy, and Mae too well since he'd only just returned to Horizon, but he knew enough to know they had a penchant for being ornery.

"Wilhelmina and Tabitha asked about you." Wouldn't that gain him favor? Didn't all women think it a delight to have others inquire about them and want to invite them to quilting parties and the like? Tyler shifted from one foot to the other. He wished he'd listened better when Pa gave him tips for being a godly husband. But Tyler hadn't cared all those years ago. All he knew was that he wanted to live a life of adventure and never get married. Settling down and being the man God called him to be hadn't entered into his thoughts. Until now.

After what seemed a lengthy time of silence, Paisley finally spoke. "Albert will need a good scolding,"

"What has that boy done now?"

"Besides the constant terrorizing of his sister for the past hour and a half and the refusal to obey authority, nothing much."

Paisley's sarcasm was not wasted on Tyler. She had spunk and he admired that. But it helped if it wasn't directed at him.

"I see."

"And we have no food in the cupboards."

"That's why I went to town—to get provisions." Had she not heard him?

"When I awoke, you were gone. I can't raise these children on my own, Tyler."

So that was what she was festered about. She thought she'd have to raise the young'uns on her own. "I don't expect you to."

"A note would have been nice."

"Sorry."

"I'm not sure what to do about Mae. She doesn't speak and doesn't even allow me to get close to her. At the first sound of chaos, she runs to a corner in the house and hides her head. Of course, chaos with Albert and Lucy commences frequently."

"I'm not sure what to do about Mae either." Tyler thought of the letter he'd found written to his parents about Mae and the life she'd lived before becoming a Shepherdson. "Maribel told me to just keep loving and praying for her and that she'll be all right. The children hadn't been here long before my parents died. It's been a lot of changes."

He met Paisley's eyes. Expressive eyes with tiny flecks of brown in them. She was beautiful even when she was mad.

"Again, Paisley, I'm sorry. I didn't want to wake you, and I didn't figure it'd take as long as it did."

Her expression softened. "I'm sorry too, Tyler. I just found it overwhelming this morning with the children and no food in the house. And I overslept, which I hadn't intended. That won't happen again."

Tyler smiled. Good. He'd made amends. He would try harder to do a better job of letting her know when he left for town. After all, he wanted this marriage to succeed.

Paisley cleared the plates of food from the table after the noonday meal. What a blessing to have received numerous food items from the townsfolk. Now if only she could find someone to give her cooking lessons. Perhaps Maribel? Paisley liked her instantly, and the sooner she learned to cook, the better. The generosity of the people of Horizon wouldn't last forever. Nor could she keep her ineptitude at making a decent meal a secret from Tyler forever.

"Paisley?"

Paisley turned to see Tyler standing by the table, his hands behind his back. "Yes?"

"I have something for you—something to make up for earlier."

"Tyler, I've already forgiven you for that, and besides, it was all a misunderstanding." He was indeed a handsome man with those convincing blue eyes and wavy dark hair.

Tyler handed her some calico. "I purchased this while in town today. I wasn't sure what you'd like, so I asked Tabitha her opinion. She's always eager to give it and told me these two patterns would suit you."

"Thank you so much! It looks like there'll be enough here to make Lucy and Mae a dress as well." Paisley fingered the lovely fabric. A new daily dress would be a delightful addition to her meager wardrobe. There was enough for a dress for her and for each of the girls as well.

Tyler's thoughtfulness touched her heart. "Thank you again, Tyler."

"You're welcome, Mrs. Shepherdson" he said with a teasing glint in his eye.

Mrs. Shepherdson. She liked the sound of it. Paisley peered down at the floor to avoid allowing him to see the blush creeping into her cheeks. "I—well, thank you." Hadn't she already thanked him? Why was she so flustered? She should change the topic of conversation. Yes, that would remedy the awkwardness. "What a blessing that Albert, Lucy, and Mae were adopted by such loving parents. I'm sure your mother was wonderful with them."

"I'm sure she was. Ma loved her family more than anything, except the Good Lord, of course."

"I'll bet she tried to help Mae. I'd love to know what she did and if she was able to get Mae to speak at all."

Regret edged his words. "Can't say as I know." He cleared his throat. "Well, I best commence tending to the crops."

A hundred pounds of relief fell from her shoulders now that she knew she wouldn't have to prepare a meal.

Chapter Twenty-Six

THE PAST TWO DAYS sped by in a blur. Paisley climbed into bed and squeezed her eyes shut, willing sleep to come quickly. The adjustment into the life of being a wife and mother had exhausted her. Lucy and Albert continued to be obnoxious, and little Mae still hadn't spoken a word. Tyler worked long days in the field and, dog-tired with exhaustion by the end of the day, wasn't much for conversation. Fortunately she hadn't yet had to cook a meal. That was one benefit at least.

Yet Paisley wouldn't give up hope. God had called her to this situation, and she would make the best of it, even if she felt as though she was failing on all counts.

Tears trailed down her cheeks. *Mama, I miss you so much. I have more respect for you than ever after seeing how difficult it can be to do the jobs of mothering and being a wife and doing them well. So much is expected of me. If only you were here to talk to and give me advice on these predicaments.*

Yes, Mama would know what to do. She'd know how to handle Lucy and Albert in a loving, yet firm and consistent manner when they failed to mind, which was often. Mama would know how to help Mae, with her vacant gaze and her aloof sadness. And most of all, Mama would know just what to do about Tyler and how to create the kind of marriage that honored God. But then, Mama hadn't married Papa after knowing him for a week and she hadn't married for convenience. She'd married for love. Paisley realized she would never be able to say she married for love. Despite that, she desired the strong, abiding love her parents shared.

She wiped away the tears and resolved to make her marriage the best it could be.

That was the desire of her heart.

Tyler was hitching the horses to the wagon when a thought occurred to him. Why not invite Paisley to travel with him to town today?

Taking long strides toward the house, he opened the door and found her washing the dishes from the breakfast meal—one of many given as a wedding gift from the townsfolk.

"I need to go to town. Would you and the young'uns like to come?"

From the way her eyes brightened at his suggestion, Tyler could tell he'd made the right choice in asking her. "I—we would love to!" She wiped her wet hands on her apron.

"How long until you're ready?" *Should I have given her more time to prepare?*

Paisley smoothed her hair with her hands. "The children are dressed and ready. I'll just need a few minutes."

"Take your time. We'll leave when you're ready."

Paisley smiled at him, a smile he hadn't seen on her before. "Thank you for inviting me. I have longed to go to town for a visit."

"I figured you might."

He should have noticed she was lonely. Church was yet a few days away and she'd see people again then, but he was sure Paisley already missed her newfound friendships with Maribel, Wilhelmina, and Tabitha. She was personable and enjoyed being around other people. That wouldn't happen much on the farm with the exception of him and the children.

"I'm going to wear my new dress," she said, more to herself than to him. "The green one I made for church." She was still smiling at him, and he wondered if she might hug him in her excitement at being invited. He should have thought of it sooner. He would welcome a hug.

"Well, then," he said, grasping for words. He gestured toward the door. "I'll be outside when you're ready."

"Would you mind rounding up Lucy and Albert? Mae is in her room and I'll bring her." The enthusiasm in her voice encouraged him.

"Sure."

"Thank you." She beamed again. Her feet appeared fixed to the floor because she didn't move. She only stood staring at him.

"Well, then," Tyler said again. "See you in a while."

"Yes, in a while."

Tyler strode from the house, hoping it wouldn't be too long of a while. He knew women could take their time when preparing for an outing to town. He recalled waiting with Pa for what seemed like an hour while Ma made herself presentable. Pa mentioned it was important since Ma would be meeting her friends in town and socializing.

"Glad I'm not a woman," said Tyler. "I'm not much for socializing."

"That's because you're only twelve. Reckon someday you'll appreciate the rides to town to see friends, especially after long hours in the fields."

"And why does Ma think she has to make herself presentable?" Tyler asked.

"My, if you aren't full of questions today." Pa ruffled Tyler's hair. "I don't know the answer to that question. Your ma is always pretty to me. Don't seem like she needs any time making herself presentable."

The interruption of Lucy and Albert chasing each other around the corner of the barn brought Tyler back to the present. Paisley certainly didn't need time to make herself presentable either.

"We're going to town, so be ready to go in a few minutes," he told Lucy and Albert.

"We're going to town?" asked Albert. "All right!"

"That means you two need to behave," Tyler said, putting on his sternest voice. "If you don't, you'll find yourselves sitting in the wagon by your lonesome while everyone else has an enjoyable visit."

"Oh, we'll be good, Tyler. We promise," said Lucy, her eyes large.

Tyler doubted it. He wondered how Ma and Pa at their ages had the energy for the two rambunctious youngsters.

He certainly didn't. Add that to the problems he knew both children encountered in their time as orphans and it made matters more difficult. He questioned for the hundredth time why his parents hadn't left the children to someone more experienced and responsible. Especially since Pa had expressed such profound disappointment in Tyler.

"Here come Paisley and Mae," announced Lucy.

Tyler diverted his gaze toward the front of the house. A slight breeze blew the loose strands of Paisley's hair, and her face shone.

He couldn't help but stare.

"Sorry that took so long," she said when she reached him.

Tyler stumbled for words. "It wasn't so long."

"I like your green dress," declared Lucy. "Don't you like it, Tyler?"

Tyler felt the red creep up his face, and he pretended to attend to an imaginary problem with one of the wagon wheels.

"Well, don't you think so, Tyler?" Lucy asked again.

Ma would call Lucy precocious. "Yes," he mumbled, again allowing his gaze to settle on Paisley.

"Womenfolk talk about the dumbest things," interjected Albert, wrinkling his nose. "Who cares about dresses? We menfolk never talk about pretty dresses, do we Tyler?"

Tyler laughed. "No, Albert, I reckon we don't."

"We talk about horses and plows and the crops and all that stuff," continued Albert. "I never say how lovely my trousers are."

Tyler chuckled again, noting it felt good to allow some humor into the otherwise-challenging past month. "I suppose we could see if there's some fabric at the mercantile. Maybe you could persuade Paisley into sewing you some dapper new trousers."

"Aw, no thanks. I don't need no dapper new trousers. These suit me fine." Albert flipped his suspenders. "I do like candy, though."

"Perhaps if you behave yourself like a gentleman, we might see to it that you receive a piece of licorice," said Tyler. He assisted Paisley into the wagon, then lifted Mae into the back. She stiffened, and it saddened him. "Would you like a piece of licorice, Mae-Mae?" he asked, inventing a new nickname for her.

Mae stared at him with forlorn eyes and nodded a nod so slight that Tyler thought he might have imagined it.

"Mae-Mae?" Lucy asked. "That's a silly name."

"I rather like it," said Paisley. "I think it fits our little Mae-Mae quite well."

Tyler grinned and his eyes once again connected with Paisley's. Little Mae was theirs now, wasn't she?

If only they could learn how to be a family. Perhaps then Mae would open her heart to them.

Chapter Twenty-Seven

THAT EVENING, PAISLEY SAT in the rocking chair and prepared to read the Bible. She'd tucked the children into bed, and Tyler was outside completing the remainder of the chores. She took a deep breath and relished for a moment the quietude, with the exception of the ticking of the mantle clock. She invited the solitude and serenity as she opened Tyler's ma's Bible to the book of Psalms.

"Paisley?"

She looked up to see Lucy standing in the doorway of her room.

"Yes, sweetie?"

Lucy offered no response but instead, in a completely unexpected action, climbed into Paisley's lap and placed a hand on Paisley's arm. She stared for a moment with large unblinking brown eyes, a slight toothless smile on her face. It reminded Paisley of the times she'd snuggle with Mama. Emotion welled in her throat.

"Paisley, have you ever been a little girl?"

"Yes, I was a little girl once not so long ago."

"Like me and Mae?"

Paisley nodded. "Yes, just like you and Mae. I had pretty brown hair just like yours."

Lucy's eyes lit. "And did you pretend like all the dolls at the mercantile were your children?"

"I did love my dolls, especially the ones Mama made for me out of cloth. I played outside often too and spent a lot of time with my papa in the fields."

"And did you give names to all your dolls?"

"Yes. Sometimes I forgot that I already gave a name to one of them, and so two of them sometimes had the same name."

Lucy giggled. "That's silly. I only have one doll, but I'm gonna ask for another one for Christmas."

"Perhaps after the harvest, we could make some corn-husk dolls, each with their own dress that matches a dress we could make for you and Mae too."

"Cornhusk dolls?" Lucy's eyes rounded. "I've never known about them dolls. Can we make four of them? Or even five?"

Paisley placed her arm around Lucy. "I think that would be a wonderful idea."

Lucy squirmed away from her. "I'm gonna go to bed now and dream all about cornhusk dolls. Good night, Paisley."

The following day, Paisley set about cleaning the house. It needed a thorough dusting, and she figured the laundry created by the children would keep her busy until dusk.

Paisley stood on tiptoe and cleaned the corners of her room. Dust particles filled her nostrils and twice she sneezed. She dusted the top of the bureau, then leaned down and reached to dust underneath. That's when she noticed something beneath the dresser.

Kneeling, she craned her neck to see under the fancy legs of the out-of-place dresser. Beneath it was a plain wooden box with a lid. She pulled it from its hiding place.

The box intrigued her. Had it been Tyler's mother's box? Had it been lost? Perhaps she would surprise Tyler by announcing she'd found it.

Paisley sat on the edge of the bed and weighed her decision. Should she peruse the contents of the box? What if it was private? Did she have a right to even open the lid and peek inside?

Well no, she didn't have a *right*, but would just a tiny peek at the contents be so bad?

She ran her fingers over the smooth edges of the mahogany box, then lifted the lid. Inside was a pocket watch, a miniature antique porcelain doll, a brooch, four envelopes, and two folded papers with no envelopes, which Paisley presumed to be letters.

Curiosity overtook her. Paisley stood and glanced out the door of the room. Mae sat at the table drawing on a slate. A peek outside the window indicated Tyler worked far in the distance in the fields, and Lucy and Albert were completing their chores.

She retrieved the first letter, addressed to Tyler Shepherdson, Boise City, Idaho Territory. Paisley carefully pulled the letter from the already-opened envelope.

My Dearest Tyler,

I hope this finds you well. I'm not sure if you are receiving the letters I mail to you as I haven't heard from you in some time. I pray the Lord is keeping you safe and under His protective hand.

We are doing well. Your pa is preparing for spring planting. We recently purchased additional acreage. Do you recall the Farrand place? Their home burned to the ground last year, and they moved back to Missouri rather than rebuild. When their land went up for sale, we purchased it. Your pa is proud of how much land he has added to the farm. He remains hopeful that you will someday return and watches for you each day, hoping you'll ride across the prairie and onto the farm again soon.

I best go for now. I love you and miss you so. Please write soon.

Love,

Ma

With tears in her eyes, Paisley returned the letter to its rightful envelope. Had there been discord between Tyler and his parents? If so, had it been resolved?

She reached for another envelope. This one had the same writing, presumably from Tyler's mother.

My Dearest Tyler,

Hope you are well. Your pa and I have some exciting news!

We decided to adopt three orphan children from an orphan train that arrived in Cornwall. Albert is nine, Lucy is seven, and Mae is four. These children have suffered much, and we are blessed to be able to give them a home. I look forward to the day when you can meet them. We've told them all about their older brother.

Love you and miss you so. Please write soon.

Love,

Ma

Another envelope was again addressed to Tyler, but with different handwriting on the outside of the envelope.

Dear Tyler,
It saddens me to inform you that your parents are both gravely ill with the fever. It became an epidemic in Horizon and many lives have been lost.
Doc says he's not sure if your parents will survive. Your father, in particular, is not doing well.
If you are able, please come to Horizon immediately.
In Christ,
Reverend Marshall

Dabbing at her eyes with a nearby handkerchief, Paisley thought of the letter. How such a letter must have devastated Tyler! To hear his parents were ill and he apparently was so far away must have caused him grief. *I remember Mama and I caring for Papa during his illness. How heartbreaking to not be able to be at the bedside of those you love when they are ill.*

Paisley stood and again checked on Mae, then glanced again outside the window. Tyler remained in the fields, and Lucy and Albert continued with their chores. Should she open another letter? The temptation was too great. So, sitting once again on the edge of her bed, she pulled another letter from its already-opened envelope.

Dear Tyler,

It saddens me to inform you that your father has passed from the fever. Your mother is not doing well and likely won't last much longer. My prayers are with you as you read this devastating news.

Did you receive my last letter? Knowing you as I do, I have confidence that you did receive my last letter and are on your way to Horizon even as I pen this one.

Hurry quickly as I'm not sure how long your mother will last. She did indicate that should you arrive after she has passed, it is her and your father's wish that you care for the children they adopted a couple of weeks ago and raise them as your own.

Hope to hear from you soon.

In Christ,

Reverend Marshall

Had Tyler made it home before his mother passed? How had he reacted when he heard that he would inherit the children?

Paisley stared at the last two folded notes. Should she read those as well? With only a brief hesitation, she reached for the first one and unfolded it.

To Whom it May Concern,

This letter is in regards to Mae Fennell. She arrived at the West Orphanage a year ago after her father was killed in a saloon brawl. Her mother passed during her birth and as such, she is now an orphan. Those who resided next to the Fennell family indicate that Mr. Fennell was a mean man with a love for alcohol. He repeatedly yelled and could not hold his liquor well. He was brusque and showed no affection toward his daughter. While he tended to his fleeting employment opportunities, Mae was left with an elderly neighbor lady. She too has passed. Mae has not spoken for some time and the doctor assures us at the orphanage that she is quite possibly mute, although she can hear.

Sincerely,
Miss Coleford
West Orphanage
New York

Poor Mae! Paisley saw the tiny pinpricks in the letter and wondered if it had been pinned to her pinafore for whoever adopted her. Her father had been a horrible man? The doctor thought her to be mute?

There was one last letter. *I might as well open it. I've opened the rest.*

To Whom It May Concern,

This letter is in regards to Albert and Lucy. Their last names are unknown. While they are not biological siblings, they were found with several other children living in an abandoned warehouse in the city. They were promptly taken to the West Orphanage where they resided until now. Albert is a rapscallion of a boy and does not obey well. He indicated that his family emigrated from Germany and his father passed away soon after arrival. He informed us that his mother has passed too.

Lucy indicates that both of her parents have passed and she ran from her home to avoid being placed with a despicable aunt. We have attempted to locate such aunt, to no avail. Lucy later confessed to fabricating the story of having a living aunt, and as such, she has no surviving relatives, making her eligible for adoption.

Sincerely,

Miss Coleford
West Orphanage
New York

The children had been through so much and had many problems, yet Tyler's parents still adopted them. How Paisley wished she had met Mr. and Mrs. Shepherdson! She sat looking at the contents of the box and at the letter she'd just read. She was so deep in thought that she didn't hear Tyler's footsteps as he entered the room.

"The things in that box are private."

Paisley jumped at the sound of his voice. Tyler stood in front of her, the corners of his mouth turned downward and a muscle in his jaw twitching.

"I'm so sorry. I didn't realize…"

"You didn't realize that this is my home and the things in that box belong to me?" His voice rose an octave, the hurt and frustration apparent.

She'd never seen him angry before.

Apprehension filled her. "I do know this is your home, Tyler, and I do know the belongings in this home are yours."

"But you pay no mind to that fact and take it upon yourself to read letters that don't belong to you?"

She never should have opened the box to see what was inside. She should have resisted the temptation to be nosy. Regret overwhelmed her. "Tyler, I honestly didn't mean to upset you. I know so little about you…"

"So that gives you a right to rummage through my things? I don't know much about you either, Paisley, but you'll never find me going through what you own."

I own nothing but two dresses, a coin purse, and two pieces of paper. "No, it doesn't give me a right to rummage through your things," she whispered.

"The contents of that box and the box itself were hidden under the bureau for a reason. They're private letters for me and my family. Just because you're now my wife doesn't make you privy to them."

She carefully placed the letters and envelopes back into the box and under the bureau. "I'm sorry," she murmured again.

But Tyler left both the room and house. Paisley watched as he stalked down the road toward the fields, shoulders stiffened and hands clenched at his side.

Her stomach knotted and a sense of heaviness rested in her chest. Tears pricked her eyes as the hurt and anguish overcame her. She'd had no right to look through his things. No right to read the confidential letters.

And now her carelessness would cost her. Would he forgive her?

CHAPTER TWENTY-EIGHT

WHY DID SHE THINK it was her right to look at the letters? Tyler stormed from the house and back to the fields. He regretted being so harsh with Paisley, but how could she go through his things without so much as a second thought? The letters were personal and no doubt she'd read each one. What must she think of him for not being there when his parents fell ill? What would her opinion of him be now after reading the words of his mother and the reverend? He didn't want her to think less of him.

Now that he was married, he shouldn't believe he'd be afforded the same amount of privacy as before his wedding vows. At some point, Paisley would have found the letters.

He stooped to pick up some tools and began again mending a broken fence, attempting to clear his mind from what just occurred. However, he couldn't stop thinking about seeing her on the bed looking through the private items in the box. Letters that only he should be privy to.

The letters. Tyler had received both letters from Reverend Marshall on the same day. Without hesitation, he rode from Boise City where he was helping to build the new assay office, to Horizon, stopping only to eat and to sleep for an hour or two. Not that he'd had an appetite. His father had already passed and his mother might too before he had the chance to apologize and tell her he loved her.

His father had already passed.

The memory clouded his mind—the memory of losing Pa without any words between them to repair the discord that occurred when Tyler left Horizon was nearly unbearable.

The sky was dark that evening when Tyler rode into Horizon. The town was deserted except for the loud commotion coming from the lone saloon. Weariness overtook him, but Tyler forged ahead to his parents' home. Ma lay on the bed, Maribel by her side.

Tyler had dropped to his knees beside Ma's bed, ignoring Doc's warnings about catching the fever. Ma's voice had been weak. So weak. He had gripped her hand, willing this to be a nightmare and not reality. Precautions were unimportant. All that mattered was Ma. How much he loved her. How much he'd disappointed her.

Beads of sweat formed on her forehead, and her red hair hung in clumps. The relentless fever had such a hold on her. But she could still survive. God could still work a miracle.

I'm so sorry. He did his best to fight the tears stinging his eyes, but he lost the battle. Gone was his robust mother. In her place lay a fragile, fever-worn shell desperately clinging to life.

Somehow Ma managed to offer him a smile. *"We missed you,"* she had rasped.

He had missed them too. Watching Ma struggle to breathe, he realized just how much. Apology after apology fell from his mouth in a desperate tone, as if he uttered those words often enough they would give Ma the strength she needed.

She only gave him another smile, saying in her weak voice how she both loved and forgave him.

And how Pa had forgiven him.

The premonition swelling in Tyler's chest quashed the joy her words brought. Later he would rejoice at being forgiven. At knowing he was still loved. But at the time, all he had to do was somehow convince Ma to live another day.

Her fingers, now so frail, had loosely tightened around his. Each word sounded like it sapped all her strength. She begged him to look after the children should she pass, to raise them as his own. The intensity in her gaze belied her feeble appearance.

He had promised not to disappoint her a second time and vowed to look after Albert, Lucy, and Mae. Then she'd told him she loved him and he'd apologized again for leaving her and Pa and not writing when he'd promised he would.

Ma also requested he marry a God-fearing woman. He agreed, ending his promise with a choked, *"I love you, Ma."*

A cough wracked her before she managed another tremulous smile. He would never forget what she said next. *"Jesus loves you, Tyler. Really loves you. Died for you. Gave His life for you."* Each word drained her, but still she persisted, insisting on Christ's love for him. *"Promise me you'll find out what it means to have eternal life."*

He promised—how could he not?

But Ma didn't hear his promise.

For she had already breathed her last.

And something within Tyler shattered that day.

A wet spot on the dirt below brought Tyler to the realization that he'd shed a tear or two during his recollection of Ma's last minutes on earth. He wiped his eyes with the back of his hand. Allowing anyone to see him at loss with his emotions wouldn't do.

He'd been so prideful. Such a fool. So worried about himself. And now what must Paisley think of him? That he truly was the lowest of low to not have written back to Ma?

To not be there in their time of need?

Tyler straightened and reached again for the tools to repair the fence, tools he'd dropped during his travel back into the worst day of his life.

He'd kept his promise to Ma that he'd look into what it meant to have eternal life. Tyler had made Jesus his Lord and Savior just hours after Ma's death, thanks to Reverend Marshall's compassionate instruction. Tyler hadn't stopped learning about the Lord since. And not only learning about the Lord, but trying to live for Him too.

And he hadn't done that for Ma—he'd made a decision for Christ for himself. At first, trusting Jesus may have been part of the promise he'd made to Ma, but in a short amount of time, his faith became genuine and became his and his alone.

Tyler now attempted to keep his other promise to care for the children and raise them as his own. In fact, some day he aimed to legally adopt them. But it was so hard to know how to be a father. He kept comparing himself to Pa and coming up short.

Then there was Paisley. He saw her in the distance hanging clothes on the clothesline. She stopped every so often to wipe her face. Was she wiping tears? Tears he had caused by using his words in an unkind manner? He hoped to be able to repair the rift that settled between them—a rift that he had caused. Did it really matter that she had seen the letters? No. If she stayed married to him long enough, she would come to know all kinds of things about him. She may have a lesser opinion of him, but he vowed to never keep anything from her. Not even what he'd done and the guilt that weighed on him each and every day.

Besides, if he wanted his new marriage to grow and succeed, he'd have to mend the tension between them, just like mending the broken fence.

Paisley had disappointed Mama on more than one occasion; however, one time had been profound. When Paisley was eight or nine years old, they'd been in the mercantile purchasing dry goods when Paisley eyeballed some candy in the glass bowl on the counter, just begging to be eaten. However, Paisley had no money and she knew better than to ask Mama for anything extra. They simply weren't able to afford additional purchases.

So while Mama preoccupied herself with asking the mercantile owner to retrieve something off of a high shelf, Paisley took the liberty of helping herself to the candy. Sticking a piece in her mouth, she savored its sugary taste.

Busy with her purchases, Ma hadn't known until they were on the way home when she'd noticed numerous pieces of candy tucked in the pocket of Paisley's dress.

All it had taken were Mama's saddened eyes and profound disappointment to make Paisley struggle with regret for many weeks following the incident. That and the hard work it took to pay for the candy and the embarrassment of telling the mercantile owner she'd unlawfully pilfered. Paisley had never stolen again.

And now Paisley faced Tyler's profound disappointment. Regret consumed her, and she longed for a way to make him see she truly was sorry. *Lord, please let him forgive me.*

Hanging the last piece of clothing on the line, Paisley lifted the metal washbasin and trudged toward the house, the disappointment in herself and Tyler's disappointment in her weighing heavily on her shoulders.

Paisley closed the door and set about finishing the remaining chores for the day. Had she had to cook a meal, she'd in no way have been able to finish the laundry. But since there were still more meals from the townsfolk, cooking had been postponed. And that was a good thing. A very good thing. Tyler may someday forgive her for her nosiness, but he'd likely never forgive her for her lack of culinary skills.

Footsteps on the wood floor interrupted her thoughts. "Paisley?"

She turned to face him. His arms hung at his sides and his eyes were red. Was he not feeling well? "Yes?"

"I shouldn't have gotten so mad about the letters." He cleared his throat and looked down at his shoes. "And I shouldn't have spoken harshly to you."

"Tyler, it's me who's sorry. I had no right to open the box and peek inside, let alone, read letters addressed to you. I am so, so sorry. Please believe me."

Tyler took a step toward her. "No, you shouldn't have read them. They are mine, but you did and that's that. I don't think a man should have any secrets from his wife, it's just that those letters, especially the ones from my ma..."

"Were yours and yours alone. I understand."

"Yes." He took another step, bridging the distance between them.

"I'll not ever so much as glance at that box again. I promise."

"I didn't want you to think less of me after reading the letters from my ma and Reverend Marshall."

"Oh, Tyler, I didn't think less of you. Not at all. My heart ached for you at the loss of your parents, and the letters from the orphanage about the children were so sad."

"You didn't think less of me?"

"Not at all."

Tyler exhaled a deep breath, and Paisley pondered his relief. He'd been concerned about what she thought of him? To think less of him as she read the heartbreaking notes never crossed her mind. Although she was curious about the details surrounding Tyler's leaving Horizon and his subsequent return.

Paisley cautiously reached a hand toward his arm. "Please forgive me, Tyler."

"I forgive you, Paisley." He held her gaze.

A sniffle escaped her. "Thank you."

Tyler put his hand on top of hers. "I left Horizon to seek adventure. In the meantime, I disappointed my parents something awful. I never was able to apologize to Pa before his passing, but I did seek forgiveness from Ma. That's how I know forgiveness is so important. She forgave me." His voice shook. "Some in town thought less of me too, but I didn't care about that. All I cared about was my own guilt and disappointing my parents, which has weighed heavier than anything I have ever carried."

"I'm sorry, Tyler." She motioned for him to sit at the table. "Would you care to share your burden with me?"

Tyler sat, but appeared hesitant.

"Sometimes it helps to share what you've been through with someone else." *Someone who cares about you.*

Within moments, Tyler shared what he'd carried since he left Horizon four years ago. And from the look on his face when he finished, Paisley sensed some of that burden had been lifted.

CHAPTER TWENTY-NINE

"IT'S SUCH A PLEASANT evening," Tyler remarked. "Would anyone care to join me outside?"

"I would!" chorused Lucy and Albert.

Mae said nothing, but attempted to drag her chair from the kitchen table and follow the others to a peaceful place outside. Tyler lifted her chair, then carried the rest of the chairs outside. He lined them up across the front of the house.

"I forgot something. I'll be right back." Tyler dashed back inside the house and returned with a thin wooden case.

"What's that?" Lucy asked.

Tyler flipped open the box and removed a metal object.

"I seen one of those!" Albert exclaimed. He jumped from his chair and stood beside Tyler. "Them's one of those harmonicas. I seen one of them in New York once. A man on the corner was playing it, and people was throwing coins into a hat he had on the ground."

Tyler nodded. "You're right, Albert. It's a harmonica."

"What does it do?" Lucy asked. She crowded around Tyler on the opposite side.

"I'll show you." Tyler motioned to Mae, who sat in her chair a good distance from the rest of the family. "Mae-Mae, would you like to come closer?"

Mae said nothing. She only stared. Tyler turned his gaze toward Paisley. "Have you seen one of these, Paisley?"

Paisley scooted her chair closer. "I have. A friend of my pa's had a harmonica he played when he served in the War Between the States."

Soon, everyone was crowded around Tyler except Mae. Was there nothing he could do to let her know she could trust this new family God had provided for her?

"Mae-Mae?" Tyler again held out his hand to her. "Would you like to see the harmonica too?" He glanced up and met Paisley's eyes. Was she wondering what could be done about Mae as well?

Mae then stood and took a step toward Tyler. He wiggled his forefinger, beckoning her to take another step, even a small one. Mae took another step and then another. Tyler attempted to hide his surprise when she not only came to stand by him but climbed into his lap, her arms firmly by her sides. Tyler resisted the urge to wrap his arm around her and pull her to him, as Pa had done so many times when Tyler was a youngster and climbed into Pa's lap. Instead, he sat still, afraid to even breathe.

His eyes again met Paisley's. Was she thinking the same thing he was about all the prayers lifted to the Lord on Mae's behalf? Was she realizing, as Tyler did, that God was already beginning to answer those prayers?

"Where did you get it?" Lucy asked, interrupting Tyler's thoughts.

"I purchased it at a mercantile last year. It got a bit lonely at times during my travels. I saw this and decided to teach myself how to play it."

"Will you play it for us?" Albert asked.

Mae reached a tiny finger toward the harmonica and fingered the raised lettering on the shiny instrument.

"It was made by a man named Matthias Hohner," Tyler said, his voice quiet. He wanted to do nothing to scare Mae.

"Ain'tcha gonna play it?" Albert asked again.

Tyler raised the harmonica to his lips and began to play a tune. When he finished, he placed the harmonica on his lap. "Does anyone know that song?"

"'Amazing Grace'?" Paisley asked.

"Yes." The fact that she'd sat so patiently this afternoon listening to him speak of his ma's last days warmed his heart toward her, and he appreciated her kindness and compassion.

"Play another one!" exclaimed Lucy.

"All right. Let's see if you recognize this one." Tyler began to play a quicker tune.

In response to the beat, Albert stood and faced Paisley. "Would ya care to dance?"

"Well, yes, I would, kind gentleman," Paisley teased. She stood and locked elbows with Albert, who took turns swinging and locking elbows with Paisley and Lucy. Soon the three of them were laughing, and when the song was over, they collapsed into their chairs.

Paisley giggled. "I can't remember the last time I danced to 'Oh! Susanna'."

"Oh, we hear it all the time," bemoaned Lucy, dragging out her words in exaggeration. "Only it's from Tyler whistlin' the song, not playin' it on his harmonica."

Tyler grinned. The lonely nights learning how to play the songs on the harmonica paid off even if he only knew those two tunes.

With the exception of a coyote howling in the distance, silence filled the air. A warm, peaceful breeze brought the scent of summer, and Paisley leaned her head back against the house and closed her eyes. For the first time, she felt at ease in her new home.

"I'm glad we live here now," said Lucy.

Paisley opened her eyes to see a satisfied Lucy leaning back in her chair and clasping her hands together. What life had she lived before coming to Horizon? What about Albert? Paisley knew hardly anything about the children, although she now knew slightly more due to reading the letters.

"I'm glad we're here too," said Albert. "I didn't like livin' in the orphanage all that much. The food tasted somethin' terrible."

"At least we didn't have to go and steal it," said Lucy.

"I only done stole once," declared Albert, giving his sister a wary glance.

"That's 'cause we were taken to the orphanage."

"The porridge there was the worst."

"I think so too."

Paisley listened as Albert and Lucy recounted their lives at the orphanage. She'd had the blessing of her parents until she reached adulthood. But the three children she had been asked to help raise hadn't been so fortunate. She again recalled the letters in the box and imagined them pinned on the children, telling what little of their pasts there was to tell to any prospective parents.

Lucy pointed a finger at Albert. "One time you stole some candy from the pantry, Albert. I saw you."

"So? I was hungry."

"It's wrong to steal, isn't it, Paisley?" Lucy asked, her freckled nose wrinkling in concern.

"Yes, it is wrong to steal," Paisley confirmed. She would make the most of the influence God called her to be in the lives of the children.

"You did wrong things too," argued Albert. "'Member when you didn't do your schoolwork?"

"That's 'cause I didn't know how."

"Children, let's not argue," interjected Tyler.

"Paisley, do you think God forgives me?" Lucy started toward Paisley and stood in front of her.

Paisley reached for Lucy. Unlike Mae who grew uncomfortable at any attempts of affection, Lucy longed for it. At the slight invitation, Lucy sat on Paisley's lap and put her arms around Paisley's neck.

Paisley brushed Lucy's hair from her face and planted a kiss on her forehead. "There is nothing you can do that the Lord can't forgive."

"Even being naughty at the orphanage?"

"Even being naughty at the orphanage. That's why He sent Jesus to us to forgive our sins," Paisley answered.

"I like Jesus. I like him a lot." Lucy snuggled closer.

"So do I, Lucy. So do I."

"You think he forgives all our mistakes, even our biggest ones?" asked Albert.

"Even our biggest ones," confirmed Paisley. She glanced up and caught Tyler's eye. She'd been so grateful for what he'd shared with her today. It had brought them closer.

"Have you ever done somethin' wrong?" Albert asked, backing away to sit by himself in his chair against the house.

"Yes, Albert, I have." She had a list of regrets and an even longer list of things she'd had to seek forgiveness for over the years. And while the Lord had forgiven her, she had things in her life she'd failed to forgive herself for. The day of the flood flashed through her mind.

"And did Jesus go and forgive you?"

"Yes, Albert, He did."

Yet if Jesus forgave her, why was it so hard for Paisley to convince herself that all that had happened to her parents wasn't her fault?

Albert rose and walked to where she sat, and Paisley put her arm around him. With Lucy in her lap and Albert at her side, she praised the Lord that two of the children were softening to their new lives.

"I think when I grow up I'd like to tell people about Jesus forgiving them," said Albert.

"Or," giggled Lucy, "you could be a bandit."

"No, not a bandit. I'm gonna be a reverend like Reverend Marshall."

Paisley had no doubt in her mind that the Lord could take a once broken little boy and give him the important task of planting seeds for eternity.

CHAPTER THIRTY

SHE HEARD HIM BEFORE she saw him.

The pounding of horses' hooves sounded in her ears. She turned from scrubbing the stain on Albert's trousers to see a familiar figure riding toward the Shepherdson farm. He was wearing his trademark brown hat, and as he drew closer, she noticed the wispy strands of black hair clinging to his neck.

Paisley willed herself to run and seek refuge, but her feet refused to move. She stood paralyzed, her heart thumping against her chest.

The rider stopped just short of where she stood and dismounted.

Ivan.

He hadn't changed in the past weeks since she'd last seen him. He still sported the same curly, black, pencil-thin mustache, and his hardened eyes still pierced through the soul with a devious probing.

"Well, well," Ivan said, striding the few short steps to where Paisley stood. "If it isn't Paisley Abbott washing laundry on this otherwise beautiful summer day."

Bile rose in her throat. Where was Tyler? She spied Mae a short distance away, but where were Lucy and Albert? "How did you find me?"

Ivan chuckled an unsettling chortle and climbed from his horse. "Thought you'd get away from me, did you?" He stroked her cheek, his touch rough and abrasive.

Paisley flinched and stumbled backward to avoid his touch. "I asked how you found me here."

Mae, who had been standing near the barn, ran toward the house.

"It wasn't too difficult. But if you must know, I'll tell you." Ivan sneered, baring his too-long teeth in a devilish taunt. "A man saw a woman of your description climb into the back of a wagon in Cornwall. Naturally, I figured you were headed toward Ingleville rather than in the other direction where there's nothing for miles. Once I arrived in Ingleville, I asked at each business if anyone had seen someone of your description or if they'd heard of a woman by the name of Paisley Abbott." Ivan paused to dust off the sleeves of his shirt. "Your name is not exactly common, although it is somewhat memorable. It was written in the record books at the hotel. Such a foolish slip on your part, Paisley.

"The proprietor mentioned that he'd heard that you and some man were heading to Horizon. Of course, when I arrived in Horizon, everyone knew about a woman named Paisley who lived on a farm with her husband, Tyler. They directed me here. Pretty friendly town if I do say so myself." His roving gaze sent a shiver down her spine. "Did you miss me?"

"You need to leave." Her legs threatened to fail to hold her upright.

"Now, now. Is that any way to talk to the man who was given a blessing by your pa to marry you? I'm here for you and I'm here for the deed to the land your pa also promised me. By the way, I don't appreciate you making a fool of me in Cornwall. There will be consequences for that."

Ivan's intimidating scowl caused the hair on the back of her neck to rise. "I am already married, and you need to leave." Paisley's voice sounded weak and shaky in her ears, unlikely to dissuade Ivan from sinister intentions.

"Annul it. You were supposed to marry me, and I intend to marry you and claim my right to the Abbott farm." He grabbed her arm and began yanking her toward his horse. "Get on the horse," he growled.

"Tyler!" Where was he? Would he hear her?

Albert peered from around the edge of the barn. "Albert, go get Tyler."

Without argument, Albert turned and ran toward the fields.

Ivan dragged Paisley toward the horse, and she again dug her heels into the ground. "You'll not give me an ounce of trouble, you insufferable woman."

"Wait. Don't you want the deed?"

He ground his jaw, and his nostrils flared as indecision wavered in his expression. He placed a tight grip on the area between her shoulder and neck and squeezed. "We'll worry about that later. Get on the horse."

Paisley winced from the searing pain and attempted to bat at him with her fists, hitting him squarely in the nose.

He muttered several curses and clutched his nose with his hand.

"Tyler!" she screamed again.

Ivan clamped a hand over her mouth and hissed in her ear, his warm, stale breath causing a nauseating twinge in her stomach. "Enough with the noise. This time you won't get away."

Tyler wiped the perspiration from his brow and started toward the house. It had been a good day. He'd achieved much in the fields and even determined he rather enjoyed the intense and fulfilling work farming brought. He hoped Pa would be proud.

"Tyler! Tyler!" Albert sprinted toward him. "Come quick!"

"What is it?"

"It's a mean man. He's hurting Paisley."

It took less than a second for the direness of the situation to be communicated from his brain to his feet. Tyler commenced to running faster than he ever had toward the house.

As he drew closer, Tyler witnessed a man forcing Paisley toward a horse.

Anger coursed through him. "Step away from my wife!"

"She's coming with me."

Tyler scrutinized the man. While he was a few inches taller, Tyler was stouter, more muscled, and likely stronger. "You heard me. Release her now." He positioned himself between the man and the horse, preventing the man from fulfilling his goal.

"Her pa promised her and the land to me," the man seethed.

Ivan. Just as Tyler suspected. But how had he found Paisley? "She's already married and the land is hers. Release her and get off my property."

"Or?"

Tyler had never been particularly prone to temper, but right now his anger flared. "Wait around and find out."

"Give me the deed to the Abbott farm and I'll be on my way."

Paisley shook her head. "No."

"Sounds to me like the lady has spoken. The Abbott farm doesn't belong to you. Best be on your way.

Ivan released Paisley and shoved her hard, causing her to stumble. Albert, eyes wide, rushed toward her.

"I'll leave this time, but you haven't heard the last of me. What Ivan Marchesi wants, Ivan Marchesi gets." He expectorated, a revolting and exaggerated sound rising from his throat, before spitting on the ground. Ivan glowered at Tyler, then forced his way past him, shoving his shoulder hard into Tyler's before mounting his horse and riding toward town.

Tyler hadn't expected Ivan to surrender so easily, but he was thankful he had. Paisley staggered toward him and he drew her into his arms, holding her close. "Did he hurt you?"

She shook her head, but from the tears dampening his shirt, Tyler surmised differently.

Tyler held her for some time, kissing her hair and re-assuring her she was safe and that Ivan couldn't hurt her now. A disturbing thought entered his mind. What if he'd been even five minutes later?

He cast a glance toward Albert who stood with Lucy a short distance away. "You did a heroic thing, Albert, in fetching me. Good job, son."

Albert puffed out his small chest and stood straighter. "Yes, sir."

"I'm proud of you."

Albert beamed. "I knew I had to do something." He rushed toward Tyler and wrapped his arms around Tyler and Paisley.

Lucy walked over and did the same. "I'm glad nothing happened to you, Paisley. I don't want to lose another ma."

Tyler didn't want to again entertain the thought of what could have happened to Paisley had he not arrived when he had. He closed his eyes and thanked the Lord for Albert's swift actions.

"Tyler…"

"Shh. It's all right. He can't hurt you now."

"But what if he comes back?"

"I'll ride into town and alert the sheriff. My thought is he'll wait before returning to avoid any trouble with the law. And I'll do whatever I can to keep you safe."

Paisley hadn't wanted to move from the comfort of Tyler's embrace. She shivered at the thought of what Ivan could have done to her had Tyler not arrived when he did. She'd not interrupt the family hug, but later she aimed to tell Albert how grateful she was to him for fetching Tyler.

A family hug. The uniting of five people into a family that God orchestrated.

Only there weren't five.

Paisley jerked her head back from resting on Tyler's chest. "Where is Mae? She was near the barn before Ivan's arrival, then I saw her run toward the house."

"She's probably inside," suggested Lucy.

Paisley rushed toward the house and searched each corner of every room. She knew Mae didn't like loud noises and likely the confrontation between Paisley and Ivan startled her.

"Mae?"

No answer, not even a slight rustle of feet.

"She's not in the house."

"We need to find her. Lucy, check the barn. Albert, check the cellar," directed Tyler.

Fear struck Paisley. "I'm worried, Tyler."

"We'll find her."

But Paisley wasn't so sure. Mae hadn't been at the farm long enough to know her way around well, and she was so young.

"I'll start toward town and get help. Paisley, you head toward the river," Tyler instructed. "I'll come for you soon."

Paisley nodded. "All right."

Lucy and Albert hadn't been able to locate Mae in the barn. Nor was she in the chicken coop or the cellar. Paisley started toward the river. *Lord, please keep Mae safe. Guard her and protect her, and please let us find her.*

Anxiety rose within her. A mother for such a short time and already she'd allowed one of her children to get lost.

"Mae-Mae! Where are you?" Desperation sounded in her voice. Had Tyler found Mae walking along the road to town? Would anyone be available to help search for her?

Paisley headed toward the river, thankful Tyler had previously given her a full tour of the farm.

Had she wandered forever? The sun began to sink below the horizon and still no sign of the child. Paisley wasn't sure if she herself was lost. The surroundings were becoming less and less familiar. Panic again rose in her throat.

She continued to call Mae's name and look for any indication she'd been in the vicinity. Concern. Discouragement. Fear. Despondency. What would she do if she couldn't find Mae? *Lord, please let Tyler have found her.*

How long had she searched? So long that she'd lost track of time. And where was Tyler? He said he would come for her. Yet, he hadn't.

Paisley inhaled the faint scent of rain. A deer ran in front of her in the distance. The rumble of thunder roared in the sky.

"Mae, please answer me!"

No response.

Paisley continued to wander, looking everywhere she could think of where a small child might hide—behind rocks, in the ravines, near the river.

Near the river. What if Mae drowned just as Mama and Papa had? No, she wouldn't think that way. The Lord would protect Mae.

Paisley combed the brush, inspected all sides of a huge rock formation, peered inside an opening likely used as a home for a critter, and again cautiously perused the rushing river. It was elevated this time of year due to the abundance of rain and showed no mercy as it lapped over rocks and swished high above the sides of the banks. She squinted toward the farthest end where the river curved around a corner when something caught her eye. She froze, dread filling every part of her. Seconds ticked by until finally Paisley forced her feet to move. Heart pounding, she hurried alongside the riverbank. *Lord, please, no...*

The sky spit random drops of rain, and the sound of the rushing water echoed in her ears. "Mae?"

Something bobbed up and down in the water, but the distance to see clearly was still too great. Paisley again hiked her skirts and slogged through the muddy areas near the river. Thoughts of Mama and Papa entered her mind, and she begged the Lord to spare Mae.

Upon closer examination, she noticed what she had seen was only a log. Her eyes flooded with tears. *Thank You, Jesus.*

Paisley pivoted to the other direction. Perhaps Mae hadn't come this way. Maybe Tyler had already found her. Or she was crouched out of sight somewhere on the farm.

She was about to return the way she'd come when she thought she heard a whimper. *Please, please, Lord, let it be Mae.* She peered to the left, then to the right. Had she imagined the noise?

Paisley strained her ear in the direction of the whimper, hoping to hear it again.

"Mae? Is that you?" *Please be Mae.*

She heard a muted sob in response. "Mae, I'm coming to help you. Please keep making noises so I can find you."

The sobs continued, but where was Mae? Something fell on her head then, and Paisley peered toward the sky. Perched in a tree about six feet from the ground, Mae clasped her arms around the trunk. Her purple calico dress was ripped and her face stained with tears. But she was safe. Paisley dropped to her knees in the dirt. "Thank You, Father!" she said, humbling herself before the One who'd answered her prayer.

"Mae, don't worry, honey. I'm going to get you down."

But how?

Climbing trees wasn't foreign to Paisley. She'd grown up climbing the trees that surrounded the farm, much to Mama's dismay. But it had been a while since she'd partaken in one of her favorite pastimes.

Wrapping her arms around the tree trunk, she sought stable footing. She was almost able to reach Mae when her right foot slipped. She slid back down the tree, stumbled, and hit her right knee on the packed earth below.

Paisley winced as the pain throbbed through her knee, but she determined she would not let that prevent her from rescuing her child. "I'm coming, Mae. Don't let go." Could Mae understand her? Paisley had no idea of how much the girl comprehended or even heard.

She again climbed to a spot where she could reach Mae. "Sweetie, carefully let go and wrap your arms around my neck. Do you understand?"

An ever so slight nod of Mae's head gave Paisley hope. "Very carefully, Mae-Mae."

The force of Mae's jump toward her nearly caused Paisley to fall again. "All right. Now we're going to get down from here," she said more to herself than to Mae.

When on solid ground again, Paisley pulled Mae to her. She held her close and kissed the top of her head. "Oh, Mae, I was so worried. Please, please don't ever run off again." Paisley's words came in choked sobs.

The emotion surged through her as she clung to Mae—Paisley's uncontrollable weeping meshing with Mae's wailing cries.

The grief overtook her as Paisley mourned for Mae and the life the girl lived before becoming a Shepherdson. For Lucy and Albert, living on the streets with no home and then taken to an orphanage. She grieved the loss of her parents and how she missed them. She mourned the loss of her farm and the vivid memories of the raging floodwaters destroying everything in its path.

Mae attached herself to Paisley, her body shaking as she wept.

And then Paisley cried in gratitude for finding Mae when so many things could have happened to her. Gratitude that Mae hadn't drowned. Gratitude that Tyler had arrived in time to protect her from Ivan. And thankfulness for the Lord's providence when she stowed away in his wagon. Appreciation to Jesus for all He'd done, the large and profound things, the seemingly minor things, and all things in between. The things she remembered to thank Him for and the things she'd often taken for granted.

She and Mae clung to each other, a bond forming between them—a bond only the Lord could have orchestrated in His perfect timing.

After some time, Paisley took a deep breath and knelt to Mae's height. Dusk was upon them and the air had cooled considerably. "Mae, we have to find our way back to the farm. Do you think you can help me?" Mae said nothing, but clamped her arms more tightly around Paisley, refusing to let go of her. Shuffling the child into a comfortable position, Paisley carried her while limping in the direction she believed to be correct.

"When I couldn't find you, I thought..." Tyler let the words remain unspoken. What if he hadn't found Paisley and Mae? What if something had happened? How foolish he'd been to send Paisley toward the river by herself. He pulled Paisley and Mae to him, holding them both tight as emotion welled inside of him.

"I'm so sorry I sent you here to find her. I should have been the one, but I was worried you might encounter Ivan on the road and I wanted to see if we could organize a search party, and..." his excuses sounded uncompelling in his own ears.

"God in His mercy led me to Mae. I thought she..." but Paisley stopped short of what were likely Tyler's thoughts as well.

He framed her face with his hands. "If anything had happened to either of you, I wouldn't have been able to forgive myself." Paisley's eyes were red and swollen, her hair tangled and mussed, and tear tracks mixed with dirt had dried on her face. He tenderly kissed her forehead. "Here, let me take Mae." He reached for the girl, but she clung tighter to Paisley and buried her face in Paisley's shoulder.

"It's all right," Paisley murmured.

"I would have been here sooner, but I was on the road toward town when I saw Reverend Marshall. He rode back into town to organize a search party and send Maribel to watch Albert and Lucy."

"I thought I wasn't going to be able to find Mae, but I did. She was up in a tree."

"In a tree? Our little Mae-Mae? I'm just thankful you're both safe."

"It started to rain, then I became disoriented. I wasn't sure I'd be able to find our way back to the farm. I'm so glad you found us," Paisley whispered.

"Me too, Paisley. Me too." Tyler held her again, noting Mae starting to squirm from the discomfort of being sandwiched between them. "Let's get everyone home."

He noticed Paisley limping toward the horse. "What happened to your leg?"

"I was climbing the tree to retrieve Mae, and I'd forgotten I'm not as agile as I was as a child. I slipped and hit my knee."

"I'll fetch Doc when we return home."

Tyler assisted Paisley and Mae onto the horse and led them to the Shepherdson farm.

During the entire way back, he praised the Lord for His protection.

CHAPTER THIRTY-ONE

IN TOWN THE NEXT day, Paisley saw Doc again for both the pain and bruising from Ivan clamping on her shoulder and neck and for her injured knee.

"As I mentioned last night when I came to the farm to check your injuries, both your neck and your knee have been badly bruised. I'd recommend you rest and stay off the knee for a few days, but with you being a wife and mom, I know that's going to be impossible."

Paisley thought about Lucy, Albert, and Mae and all the chores that awaited her. And today would be the first time she'd have to make supper.

The thought terrified her.

"Just take it as easy as you can," Doc continued.

"Thank you, Doc." Paisley pondered her next question. "I've been meaning to ask you about Mae."

"Yes?"

"Do you think she's mute?"

Doc folded his hands over his protruding belly. "Tyler's ma, Ruby, brought Mae in to see me shortly after the Shepherdsons adopted her. As you know, the Shepherdsons had such a short amount of time with their newly-adopted children before their untimely deaths. Thankfully, none

213

of the children caught the fever, which led me to believe they'd all been exposed to it at some point in their lives. Likely the orphanage."

"I can't imagine them dying so soon after adopting the children."

"Nor can I. It was devastating to be sure. You and Tyler now have three children, all of whom have suffered much in their young lives. Who knows what kind of lives they lived in the orphanage as well? Some orphanages are good, some not so much. And Mae's pa often partook in whiskey and was prone to temper. Did he take out that wrath on Mae? We may never know." Doc paused and reached up to adjust the round spectacles on his nose. "Do I think Mae is mute? No. Do I think that she has suffered much hurt and trauma in her young life? Yes. However, I serve a God who is the Author of miracles.

"Had Ruby and Zeke had the opportunity to raise Lucy, Albert, and Mae to adulthood, there's no telling how God could have used their love and devotion to heal those children, especially Mae. The Shepherdsons were wonderful, God-fearing folks. I was sorry He took them home so soon. But now it's yours and Tyler's chance to pray for, love, and nurture the children. And who knows? Mae just might surprise us."

Paisley smiled. Doc's words about Mae comforted her. "Thanks for everything, Doc." She accepted Doc's arm as he assisted her to her feet.

"You're welcome, Paisley. Take care of that knee, and if it doesn't feel better in a few days, be sure to have Tyler fetch me."

Paisley glanced at the schoolyard. Albert and Lucy had joined in playing a game with a few other children. Mae sat beneath a tree, seemingly content. Paisley limped toward the mercantile. She had a few items to purchase before she met Tyler and returned home.

"Good afternoon, Tabitha," greeted Paisley as she hobbled through the door.

Tabitha looked up from her work. "Well, good morning to you too, Paisley. I was so glad to hear Mae was found. What a frightening ordeal!"

"I'm so thankful she was uninjured. Who knew being a mother would be such an adventure?"

Tabitha laughed. "For certain. How's your knee?"

"It'll heal in time. Please thank your husband for being willing to join the search party to look for Mae."

"He's glad to help. I heard that a man came to the farm and threatened you. My husband serves as a deputy when needed, so he was informed of the situation."

"Yes, Tyler stopped by to see the sheriff. He said he'd keep a lookout for Ivan, whom I hope has returned to Pringle."

Tabitha firmed her hands on her hips. "He will if he knows what's good for him." She paused. "It is our prayer as well that he has left Horizon and that he'll leave well enough alone. My husband said the sheriff plans to apprise the entire town about this Ivan fellow so we can all be aware. That's one of the things I like best about Horizon—folks all care about each other here."

Paisley added the fact that the Lord had led her to such a benevolent town to her list of things she was thankful for.

Tyler had just the surprise for Paisley. "What about supper at the restaurant before we head back to the farm?"

"Supper at the restaurant? Really?" Paisley's countenance lit with enthusiasm. "Yes, that would be delightful!"

"An early supper at the restaurant it is then. I'll fetch the children."

At first he'd thought better of his decision because, at some point, he would run out of the funds he'd saved from his previous employment. But when she'd so enthusiastically responded, he couldn't change his mind. Although it would be pricey to feed a family of five at the restaurant, it would be worth it.

Had Tyler known such a minute gesture would have meant so much, he would have suggested it first thing that morning. But his mind had been on so many things: the gratitude at finding Mae, Paisley's injuries, and Ivan's untimely visit yesterday. Would the man return? Was Paisley in danger? He'd for sure do whatever it took to protect her. A visit with the sheriff had eased Tyler's concerns somewhat. It never hurt to inform the law when things were amiss.

Tyler held the door to the restaurant open while Paisley, Albert, Lucy, and Mae shuffled inside.

"Well, if it isn't the Shepherdson family. It's so nice to see you all." Wilhelmina embraced Paisley. "How's the knee?"

Tyler watched the interaction between Paisley and Wilhelmina, marveling at how quickly they'd become friends. The two women couldn't be more opposite. Wilhelmina was well into her forties, short and rotund with red hair. Paisley was twenty-two and tall and slender with brown hair and hazel eyes. Wilhelmina never met a stranger and Paisley was more reserved.

Wilhelmina had been Ma's best friend, so he wasn't surprised that Wilhelmina liked Paisley as well.

"Now, I know Tyler will want pumpkin pie for dessert, but what can I fix for you all for supper?"

"We ain't never been to a rest-er-ont before," said Albert.

"Haven't ever been," corrected Paisley.

"Haven't ever been," agreed Albert. "I think I'll just have pumpkin pie."

Wilhelmina laughed and ruffled Albert's hair. "You sound like Tyler. Remember when you ate too much pumpkin pie that time you and your folks came here? You were so sure you wouldn't get a bellyache afterwards."

"I do remember that. We'd just moved to Horizon and we came here for Ma's birthday."

"You prit' near ate an entire pie in just a few minutes. What were you, sixteen years old or so?"

"Almost seventeen, and while I had a bellyache something fierce all the next day, it didn't stop my love for the best pumpkin pie at Wilhelmina's Restaurant."

Wilhelmina brushed aside his compliment. "I'm sure you had some fine cooking when you were away from Horizon."

"Reckon not. I'd be dishonest if I said I had any decent cooking while I was away. Some of the meals were just plain distasteful and unfit to eat. Once in a while they were edible, but not often." He and Wilhelmina laughed, but Paisley blinked excessively and bit her lip.

Tyler's comment caused her distress. Would he think her cooking, or lack thereof, was "just plain distasteful and unfit to eat"? How could she have forgotten to retrieve an important item when she was at Tabitha's earlier today? "I need to go back to the mercantile for a moment if it's still open."

"We can all go now before the meal, if you'd like," suggested Tyler.

She moistened her lips. How would she be able to accomplish her surprise for Tyler if he was present when she made her purchase? "Actually, I was wondering if Mae-Mae would like to go with me."

Mae said nothing, but nodded.

"Why does Mae always get to go?" whined Albert. He crossed his arms and pouted.

Lucy shrugged. "I'm fine if Mae goes. I'd rather have some supper."

"Perhaps you can go next time, Albert," suggested Paisley. "Are you ready, Mae?"

Tyler's brow furrowed. "Are you sure I can't retrieve it for you, with your knee and all?"

"Thank you kindly, but Mae and I don't mind. We'll return soon." Did she sound as nervous as she felt? This might be her last chance to fetch the item that might make all the difference in the success of her new marriage. She held out her hand to Mae. Without hesitation, the little girl grasped her hand. Paisley was overcome with emotion at Mae's action and how far she had come in such a short time.

A few moments later, Paisley and Mae entered the mercantile.

"Hello again," greeted Tabitha.

"Tabitha, hello. I forgot one item when I was here before." Paisley lowered her voice. "Please may we keep this purchase just between us?"

"Absolutely. I just *love* secrets." Tabitha leaned closer, her eyes wide.

"I'm looking for a recipe book."

"A recipe book?" Tabitha sounded disappointed.

"Yes."

"Oh. All right then. Right this way." Tabitha led Paisley and Mae to a shelf that housed books toward the back of the mercantile. "I only have two at the moment, but I can order you one from the catalog."

"No, thank you. I need it today." Did her desperation show?

"This one is a good one. I've leafed through it myself." Tabitha handed Paisley a thick book with a brown and orange cover titled *Recipes from Augusta's Kitchen*.

"Who's Augusta?"

"I have no idea, but apparently she cooks a lot. There are enough recipes in here to keep one busy the rest of the year."

Surely such a thick book would be costly. But it would be even costlier to have no idea what to cook for tomorrow's meals. "Should we buy the book, Mae?" she asked.

Mae gave a hint of a smile and again reached for Paisley's hand. Paisley limped to the counter to purchase the item when she saw Maribel.

"Hello, Paisley. How delightful to see you. I see you and Mae are purchasing a book today."

The warmth of a blush suffused her cheeks. "Yes."

Maribel placed a hand on Paisley's arm. "What a thoughtful wife you are to make sure you have some delectable meals for your new husband."

"Would you like me to add this to Tyler's charge account?" Tabitha asked.

"Yes, please. Thank you, Tabitha." Hopefully it would be worth the cost since Paisley planned to be just as proficient a cook as Augusta was—whoever she might be.

Maribel peered down at *Recipes from Augusta's Kitchen*. "That sounds like a delightful book. Speaking of cooking, Tyler's ma, Ruby, outshone everyone in Horizon with her scrumptious meals. She was especially known for her meatloaf recipe. Every year at fair time, she won a blue ribbon." Maribel paused. "Come to think of it, meatloaf is Tyler's favorite meal. Ruby was gracious enough to write the meatloaf recipe down for me, and it has become one of Marshall's favorites as well. I have it at home. May I copy it for you?"

"Tyler's ma's recipe?" Paisley again chastised herself yet again for not paying closer attention when Mama was attempting to teach her to cook. At the time, the outdoors proved far more important than being confined to the kitchen.

"Ruby never wrote down one recipe. She had it all in her mind." Maribel tapped her head with her forefinger. "She knew exactly how much of each ingredient and how long to cook each meal. I had to beg her to write it down for me."

Paisley did her best not to allow her shoulders to slump at this latest news. Ruby was an accomplished cook, likely even more skilled than Augusta in the recipe book. How could Paisley ever hope to compare? The odds of winning Tyler's heart with her cooking grew bleaker by the minute.

"Of course, I'm sure you're a good cook too, Paisley, and we didn't mean to make you feel inferior to Ruby. It's just that she was exceptional. Nearly as good as Wilhelmina." Tabitha patted the top of the book. "It's all charged to Tyler's account."

"I wish I could have known her. She sounded like a wonderful woman."

"One of the kindest and most gracious you ever met," said Maribel. "And one of our dearest friends."

"Indeed. Do you want me to wrap this for you, Paisley? We wouldn't want Tyler to see his surprise."

Maribel placed a hand over her heart. "How sweet that you want it to be a surprise for Tyler. He is blessed to have chosen you."

Paisley hoped Tyler felt that way *after* her first attempt at cooking. "Thank you Maribel for your encouragement. Would you mind keeping this surprise between us?"

"Most certainly."

CHAPTER THIRTY-TWO

TYLER'S SUGGESTION TO EAT at Wilhelmina's tonight and the many meals from the townsfolk had been a blessing. But it only delayed the unavoidable. On the way back to the restaurant, Paisley contemplated what she would say if Tyler asked about the parcel. All she needed was abundant prayer and several weeks to increase the chances she could cook a worthy meal. When she and Mae entered the restaurant, Wilhelmina hadn't yet delivered their food. Tyler stood and pulled out Paisley's chair. "Thank you," she said and stowed the parcel beneath it.

He nodded and offered her a crooked grin that made her heart beat a little faster. "How was the mercantile?" he asked.

"What's in the parcel?" Lucy inquired.

"Glad our food is gonna be here soon. I'm starvin' somethin' fierce," declared Albert.

Paisley would answer Tyler's question, but somehow avoid Lucy's. "Tabitha certainly offers a plentiful variety of items."

"That she does," agreed Tyler. His eyes darted in the parcel's direction. Would he ask about it? If so, what would she say?

Wilhelmina placed heaping plates of food on the table. "Enjoy your meal and do let me know when I can bring the pumpkin pie."

Tyler said grace, and Albert shoveled an enormous bite into his mouth. Paisley cut Mae's meal into small pieces before eating her own.

Albert piled another spoonful into his mouth. "This is a lot better than what Tyler makes."

Paisley shuddered to think what Albert would think of the fare she would be preparing tomorrow morning.

Lucy's plate of food was bigger than she was. "Tyler says we can have dessert if we eat all our supper." She beamed. "I can't wait to try some of that pumpkin pie."

"Why would you want a bellyache?" Albert asked.

"If you're not gonna have any, that leaves more for the rest of us," said Lucy.

Albert shook his head. "I didn't say I wasn't gonna have any, I'm just only gonna have three pieces instead of four."

A tiny giggle erupted from Mae before she tilted her head shyly and took another bite of her food.

After they'd finished eating and Albert and Lucy declared they had bellyaches from consuming too many slices of Wilhelmina's delicious pumpkin pie, they prepared to return home. Paisley was grateful Tyler hadn't asked her what was in the parcel. Lord willing, she would learn how to prepare a meal from *Recipes from Augusta's Kitchen* in time for tomorrow's breakfast. And hopefully, by the time Maribel delivered Ruby's recipe, Paisley would have begun her journey toward being a seasoned cook like Augusta.

Regardless, Tyler mustn't discover her ineptitude when it came to culinary skills.

Tyler wondered what was in the parcel, but he decided not to ask. He recalled one time when Ma brought home a parcel from the mercantile when they lived in Missouri. Pa told him that while he was curious about what was inside, he'd leave his wife to her own business. It was a good thing he did because it had been a surprise for Pa.

He climbed into bed that evening, his belly full of the savory beefsteak Wilhelmina prepared. While Wilhelmina's reputation for cooking had few competitors, he missed his mother's meals. Tyler hoped once the food from the townsfolk was gone, Paisley could cook as well as Ma had.

Yesterday and today had been eventful with sending Ivan on his way and notifying the sheriff about him, finding Mae, and then taking the family to Wilhelmina's.

He also recalled how Paisley felt in his arms yesterday.

Like she'd always belonged there.

The sheriff hadn't been concerned about Ivan returning, and Tyler vowed he'd be vigilant in making sure Ivan caused Paisley no further harm.

He'd grown to care for her in a short amount of time and appreciated her tenderness with Mae, her compassion toward the children, and her dedication to making their unorthodox situation successful. Her love for the Lord was apparent, and she was gentle, kind, and beautiful.

Tyler clasped his hands behind his head and thanked the Lord again for keeping his new family safe. He thanked Him for Ma and Pa's consistent instruction in God's Word when he was a youngster and that God hadn't given up on him.

Pa had read from the Bible each night without fail during Tyler's growing-up years. But when Tyler decided to seek his own way, there was no time for the Lord. Any knowledge of Jesus quickly became an afterthought, and there had been no relationship between Tyler and the Lord. Only a knowledge.

Tyler had a long way to go before he would be the man he hoped to someday be, but now, after surrendering his life to Christ, Tyler experienced a faith he'd never before had. He prayed often and sought to trust God with every detail of his life, from his choice of a bride, to Mae and her lack of speech, to the harvest. Tyler now knew what Ma meant when she said she loved the Lord with all her being and trusted her very life to Him.

Chapter Thirty-Three

GRAY CLOUDS FILLED THE sky, an indicator of imminent rain. Paisley wiped the tears from her face and forged ahead as quickly as she could down the road toward Horizon. She had to get away from him.

Hadn't she been through this once before?

True to his word, Ivan hadn't stopped his attempts to make her his wife. And this time, he'd almost succeeded.

If she hadn't escaped.

Tyler had been in town when Ivan returned to the farm to take what he believed was his.

Lucy and Mae cried, and Albert began to hit Ivan on the back with his fists. "You can't take her!"

"My first ma and pa died. My second ma and pa died, and now my third ma is leaving," wailed Lucy.

Mae slunk to the ground and covered her face with her hands.

And then Ivan had grabbed her and had taken her by force.

It hadn't been long before Paisley escaped, but she knew it wouldn't be for good. Ivan's relentless pursuit would ensure that.

Paisley continued down the road, hopeful that a wagon would stop and give her a lift part of the way to Ingleville. Her knee throbbed and with each step, grew worse. Would she ever make it back to Horizon?

Back to Tyler?

She smelled the scent of rain in the air and felt the first raindrop.

Paisley used her hand to help drag her leg along sideways. She found that if she didn't assist her leg, she couldn't walk. The side of her boot caught in the dirt, and she stumbled and nearly fell to the ground.

How much farther could she go?

Would she make it to Horizon before dark? And if not, what would become of her?

Glancing behind her, she saw Ivan again riding toward her on his horse, his evil grin matching his malicious laugh. "Did you think you could escape that easily, Paisley?" He climbed from his horse and reached for her with no tenderness in his touch. "Not this time," he sneered.

Paisley's heart raced and sweat lined the back of her nightgown. Her breath emerged in gasps, and she bolted up to a sitting position and stared into the darkness. Where was she? Was she in Pringle at Mama and Papa's house? Miss Greta's boardinghouse? In Cornwall?

She swung her legs over the side of the bed and toddled toward the kitchen. When she reached the table, she dropped into the chair, her mind full of confusion. Her fingers fumbled as she lit the lantern. The light flickered, and she watched the bouncing shadows on the walls.

Where was she?

Then realization hit. She was in the Shepherdson home. Tyler's home.

Paisley heard the rhythmic sound of his snoring and the pitter-patter of raindrops on the roof. One of the girls tossed and turned in her bed, and Albert mumbled something in his sleep.

She closed her eyes and breathed a deep sigh. The wedding ring rested on her left ring finger where it had been since she'd married Tyler. She slipped it up and down her finger to be sure it was real.

It was.

Paisley opened her eyes again. In the dimness of the lantern, she recognized the fireplace with the mantle housing two tintypes: one of Tyler's mother and one of his father. The family Bible sat in the middle of the mantle. She squinted in the dimness. Dishes lined the shelf in the kitchen, dishes Ruby Shepherdson had lovingly used to serve meals to her family. Everything was as it had been when she'd first arrived.

A long breath escaped her lips. She'd only dreamed Ivan had kidnapped her.

Relief flooded her.

Paisley wasn't sure how long she sat at the table thanking the Lord that she lived in reality rather than a nightmare.

Tyler was surprised to see Paisley asleep at the kitchen table the following morning. He softly tapped on her shoulder. "Paisley?"

When she didn't respond, he tapped again, careful not to shock her awake.

Paisley awoke from her slumber, her bleary eyes blinking rapidly, and a large red mark on her forehead from where she'd rested her face on her arm. A small puddle of drool had collected on the table. Tyler attempted to hide his amusement.

Paisley rubbed her eyes and appeared as though she willed them to focus in his direction.

"Good morning, Paisley."

"Good morning."

When she blushed, Tyler diverted his eyes toward the fireplace and away from her nightdress.

He hadn't meant to embarrass her.

Tyler removed the coat he'd donned in preparation for early morning chores and slipped it around her shoulders. He'd tend to chores later. For now, he was curious as to how she found herself sleeping at the table.

"Thank you."

"I thought maybe you found the bed to be less than comfortable?"

"No. I—I'm not sure how I came to sleep out here." Paisley reached up and massaged the side of her neck not bruised by Ivan. "I must admit it's not the most comfortable place to sleep."

"A crick in the neck?"

"Yes."

Awkward silence filled the air. Should he leave? He didn't want to. He wanted to spend the precious morning minutes with her before the children awoke. There had been so little time to converse with her.

And he longed to know her better.

Should he talk of the weather? Isn't that what most folks did when they couldn't think of anything else to say? "Fixing to be a nice day today."

"I think I may have heard rain outside. Or maybe I dreamed it rained."

Tyler shifted in his chair. "Yes, it rained. Just the right amount for the crops. So far it's shaping up to be a plentiful harvest."

"That's good." She reached up to massage her neck again.

Maybe he should do something to help alleviate the pain. He placed a hand over hers. "I could rub your neck for you," he suggested.

"I would appreciate that." She spoke softly and he strained to hear her.

Tyler pulled another chair from the table and sat behind her. Then leaning forward, he tenderly massaged the right side of her neck. "Is that where it is?"

She flinched at his touch and he considered removing his hand. The last thing he wanted was to make her uncomfortable.

"Yes, that's where it is," Paisley whispered.

How many times had Pa done this for Ma? After a hard day himself, Pa had graciously sat in one of the chairs, much as Tyler was doing now, and massaged Ma's sore neck muscles. Then he'd wrapped his arms around her, kissed her, and told her he'd always love her.

And Zeke Shepherdson had loved her until his dying day.

Tyler gulped. Why did memories of his parents come to the forefront of his mind at such unexpected times? He missed them more than he could articulate. Tyler missed the love they had for him and the love they shared for each other.

If only he could go back in time and change things, he would.

Would he ever be able to share a love for Paisley like Pa had for Ma? While his parents' marriage hadn't been perfect, Tyler grew in the knowledge that for each of them, there was no other.

His face was close to hers, and she had closed her eyes, completely relaxed. Would she be amenable if he kissed her? What did she think of living on the Shepherdson farm? Of the children? Of him?

Especially of him. What did she think of him?

From as close as he was, he could see the way her hair had formed to her forehead during her sleep. He could see the slight dimple in her right cheek, her round nose, and her full lips. He'd never been this close to her, and a pinch of guilt washed over him at the liberty he took at staring at her without her knowledge.

"That's why," Paisley said, an answer to an unknown question.

Tyler jolted from his thoughts of her. Her eyes flung open and for a moment, she appeared to hold her breath as she stared straight ahead.

Had he embarrassed her by his closeness?

Tyler removed his hand from her neck and placed it at his side. He then leaned back in the chair. "What's why?" he asked.

"I just remembered why I slept out here last night."

He waited for her to continue. When she didn't Tyler asked, "And why was that?"

"I had a dream. A nightmare actually."

Tyler yearned to stare at more than the back of her head, so he inclined forward once again and placed an elbow on the table. "Are you all right now?"

"Yes."

"Would you like to share what it was about?" Did Tyler have a right to ask her that? Maybe dreams were too personal to share with one's husband. But how could he know? He'd never been a husband before.

Her gaze darted about the room. "Just about Ivan returning to the farm."

"Paisley, I will do everything I can to protect you from him. The sheriff and several of the townsfolk are also keeping a lookout for him." Tyler took her hand in his. "I promise Ivan will never hurt you again."

She said nothing. Did she believe he'd do everything he could to keep her safe?

"I suppose I should set about preparing breakfast."

"How's your neck?"

Paisley stretched her neck from the left side to the right side and again to the left side. "Still a bit sore, but it'll be fine."

"Here," Tyler said, shifting himself closer to her again. "Allow me to rub it again for you. Sometimes that helps."

Surprised that she didn't resist him, Tyler again massaged her neck. But this time she didn't close her eyes, and this time he didn't stare at her.

It occurred to him how little he knew of her and her of him. He longed to know her hopes and dreams and everything about her.

Mae entered the room then and stood before them. She uttered no words, only fixed her eyes on both of them.

"Good morning, Mae-Mae." Would Mae ever heal from the wounds that had broken her heart?

Tyler watched as Paisley motioned to Mae to come toward her. Mae climbed onto Paisley's lap and nestled her head against Paisley's shoulder. Then Mae reached up for Tyler's hand and intertwined her small fingers through his.

No expression on her face and no words. Just the unanticipated action.

Tyler's eyes met Paisley's. Her brow furrowed and she peered down at the top of Mae's head, then back to Tyler. She appeared as shocked as he.

Instinctively, Tyler reached his other arm around Paisley and held both Paisley and Mae in a loose embrace.

Neither resisted.

Lord, I pray for Mae that You would bring healing to her and that You would lead me as a husband and father. Help me be the man You want me to be.

Paisley sat as still as she could for fear that even the slightest movement would frighten Mae.

There was something natural and comforting about Tyler's arms around her. Emotions flurried in her heart. He'd shown such concern, and not only concern, but affection. And what of the moment she caught him staring at her? He'd been so close. From her peripheral view, she had seen every detail of his handsome face.

Tyler Shepherdson was an attractive man, but she was even more drawn to his character traits than his appearance. Godly, thoughtful, strong yet tender, and determined. It was no longer just for the children that Paisley wanted their marriage to succeed.

Mae snuggled closer, and Paisley slowly wrapped her arms tighter around the girl, placing a kiss on top of her head. She prayed her actions would not cause Mae to leap from her lap and find a place to hide.

Tucked in Tyler's arms holding Mae, peace settled over her. Mae would be all right because, as Doc had said, God was the Author of miracles.

Lord, please show me how to be a wife to Tyler and a mom to the children.

"What's for breakfast? I'm starvin'!" Albert said, rushing from his room. He rubbed his stomach.

"How about a 'good morning' before your breakfast request?" Tyler suggested.

Paisley watched to see Mae's reaction at the interruption. She hoped the girl would stay and allow Paisley to hold her for a bit longer. She also hoped Tyler would remain with his arms around her.

"Breakfast will be soon," Paisley promised.

"Good thing or I might starve to death!"

CHAPTER THIRTY-FOUR

TYLER LEFT TO START his morning chores, and Paisley hastily dressed and prepared to make her first-ever meal. Anxiety plagued her, and she hoped she didn't fail what she deemed a test.

She unwrapped the parcel and ran her fingers over the cover of *Recipes from Augusta's Kitchen.* Paisley opened it to the first page and read the inscription: *To my beloved Earl who inspired me to create only the most decadent of dishes for supper.*

While not normally given to fanciful notions, Paisley did attempt to imagine what it would be like if she were a professional cook like Augusta. She would have her own thick four-hundred-and-fifty-seven-page book. For a moment, she allowed the delightful daydream to permeate her thoughts.

"Mrs. Shepherdson, I have here a copy of your most recent book Recipes from Paisley's Kitchen. *Tell me, how did you come to be the world's most famous chef?" The reporter for the* Horizon Herald *inquired.*

Paisley smoothed the imaginary wrinkles in her satin dress. "I became world-renowned with abundant practice cooking meals soon after my wedding day."

"Is that why you dedicated each of your three-hundred-and-ninety-nine volumes of books in your recipe series to your husband, Tyler?" the newspaper reporter asked.

"My, but yes. Can you believe that I once was so frightened I wouldn't be able to cook a decent meal? How incorrect I was!" Paisley placed her hand over her heart. "From the very second I began on my quest for the perfectly palatable meal, I was a success. Soon, I was known, not only in the Idaho Territory, but throughout the United States, all of her territories and beyond, and to England and France for my knowledge of cooking."

"Congratulations on your well-earned success, Mrs. Shepherdson. You have become far more famous than even Augusta Terhune." The reporter was clearly impressed. "I understand your four hundredth volume is to be published soon."

"Here are the eggs," Albert said, placing the pail on the table and interrupting Paisley's daydream.

"Eggs?"

"Yes, the ones you asked me to collect from the coop," muttered Albert, shaking his head.

"Oh, yes. The eggs. Thank you, Albert. Now run along and complete the rest of your morning chores while I prepare breakfast."

"Can't we eat breakfast *before* chores? I'm starvin'!"

"Not today." Paisley smiled at him and gave him a slight push toward the door. "I'll call for you when breakfast is ready."

Full of vigor and optimism, Paisley flipped to the index where she located the recipe for Augusta's Famous Flapjacks. Careful to pay attention to details, Paisley measured the flour and other dry ingredients and poured them into her mixing bowl. She added the eggs and the milk and exuberantly stirred the mixture. Why had she thought cooking to be such a vexatious chore? Perhaps all those times she'd failed miserably at cooking with Mama were in the past. Perhaps all those times she'd preferred helping Papa in the fields as opposed to assisting Mama in the kitchen would not impede her in her quest to be able to cook any type of meal.

Yes, today Paisley had renewed confidence that she, with Augusta Terhune's help, would be able to make a meal that would please even the most skeptical of breakfast-eaters.

Paisley hummed while she completed the task set before her. She placed a cast iron skillet on the cookstove and counted the eggs. There were just enough left to prepare fried eggs to accompany the flapjacks.

When the pan heated, Paisley poured an amount of flapjack batter into the skillet, then busied herself with the fried egg preparations. Cracking the first egg onto another skillet she'd found on the shelf, Paisley watched the heat of the stove cause the yolk and the white to bubble and sizzle. Thankfully, she had lit the old stove and it had had plenty of time to heat before she'd started her cooking. *It shouldn't be long now.* Wouldn't Tyler be so pleased when he tasted her savory cooking? He might even think she cooked as well as his ma or Wilhelmina.

Paisley wandered over to the window and gazed out at the day. Sunny and bright, everything was even greener from last night's rain. Today was going to be a perfect day.

She returned to the stove and carefully flipped the first flapjack. However, instead of landing back in the pan, the flapjack splattered in a doughy mess on the floor. *Oh, dear. There's not enough mixture to be wasting it.* Paisley poured more batter into the pan, then tended to the mess on the floor. There was no way to salvage the mutilated heap of flapjack.

A burning smell alerted her to the frying pan that held the egg and she, with much more care than she had with the flapjack, flipped the egg. It was burnt to a crisp, and the smell of smoke permeated the room. Paisley held back a cough. Another breakfast item ruined.

Maybe today wasn't the day she would prove her ability in the kitchen.

She discarded the egg, knowing no one would eat something so badly scorched. Smoke billowed in the air. Fearing Tyler would think the house on fire, Paisley propped open the door with a chair. She peered around, ensuring Tyler was nowhere in sight before fanning the air toward the door. No sense in allowing anyone to grow suspicious of her attempts at making breakfast. She then stood outside on the porch and fanned the fresh outdoor air into the house.

But when she returned to her cooking, she noticed a problem. She was now an egg short.

"Albert!" she called.

Albert moseyed toward the house. *Those children really need to learn some manners. Never would I have been allowed to slowly saunter toward the house when Mama or Papa needed something.*

"Where's all the smoke coming from?" Albert asked when he reached the door.

"Albert, can you please retrieve another egg for me from the coop?"

"I done already did that."

"Albert, I need you to please go see if there are any more eggs in the henhouse."

"There aren't."

"Please do not argue with me. You need to learn to mind. Now, go to the chicken coop and fetch another egg and please don't dawdle." Paisley placed her hands on her hips. Raising youngsters was harder than she'd ever imagined.

Especially obstinate ones.

"All right, all right. But I'm tellin' you, there ain't any more eggs."

"If you find two, bring them both back," Paisley returned to the stove.

Albert shook his head and left the house, only to return a few moments later. "There ain't no more eggs. Like I done said before, I got 'em all the first time. Why does it smell like smoke in here?"

"Albert, are you sure? Absolutely sure?"

"I'm sure."

"Because I need one more egg if you are to have one."

Albert straightened his narrow shoulders. "Well, you didn't say you was short one. I'll go look again."

This time, Albert returned with an egg. "Reckon it was hidin' from me."

"Thank you." Relief flooded over her. She'd have to be more careful not to burn this one.

Sometime later, Paisley had prepared six fried eggs, a sizable stack of flapjacks, and a pot of coffee. Feeling rather proud of herself after what seemed at first to be defeat, Paisley stood back to admire the table which held the breakfast meal. If only she had a tablecloth.

She'd just have to find time to sew one. Now sewing was something she could do. And do well.

Taking plates from the shelves, Paisley distributed one to each place setting. She added five cups for milk or coffee and a fork for each person.

It looked almost as professional as the table settings at Wilhelmina's Restaurant and for certain as lovely as something Augusta Terhune herself would have created.

Now to present her delectable meal to her new family.

And hope that Tyler, above all, enjoyed the meal.

Paisley called to Lucy to let everyone know it was time to eat, and the stampede arrived shortly after.

"I'm glad it's time to eat," said Albert, as he washed up in the wash basin. "I was growin' mighty hungry out there with all that hard work."

Tyler grinned. "You're learning a lot about farm work and you're doing very well, Albert. Perhaps you might want to be a farmer someday."

"Naw, I want to be a reverend."

"Well, then, you will make a fine reverend someday." Tyler patted his shoulder. "That's one of the most important jobs a man can have."

A relaxed smile crossed Albert's face. "I think so too, and when I am, we're gonna sing lots of hymns before the sermon."

Lucy's countenance bubbled with excitement. "You can talk all you want about hymns, Albert, I just can't wait to try them flapjacks."

Paisley stood tall, filled with pride at a job well done. Who said she couldn't learn to cook? Thankfully she had hidden the recipe book under the bed before everyone arrived for breakfast.

No sense in sharing her secret.

After Tyler led the prayer, mass commotion ensued. "Now, now, children. There's plenty for everyone," said Paisley. "Please remember your manners." What manners? Albert and Lucy surely didn't have a manner to speak of. At least Mae was sitting quietly.

Paisley watched as Tyler eyed the flapjacks. The tops of the pancakes glimmered a golden brown. He seemed pleased. The eggs didn't look quite as delicious, but they likely tasted good because Paisley had followed Augusta's recipe from beginning to end. Thankfully she had hidden the evidence of the one scorched egg. And for the most part, the room no longer emitted a foul smoky odor.

Satisfied that there was enough for everyone, Tyler retrieved three flapjacks and two eggs. He forked the flapjacks and placed them directly on his plate as they had been on the platter—golden side up. Albert and Lucy also gave themselves generous portions of food. Paisley served Mae and then herself.

"May I take the first bite?" Lucy asked.

"Sure, Lucy." Pleased that the meal had become a special occasion, Paisley watched as Lucy took a bite of flapjack. She'd barely placed it in her mouth when Albert and Tyler followed suit.

After Tyler's first bite, he flipped over the flapjack and viewed the underside. Instead of a golden-brown, it was a dark brown—almost black—and burnt.

"I forgot the syrup," Paisley announced. She stood and fetched the special syrup from a recipe in Augusta Terhune's book and handed it to Tyler. He seemed all too eager to drench his flapjacks.

CHAPTER THIRTY-FIVE

"MUCH OBLIGED," TYLER SAID and poured an abundant amount over the top of his stack of flapjacks. He knew Paisley worked hard to prepare the meal, and he didn't want to ruin an ounce of enthusiasm he'd seen on her face when he entered the house

As quickly as Tyler had opened his mouth to ask about the smoke, he closed it. Some things were likely better left unsaid, even if it was a struggle not to make mention of those things. Besides, while at first he'd feared the house was on fire, after a quick peek into the window, he noticed no flames and had continued his morning chores.

"These flapjacks are two different colors," announced Albert. "Reckon they're black on the one side and brown on the other."

Lucy scrunched her nose. "I ain't never tasted nothin' like these kind before."

Downing the bite of flapjack with a bountiful amount of coffee, Tyler decided to try the eggs. Anything had to be better than the burnt-on-one-side-with-a-golden-top flapjacks.

Minutes later, he chewed what seemed like forever on his first bite. The eggs, rubbery and tasteless, seemed to never be ready to swallow.

He'd never tasted anything so awful. Not even during his time away from home. Tyler resisted the urge to retch.

Tyler could see the expectation in Paisley's eyes.

Expectation of a compliment for her fine cooking.

Should he lie? Should he say he'd never tasted anything finer? Or should he be forthright with her and risk hurting her feelings? Didn't wives want to know when something wasn't right and needed to be improved? How else could they do a better job next time?

The next time?

The thought of the next meal she prepared frightened him worse than a pack of wolves chasing him.

Tyler pondered what to say. He hadn't said anything about the burnt bottoms of the flapjacks or the smoke. But perhaps he should make mention of the eggs. He certainly hoped she didn't use the same recipe in the future.

Living a lifetime of eating the thick, bland, rubbery eggs would be a lifetime too long.

"How are the eggs?" Paisley asked, as if to read his mind.

"Is that what they are?" inquired Albert.

"How are the eggs, Tyler?" Paisley asked, seeming to ignore Albert's rude comment.

"The eggs?" Tyler asked. He swallowed a bite and re-swallowed, just to be sure it was safe to take another bite.

"Yes, the eggs. Are they as delicious as your mother's eggs? Or Wilhelmina's?"

Hunger won the battle within his stomach, and Tyler took another bite. Were they better than his ma's eggs? No. Not even close. Or Wilhelmina's? No. She would never serve scorched, overcooked eggs at her restaurant. He met Paisley's gaze.

She awaited his answer.

"You don't like them."

Was it more of a question or a statement? Whatever it was, she was correct. "I—they're different than what I'm accustomed to." There, that answer wasn't so bad. It was the truth.

"So you don't like them." Paisley pursed her lips.

Tyler gulped. The pursed-lip look couldn't be good. "I—Paisley..."

But Paisley turned her gaze downward and took another bite of her meal.

"The milk is good," Lucy offered.

"Thank you," Paisley mumbled.

"The coffee is good too," Tyler added.

Silence greeted his comment, and Tyler choked down another bite of egg. He couldn't afford to starve. Hard work awaited him. He settled into the lengthy chewing process. At least one side of the flapjacks had been good.

One side.

Perhaps mentioning the coffee hadn't been the thing to say, especially since she provided no answer. But it did take talent to make a good pot of coffee. He recalled a cook the foreman hired who couldn't even make a decent pot of coffee. Tyler remembered that day as if it happened only moments before. When Tyler had brought the cup of coffee to his lips, he'd almost regurgitated. It had tasted like dirt. Tyler shook his head in disgust at the thought. That cook hadn't lasted long.

"I thought so."

Tyler caught Paisley's eye. "I beg your pardon?"

"I saw the look you just made when you took a sip of your coffee."

"What look?"

"The look of loathing as if you'd never tasted anything so hideous."

"Paisley, it wasn't the coffee."

"Then it was the eggs. You didn't like the eggs." Paisley stood. "I'll have you know I prepared those eggs according to a recipe from a very famous chef. I'm sorry you found them to be lacking."

Tyler didn't know what to say.

Albert muttered something about thinking the eggs were hideous and was promptly scolded by Tyler. Lucy asked for a refill of milk. Mae pulled her knees to her chest and buried her face in the midst of all the commotion.

And Paisley left the house.

On her way out, she locked her gaze with Tyler's. "I need a few minutes to myself. No need to worry. I'll be back shortly." She flipped her long braid over her shoulder and, without another glance, left the house.

Tyler finished his meal and cleared the table of the dishes. He figured that would give Paisley some time to think about things and hopefully not be so angry with him. Being a married man sure was a challenge.

That fact became clearer and clearer to him with each passing day.

Especially since he had a penchant for speaking before thinking.

Tyler gave the children some simple chores and then went in search of Paisley. He realized that on a farm the size of the Shepherdson farm, it may take him some time to find her. Or should he even try to find her? Maybe she desired to be left alone. If that was the case, chores beckoned him and he couldn't afford to waste any time. On the other hand, if she wanted him to come find her, he should do so.

Tyler sighed. He tried to recall when his mother had grown frustrated with his father. To Tyler's knowledge, it hadn't happened often, but when it had, Tyler's parents always discussed the matter in private.

He set off toward the northern end of the property. After a time of not locating her, he turned and walked in the opposite direction. Before long, he noticed her pale purple dress, the skirt blowing in the breeze. He waved, but received no indication she had seen him.

"Paisley?" Tyler called as he drew nearer to her. He stopped then and took in the sight of her. Wisps of loose hair had fallen from her braid and blew from her face in the slight breeze. Her eyes were closed.

His wife was a beautiful woman.

Should he call out to her to warn her he was nearby?

Paisley closed her eyes tighter and rested in the breeze. The growing crops and the endless blue sky reminded her of her parents' farm as a child. She missed those days.

She thought of the breakfast and how she'd failed miserably in her quest to cook the perfect meal for Tyler. He'd found it detestable. But why shouldn't he? Paisley knew full well she couldn't cook. *And to think I imagined myself a famous chef like Augusta Terhune. Such nonsense!*

She'd seen his face when he'd tasted the eggs. She wanted so badly to make Tyler proud. To make him grateful he'd chosen her for his wife.

The thought of supper filled Paisley with dread. In her anger, she'd left the house without starting the bread. Now it would likely not be ready in time for supper, unless it was a late supper.

Why did she feel as though she was failing at her new life?

She sensed someone watching her then and opened her eyes. Sure enough, Tyler stood a short distance from her. How long had he been there?

"Paisley? Can we talk?"

Goodness if he wasn't a dapper man! A lock of his dark brown hair had fallen over his forehead in a curl, and he'd rolled up the sleeves on his shirt to his elbows exposing strong forearms.

She needed to apologize for her lack of cooking skills.

"Look, Paisley, about the eggs. I wasn't even thinking about your cooking when I made that face. I was thinking back to a time when I drank the most disgusting coffee I ever tasted. It had nothing to do with the eggs or flapjacks."

"But you have to admit it wasn't the best meal you've eaten."

Tyler kicked at a dirt clod. "No, it wasn't the best."

"I thought so." Paisley sighed. "I'm sorry. I'm not the best cook, but I did try. I wanted so badly to succeed."

"I know you did. And I'm not the best farmer." He paused, his eyes twinkling. "Some pair we make."

"Add that to the fact that we're now parents."

Tyler chuckled then, his laugh low and comforting. "You're right. Don't you sometimes wonder about this predicament?"

His laugh was contagious and she joined him, grateful for the diversion from the otherwise distressing topic. "I do wonder that. And I am sorry about my cooking inadequacies. Mama tried her best to teach me how to cook, but she wasn't the least bit successful. I always preferred being outside, even if it meant helping Papa with the farm rather than being stuck inside learning to bake a cake. Now I see why Mama tried her best to teach me how to cook. It comes in handy when you have a family." She sighed. "It just seemed so easy for Augusta Terhune."

"Who's Augusta Terhune?"

The look on Tyler's face, one of bafflement with his eyes wide and his head tilted to one side, made Paisley laugh. "Augusta Terhune is a famous chef. I purchased her book so I could learn how to cook."

"You purchased her book?"

"Yes. It was the wrapped parcel yesterday from the mercantile."

"Oh. So that's what it was. I wondered."

"Sadly, I won't be competing with Augusta anytime soon." Paisley took a deep breath. "Sorry, Tyler. I know you would prefer a good meal, but alas, I have some learning to do."

He said nothing, but instead took a step toward her. He reached up and stroked her cheek with his thumb, and a peculiar fluttering took up residence in her belly.

"You sure are pretty today, Paisley."

Tyler was standing so close to her that she feared if she even breathed a tiny breath that this special moment would cease.

The morning's events reentered her mind. His kind gesture when massaging her neck muscles and then declaring his protection over her had made her realize for the first time that her choice in marrying him was no mistake.

It had been God's divine plan.

His eyes settled on her lips and her heart turned over in response. Would he kiss her? Would this kiss be different than the one at the wedding—the one done as a rushed obligation?

She held her breath and willed her knees not to buckle beneath her.

And then, in a moment Paisley could never have imagined, Tyler's lips met hers.

It didn't take long for Paisley to realize that this kiss had nothing in common with the wedding kiss.

He hadn't planned on kissing her.

Really, he hadn't.

It just happened. One minute they were discussing how she wasn't a world-famous chef and the next he was declaring her beauty. And then, while he stood there taking in how pretty she was, Tyler did something he'd wanted to do that morning. He'd taken the step toward her and pulled her into his arms.

So different from the kiss they shared at their wedding. Instead, it was passionate and, he hoped, expressed the way he was beginning to feel toward her.

Yes, Tyler cared about decent meals. Cared a lot because food was important to him. But cooking skills could be learned. He was beginning to love her for who she was.

Tyler took a step back and caught both of her hands in his. "There are more kisses where that one came from," he teased. "And, Paisley, don't worry about the meal. You have a lifetime to cook for me, if I'm so fortunate."

She released a sigh and closed her eyes. He could easily kiss her again.

And he did.

That night, Tyler moved from his bed in Albert's room into the room he would now share with his wife.

253

Chapter Thirty-Six

PAISLEY AWOKE WITH EXCITEMENT. Today would be the day she would put her plan into action. Well, if Wilhelmina was amenable. Hopefully the jovial woman would agree to teach her how to cook in exchange for Paisley sewing curtains for the restaurant.

After a breakfast of coffee and toast with preserves from Ruby's cellar, Paisley kissed Tyler goodbye, left Albert and Lucy with strict instructions to help him with the chores, and loaded Mae into the wagon.

Would Wilhelmina be agreeable to Paisley's suggestion? Paisley had barely been able to sleep last night just thinking about it. While Augusta's book had helped a bit in making a few suppers the last couple of nights, Paisley still had a great distance to go before considering herself an adequate cook.

Mae clutched the rag doll that Ruby had sewn for her upon the children's arrival from New York. Paisley had also brought along a slate and chalk to keep the little girl entertained.

"Good morning, Paisley. So nice to see you."

"Hello, Wilhelmina. I was hoping to discuss something with you."

"Do come in." Wilhelmina stepped aside and ushered Paisley and Mae into the restaurant. "Have a seat at the table and I'll bring you some coffee. We don't open for another hour yet, so I'd love to visit."

The aroma of baking bread lingered in the air. That was an item on Paisley's list as well. Thankfully Maribel had delivered three loaves of bread yesterday when she'd stopped by for a visit. But the time was soon arriving when Paisley would make her own bread.

Mae settled quietly into the chair. She'd propped her dolly against the flower vase on the table and was scribbling on the slate. Occasionally, Mae would show the dolly the slate, her head bobbing, as if teaching the doll. Her mouth moved but she said no words.

Wilhelmina brought two cups of coffee to the table and took a seat across from Paisley. "It appears Mae is doing so much better."

"She is. The Lord is working a miracle."

Wilhelmina's face brightened. "Yes, He is. Now tell me, what brings you to the restaurant?"

"I was hoping I might offer to make you some brand new curtains for the restaurant in exchange for cooking lessons."

Her friend's gaze traveled to the windows. "What a fantastic idea!"

But she was nowhere as thrilled as Paisley. "Thank you, Wilhelmina."

"Of course! Although I think I might be benefiting the most. Sewing has never been my forte, and just take a gander at those windows. I've been fretting something awful about how faded the curtains are. I believe one of them even has a small hole in it." Wilhelmina shook her head. "Hubs would say I've been procrastinating something fierce about making new ones. He might be right."

They both laughed, and Wilhelmina reached across the table and clasped both of Paisley's hands. "Now, tell me, how are you adjusting to being a wife and ma?"

"I'm doing better. At first, I was worried." Paisley had never shared with anyone else how she and Tyler had met and their agreement for a marriage of convenience.

Some things were better left between a woman and her husband.

"And now?"

"Things are starting to get easier. Tyler and I have been listening with intent to Reverend Marshall's sermons about raising a family. We've also discussed how to be united in how we discipline Albert and Lucy. It hasn't been easy. Those two cause quite a ruckus. And then there's the whole issue of being a wife. I've never been one before, so…"

"And Tyler's never been a husband before."

"True. One thing is that we've been able to talk about our differences, which has helped."

"That's how Hubs and I are. We don't see eye to eye on a few things. All right, more than a few things. At first in our marriage, it caused some bickering and still does from time to time. But over the years, we've learned to try seeing things from the other's perspective. Not easy, but it can be done. The fact that you both are recognizing the need to discuss your differences bodes well for your life together."

"I hope so, Wilhelmina. I know I need to start learning how to cook. The last few days have been a disaster. Tyler nearly broke his tooth on a biscuit I made with supper and don't even ask about the breakfast meal. Good thing our hens lay a lot of eggs as I've messed up plenty of them."

"That's all about to change. Once we begin your cooking lessons, you'll be making blue ribbon preserves and meals fit for royalty."

"Will you teach me how to cook Ruby's famous meatloaf?"

"I can, but remember, Tyler loves you no matter if you can make his ma's famous meatloaf or not. Have you considered making a meal for him that's all your own idea? Something that can become a favorite of his that you make?"

Paisley nodded, but she wasn't sure if Tyler *loved* her as it was far too soon for that. In the past few days, something *had* changed between them. He hadn't declared his love to her in words, but if actions were any indication, Tyler's feelings for her had grown, just as hers had for him. "Do you have a suggestion I could make for him that would become a favorite?"

"What about beefsteak? I know he ordered that the other evening for supper and, from all appearances, seemed to like it."

"If it wasn't for the beefsteak and the delectable meals from the ladies at church, Tyler would have been half-starved by now if he'd had to depend on my cooking skills."

Wilhelmina laughed. "That's all about to end. Let's start on learning how to make perfect eggs. Even better than Augusta Terhune's recipe. Then we'll proceed from there."

God had given her a husband, and Paisley meant to do all she could to glorify God in the way she cared for him. Whether she made beefsteak or Ruby's famous meatloaf, Paisley was willing to learn how to cook because it was important to her new husband.

"Are you all right?" Wilhelmina asked, concern etched in her face.

"Sorry, Wilhelmina. I was deep in thought for a moment."

Wilhelmina tapped her chin with her finger. "I remember when Hubs and I were first married. It was a special time to be sure. But nothing can compete with the exceptional kind of love between a couple who's been married for years and has shared memories of good times and bad. It's more than those special early days. Much more. Someday you and Tyler will have that."

"I hope so. You and Hubs are such an inspiration."

"You're sweet for saying so and I'm honored. Truly, it's by God's grace alone that any marriage survives seeing as how two completely different people have to adjust to living with each other and sharing their lives. I love Hubs more than anything, even if there still are days when that little Dutch husband of mine can be quite stubborn. Ornery too."

Paisley giggled at Wilhelmina's statement. And as she sat there with her friend, she marveled again at God's providence of providing her with the close friendships she so desperately sought.

Tyler tied his horse to the hitching post and walked toward the church. The humble-sized whitewashed building boasted two windows in the front, a tall steeple with a cross, and three steps leading up to double doors. How many times had Tyler entered the doors of this church since moving to Horizon before he left town?

Too many times to count.

"Hello? Reverend Marshall?"

"Good afternoon, Tyler. I was just finalizing the words for Sunday's sermon. What brings you here?"

Tyler removed his cowboy hat and tapped it against his thigh. Maybe it wasn't the right thing to be here. Maybe he ought to leave as quickly as he'd entered. After all, who talked to the reverend about such delicate matters?

He decided not to broach the subject on his mind. Not just yet. "So what are you working on for your sermon? If you don't mind me asking."

"It's a sermon on the parable of the prodigal son."

A topic a bit too close to his own life. Perhaps he'd see about missing church this Sunday. But just as swiftly as the thought popped into Tyler's mind, he dismissed it. If he yearned for a closer relationship with Christ, he couldn't very well skip the sermons that prompted conviction in his heart.

"I'm thankful God never gives up on us," said Reverend Marshall. "That He is a Father who welcomes us with open arms. That He leaves the ninety-nine behind to find that one missing sheep."

"Yes, me too."

"Tyler, I'm sure you didn't come to speak about my next sermon. How are things at the farm?"

"Good. Things are good."

"Would you care to sit?" Without waiting for an answer, Reverend Marshall led Tyler to the first row of pews on the left-hand side.

Tyler took a seat next to the reverend.

"Is there something on your mind, son?"

"Yes, Reverend, there is."

"Go ahead."

Tyler traded his hat to his left hand, then back to his right, then finally back to his left again. Where should he start? How should he start? "I—uh—I wanted to speak with you about something."

"People tell me I'm a good listener." Reverend Marshall's eyes twinkled.

Tyler took a deep breath. The reverend's hospitality did little to ease his apprehensiveness. "I was meaning to speak to you about Paisley."

"Yes. How is Paisley?"

"She's fine."

"Good. I understand you folks are thinking of taking a visit to Cornwall for a delivery. That's a grand idea to make a family trip out of it. I bet Lucy, Albert, and Mae will enjoy it. If they're anything like my children were as youngsters, they make everything into an adventure."

Tyler chuckled, noting that his voice echoed in the empty building. "We plan to take them for ice cream after I retrieve the orders for the Horizon folks."

"You and Paisley are doing a fine job raising those children. Your parents would be proud."

"I hope so. It hasn't been easy. Lucy and Albert are a mite bullheaded and rebellious. But they're improving."

Tyler didn't add *slowly*.

"Sometimes all young'uns need is to know they're loved. And to have a stable home. Your parents started those three kids on that journey after the adoption. Sadly, your ma and pa passed on so soon after the adoption. They never had a chance to really make a difference in the lives of those youngsters. You and Paisley are doing that now, and I couldn't be prouder of the both of you."

"Thank you, Reverend. Always did appreciate your encouragement."

"Anytime. Now tell me, Tyler, what's weighing heavily on your mind?"

"It's Paisley. I need to ask a few questions. Between you and me." Wasn't the reverend obligated to keep his confidence?

"Of course. You have my word."

"All right then." Tyler took a deep breath. "Not sure if you know this or not, but Paisley and I weren't able to have a long courtship before our marriage."

"I figured as much."

"You did?"

"You never mentioned courting someone before you went to Cornwall."

Relief flooded him at Reverend Marshall's correct assumption. He thought his words over carefully before continuing, although it would be easier now to discuss the matter on his mind. "Because I never was able to properly court her, I was wondering if you could give me some advice. I love her and I wished we'd had a proper courtship. You know, women like all that romantic stuff and all." Tyler felt the heat rise up his neck and face. Wasn't it unmanly to blush?

"Have you told her you love her?"

"Not exactly—no, not yet."

"That's fine. Those words will come."

"I know it's too late for courtship seeing as how we're married and all, but... How does a man go about wooing his wife?" Tyler kept his eyes pinned on his brown boots. Mud from yesterday's rain caked the edges.

When Reverend Marshall didn't answer right away, Tyler cautiously lifted his eyes to the reverend's face. Instead of judgment or amusement, Tyler saw nothing but kindness and understanding. Much like the face of a father who cared for his son. Or a pastor who cared about the needs of each member of his congregation, no matter what those needs were.

"Tyler, you bring a valid question. I wish more men would concern themselves with how to love their wives as Christ commands us. Many would say they're too busy or too concerned with their work to give a moment's thought to their wife's feelings. Some husbands would say their wives know they love them, and they need to do nothing more to affirm that love."

Tyler nodded. What else could he do? He didn't know what other husbands did or thought.

He didn't even know what he thought half the time.

Tyler had no training on how to be a husband. Not really. His pa had set a good example, but Tyler hadn't paid much attention back then, although he wished he would have. And then there was the fact that Tyler hadn't even anticipated getting married so soon. He hadn't had time for the ridiculous notion of courtship. There were adventures to be had and dreams to fulfill.

In his mind, women only took from those dreams.

"You can tell your wife you love her, and I would recommend that often. Women never tire of hearing those special words. Believe me. I've been married over thirty years and my Maribel still longs for me to say them to her. But there's a second part of it. You must also *show* your wife you love her, and this can be accomplished in many ways. Thoughtful things like a handpicked bouquet of flowers, allowing her to have a few moments to herself, offering to help her with a chore, or presenting her with a small trinket are all considerate gestures. Holding her hand and going for a walk with her—that works well too."

"Thank you, Reverend, I never would have thought of those things." Tyler stood, preparing to leave.

"You don't have to leave just yet, son. There's a bit more."

Tyler sat back down and set his hat beside him. He'd heard enough. Really. Besides, he'd never before been so embarrassed.

"The other thing is that you don't have to leave courtship behind when you marry. This is a misconception. Women like to be courted long after they're married. Ask my wife.

She'll tell you the same thing." Reverend Marshall shook his head. "I wished I would have learned this sooner. For the longest time, I didn't realize how to treat my wife like the special jewel that she is. Yes, I was kind and loving and how God calls us as husbands to be, but I never went that extra step. I never courted her after the wedding. Several years ago, I started doing just that."

Reverend Marshall held up his hand as if to count the suggestions he was about to make. "Besides the things I mentioned above, take Paisley for a picnic, read the Bible and pray with her, sit and stare at the stars at night, just the two of you. Discuss your hopes and dreams and where you hope to find yourselves ten years from now. Tell her how beautiful she is and how she's the only one for you. Spend time talking about things you would have talked about had you courted. Get to know her. Really get to know her. What makes her happy? What is she afraid of? What bothers her?"

"I think I know what bothers her. Reckon she's let me know on more than one occasion. She's mighty feisty at times."

"Feisty is a good thing. It keeps us men in our place when we start getting ornery."

Tyler rubbed his palms together. "All right, Reverend. I think I've gained some knowledge." He suddenly felt grateful he only had one wife. They were a lot of work.

"Thank you for stopping by, Tyler. May the Lord guide you as you seek to be the husband He designed you to be."

Tyler shook the reverend's hand. Then, armed with knowledge, he set out to *show* Paisley he loved her.

Tyler mounted his horse and headed out of town. He wished he had taken notes as Reverend Marshall spoke. How would he ever remember everything the reverend mentioned? He ran over a few things in his mind. Yes, he would start today on his quest.

Sometime later, he stopped alongside the road to search for some wildflowers. He recalled how much the flowers at the wedding meant to Paisley.

Proud of himself that he'd already thought of two things on Reverend Marshall's "list," Tyler grinned. Perhaps he'd been too uptight about the whole thing.

Tyler spied a patch of purple wildflowers. Hastily yanking them up nearly by their roots, Tyler took the handful and mounted his horse. Wouldn't Paisley be thrilled when she received the flowers?

When he reached the farm, Paisley was in the garden. The children appeared to be preoccupied. Good. He needed time alone with his wife to present her with the bouquet. Hiding the wildflowers behind his back, Tyler strode toward her.

"Hello, Paisley. My, but don't you look beautiful today."

Already one thing accomplished that Reverend Marshall had suggested. Now for the second item.

Paisley eyed him with suspicion. Did she not believe him? Sure, she had a smear of dirt on her face and her hair was plastered to her head, but she was lovely. "Thank you," she finally said.

"You're welcome. Say, I was in town today and decided to bring you a gift."

Paisley's eyes lit up. A good sign. This was going to be simple. "Really? That's very sweet of you. I have been eyeing something in the mercantile." Paisley's countenance lit up like sunshine.

"At the mercantile?" She wanted something from the mercantile? For a moment, Tyler panicked. But then, a thought occurred to him. Nature was better than man-made gifts any day. After all, God had made the wildflowers. People made the stuff at the mercantile.

"Close your eyes and hold out your hand."

When she did as he had asked, Tyler placed the bouquet in her hands. He tried to hide his shock when he noticed the flowers were wilted.

Paisley gave him an appreciative look and brought the wildflowers to her nose to inhale their fresh scent.

"Aren't they pretty?"

"Yes they are."

Tyler watched her close her eyes and inhale another scent of the wilted flowers. He wanted to take a step forward and kiss her sweet lips. "I picked them for my beautiful wife."

He'd told her she was beautiful twice in a matter of a few minutes. Add another point for the "courtship project".

Paisley's eyes fluttered open and met his. "Thank you, Tyler. This means a lot to me."

In an instant, she was in his arms, and through a kiss, Tyler showed her for the fourth time in a matter of minutes that he loved her.

CHAPTER THIRTY-SEVEN

PAISLEY STOOD BACK TO admire the garden. The tomatoes, squash, and zucchini were growing quite well. She raised her chin in pride. Her new life was coming together more than ever with the Lord's help.

Not only was the garden growing well, but she was falling in love with Tyler. In the past couple of days, they'd taken a long walk together while the children played in the fields. They'd also spent the past two evenings reading the Bible.

To make matters even better, Paisley's cooking had improved. *Not a lot, mind you, but with Wilhelmina's help, my cooking has finally become edible.*

Paisley's thoughts were interrupted when she glimpsed a horse and buggy approaching the farm. An unfamiliar older man stepped from the buggy and sauntered toward her. "Good afternoon. You must be Mrs. Shepherdson."

"Yes." Paisley warily eyed the tall, lean man.

"I'm Waylon Dowell from First Bank of Cornwall." Mr. Dowell removed his hat and bowed slightly.

"Nice to meet you."

"Likewise." Mr. Dowell scanned the farm. "It's been some time since I've been here. It appears the farm is doing well."

"Yes, Tyler says the crops are growing ahead of schedule."

"Good to hear that. I always did know that boy had a knack for farming, just like his pa, even when Tyler denied it. Speaking of Tyler, is he here?"

"He's in the field. I can have Albert fetch him for you if you'd like."

"I'd be much obliged."

Paisley saw Albert near the barn doing the chores Tyler had assigned him for the day. "Albert, could you please come here for a moment?"

Albert's head jerked up, and he dropped an armload of rocks and headed toward Paisley. "Albert, Mr. Dowell is here to see Tyler. Would you please find him and let him know?"

"Yes, ma'am."

Paisley smiled. Albert and Lucy had improved in their manners in the past couple of weeks. She offered a prayer heavenward. Yes, she was certainly succeeding at more than the garden. She redirected her attention back to Mr. Dowell. "May I offer you some coffee while you wait?"

Mr. Dowell followed Paisley into the house and sat at the table. "The children seem to be doing well."

"They are doing better. It's been rough for them."

Mr. Dowell took a drink of his coffee. "I recall the day Ruby and Zeke adopted them. The orphan train had just arrived at the Cornwall train station. I don't think Ruby and Zeke had any intentions of adding to their family that day, but the Lord had other plans."

Paisley silently hoped Tyler would take his time coming in from the fields as she wanted to learn all she could about the day Lucy, Albert, and Mae were adopted into the Shepherdson family. "Did you know Ruby and Zeke well?"

"I did. Wonderful, godly folks."

"I wasn't privileged to meet them before their deaths, but I've heard many good things about them."

"Indeed." Mr. Dowell looked thoughtful. "They were a fine couple, those two, and they raised a fine son. They were getting on in years, so I'm sure being parents again wasn't in the plan." Mr. Dowell shook his head. "Most unfortunate about the fever claiming their lives."

"Mr. Dowell, I would be interested in hearing more about the day Ruby and Zeke adopted the children from the orphan train."

"Well, I don't have a lot to tell, but I was conversing with Zeke outside a restaurant next to the railroad station. A group of children stepped off the train with their agents—the adults who traveled with them from the orphanages. The children's clothes were rumpled and their faces tired, but other than that, they appeared in good condition. A church offered to set up the adoptions. I remember seeing Ruby's face light up at the sight of the children. I know she missed Tyler something fierce when he left to strike out on his own." Mr. Dowell stroked his beard. "She politely interrupted Zeke and me and asked if she could speak to Zeke in private. I stepped aside, and after their discussion, they prayed. I'll recall as long as I live the peaceful sight of those two praying together outside the restaurant, their heads bowed as they held hands."

Paisley tried to imagine Ruby and Zeke praying for guidance on the busy streets of Cornwall. She had memorized their faces from the photograph on the mantle—Ruby with her sweet face and Zeke, an older version of Tyler. "They seemed to be strong in their faith."

"Very strong in their faith. They weren't perfect, but they lived in a way that exhibited the love of Christ to all they met. I think of them often."

"So did they know which children they wanted to adopt right away?"

"I don't think so. I felt privileged when they asked me to accompany them to the church. I wished my wife could have joined us. Of course, if she had, we might have adopted a few ourselves." Mr. Dowell chuckled. "Anyway, at the church, it was obvious which children would be adopted first. Crowds filled the building, and the babies—there were two if I remember correctly—were adopted first. Then the strong, able boys. They were next. There were two or three of them. Albert, he was a skinny, scrawny boy with a scowl on his face. Not much of a way to persuade someone to adopt him."

"I can imagine Albert's scowl." It was the same scowl he exhibited frequently when asked to do chores.

"Third went the older girls whom many parents adopted because they could help with the household chores and the younger children. Of course, no matter what the age, the cute ones were adopted quickly. Lucy wailed up a storm the entire time. Just cried her little eyes out. Her hair was in disarray, and every time someone attempted to comfort her, she pushed them away. And then there was Mae. She didn't present well either. A pretty little girl, but she just sat with her legs pulled to her chest and her head buried. Never did speak. I think folks would have adopted her ten times over if she would have said a word or two."

"Those children have suffered more than we will ever know."

"Yes, I think so," agreed Mr. Dowell. "Especially Mae. Of over two dozen children from the orphan train that day, only three were left with no family to call their own."

"Albert, Lucy, and Mae."

Mr. Dowell nodded. "It was a sight that, I'm sure, brought a tear to even the toughest demeanors. When everyone else had left, the agents said they'd take the children back to the orphanage in New York and try again. The pastor attempted several times to convince folks to take at least one of the children. There were no takers, what with Albert's scowl, Lucy's incessant whining, and Mae's reclusiveness. There the three sat, unloved, unaccepted, and unwanted. That is, until Ruby and Zeke walked, hand in hand, to the front of the church. Zeke told the pastor they'd take all three. Albert attempted to run away, said he didn't want anyone to adopt him." Mr. Dowell shook his head. "But as I always say, the Lord had other plans."

"It is a shame they died so soon. It must have made the children feel more abandoned."

"I would say so. But now you and Tyler have the opportunity to raise them. I've prayed for those children since I first laid eyes on them, and I'll continue to do so. From what I saw, Albert's demeanor appears to have improved."

"Yes, just in recent days."

"And Mae—has she spoken yet?"

"She hasn't uttered a word, but I have faith the Lord will heal her broken heart."

On his way in from the fields, Tyler saw a buggy parked by the barn and recognized it as one available for rent from the livery in town." He heard the murmur of voices inside the house, and as he drew nearer, he saw a familiar man sitting at the table. Tyler stepped inside the house and confirmed his suspicions.

"Well, I'll be! Is that you, Waylon?"

"That it is." Waylon stood and gave him a fatherly hug and a slap on the back. "How have you been?"

"I've been well. You?"

"Doing well."

"That's good to hear." Tyler took a seat at the table. "What brings you to Horizon?"

Waylon's face grew somber. "Not good news, I'm afraid."

"Oh?"

"Tyler, did you know that your parents had a rather large note on the farm?"

"I didn't know that. All I knew was that they acquired the Farrand place at a reasonable price. I always assumed because they did that, they were fine financially."

"They have always paid their payments on time and when they came to me and asked about acquiring the Farrand property, I knew they were worth the small risk. I'd always appreciated that they came to me, even when the new bank here in Horizon opened. Or maybe they went there first and were turned down. I have no way of knowing. Anyhow, in the few months leading up to your parents' passing, they were unable to make full payments and slowly fell farther behind. Last year's crop was bad, they were already in arrears by a nominal amount. As of today's date, they are a full five months behind."

"How come you didn't come to me sooner?"

"It wasn't until the main bank in Boise City contacted me with a harsh letter that I realized things were amiss. With the death of your parents, I convinced the bank owners to give you a chance to make the payments and turn things around."

"I made a payment when I went to Cornwall."

"I know you did. But the owners in Boise City were not satisfied. They've given you thirty days to remit the balance owed in full or they'll seek foreclosure."

"Thirty days?"

"I'm sorry, Tyler. I did convince them not to charge any additional interest or late fees. However, they are holding to their decision on wanting the entire amount."

"I can't believe this."

"Again, I am so sorry. If there was anything I could do..."

Tyler pounded his fist on the table, frustration permeating his thoughts. "You were one of my father's closest friends. You could have done something more."

"Believe me, I tried."

"So now if we don't come up with that money, we stand to lose the house, the farm, everything?"

"Yes." Waylon presented Tyler with a piece of paper. "Here's what is due," he said, pointing to an amount at the bottom of the document.

Tyler stared at the signatures of his parents. They'd been so excited the day they took out the loan on the farm. Tyler even remembered that day. After the signing of the papers in Cornwall, he and his parents had celebrated by eating ice cream at O'Dell's Soda Fountain and Confectionery, something they never could afford to do again.

Tyler traced, first the name of his father, then the name of his mother, with his finger. How could they have been there one day and gone so quickly the next?

He gaped at the amount due. "Where am I going to come up with that amount? I have some of it, but not all of it."

"I tried my best to get it reduced. I even offered to promise you'd pay it in full to receive some sort of discount. The bank owners wouldn't hear of it. They said they'd already done you a favor by removing the penalty amount they could have imposed."

"So all that my parents have worked so hard for will be lost if I don't pay this full amount in a month? Can't they wait until the harvest? It's looking to be a fine one this year."

Waylon shook his head. "I already asked. When they sent a bank representative to discuss delinquent accounts, I even inquired if I could pay a small amount of your parents' debt given what happened. They informed me that would cost me my job. I'm sorry, Tyler."

Tyler rose from his chair and pushed it into the table a little too hard, causing the table to jolt. "I can't believe this. All they have worked so hard for, all those years of paying, and it's come to this? And you're telling me there's nothing that can be done?"

"Tyler…" Paisley reached for his arm, but he set off pacing the floor.

"I can't believe this," he repeated. "Thank you for stopping by, Waylon." He paused long enough to shake Waylon's hand. It wasn't his fault money was owed on the loan.

"We'll find a way," Waylon reassured him.

Tyler didn't want to think of the alternative, especially since acquiring that amount of money seemed impossible. "If you'll excuse me, I have work to do."

He headed out the door and toward the fields. *Father, tell me this isn't happening. Not now. Not when things are going so well. Paisley, the children, and I are finally settling in as a family. Please let there be something that can be done.*

For the past four years, he'd done everything on his own—had only counted on himself. It was an adjustment to have someone care about him besides his parents. Someone with an interest in his life.

He gazed at the crops. He turned back and took in the sight of the house, the barn, and Paisley's garden. For the first time in his life, Tyler realized how important the farm was to him —the farm his parents had worked hard for so he could one day inherit.

There had to be a way to save it. There had to be.

Chapter Thirty-Eight

IT WAS SOME TIME after Waylon Dowell left that Tyler returned to the house. "Don't worry about me when it's time for supper," he said.

"Tyler, wait. Can we talk about this?"

He said nothing, but strode back toward the barn.

Tears misted in Paisley's eyes. She could only imagine how Tyler must feel after hearing Mr. Dowell's news. The farm had meant so much to him, and she knew what it was like to lose your home. Where would they go if they weren't able to secure the funds?

And not only that, but Tyler had already lost his parents. Now he must lose his farm too? If only she could bring in enough income with her sewing to assist with the payment. She followed Tyler to the barn. "Tyler?"

Tyler didn't acknowledge her, but continued to saddle his horse.

"Tyler, I can make some money between now and when the note is due from my sewing. It would help."

"It wouldn't help enough, Paisley."

"There must be something we can do."

"I appreciate what you're trying to do. Right now, I need to go to town and pay a visit to the bank in Horizon. I'll be back soon."

Tyler climbed on his horse and rode through the open barn door, leaving Paisley helpless to assist him in a problem that affected both of them.

She found a crate in the barn, sat down, and buried her face in her hands. *Lord, I don't know what to do. Please give us wisdom and the strength to endure whatever Your will is. Let there be a way to keep the farm.*

She shifted her sitting position on the crate when she heard a crinkling noise. She lifted her head and stood. There underneath her was a now-wrinkled piece of paper. Paisley picked it up and sat down again on the crate. Pressing the crinkles from the paper, her heart raced as she read the words it contained.

Gold discovered on Caribou Mountain! Come one, come all to discover the wealth to be had.

The announcement contained a drawing of a man holding a gold nugget.

Was Tyler considering taking the family and moving there? Was the visit from Mr. Dowell confirmation for Tyler that his time and life was better spent somewhere besides the farm his parents bequeathed to him?

Paisley set the paper beside her. She and Tyler had been married for such a short amount of time. But in that time, she was growing to love him and care for him. And she needed him.

The children needed him as well.

She would follow him to Caribou Mountain if that's what he thought was best.

Tyler walked through the doors of Horizon's lone bank. When he'd first returned home, he'd placed his money in the bank, hoping to someday use it to start a new life elsewhere. Months and months of hard work and saving nearly every penny resulted in a tidy sum, but it wasn't enough to save the farm.

And did he want to even save the farm? Maybe he should let it go and move the family elsewhere. There was gold to be found in Caribou Mountain. He and Paisley could start a new life there with the children.

But something about the farm had drawn him into staying here. Was it because of the promise he'd made to Ma and her assumption that he'd raise the children here? Was it because of Pa's profound disappointment in him that he desired to run the farm Pa had worked so hard to build? Or was it because this was where he belonged?

Tyler discreetly hid the money in his saddle bag. Tomorrow he'd make plans to go to Cornwall and pay all he had toward the loan.

After that, it would be in God's hands.

Paisley fed the children and cleared the table. Keeping a plate of food for Tyler just in case, she set it to the side in the hopes he'd be arriving home soon.

A fleeting fear had filled her mind. Why hadn't he shown her the paper advertising gold in Caribou Mountain? Why hadn't he discussed with her the possibility of moving? Was it because he had planned to go by himself?

No, I won't believe it for a minute. Paisley brushed aside the temptation to believe that Tyler would ever do anything to jeopardize the new life they were building together.

She trusted him.

"Tyler?" She rushed toward the door the second it opened and he walked in. She noticed a bag in his hand.

"Smells good in here."

"I saved you some supper. I know you said not to, but..."

"Much obliged for that, Paisley. And now that you mention it, I'm a mite hungry." He said grace, then took a bite. "This is the best beefsteak I've ever tasted."

"Even better than Wilhelmina's?"

"Even better than Wilhelmina's."

His words endeared him all the more to her. She waited a few more minutes before she shared the concerns of her heart. "Tyler, I meant what I said about helping to pay the note on the farm. I'm a good seamstress, and I could place items in Tabitha's mercantile for sale." She'd seen other women leave their sewn items for sale at Tabitha's. Surely she could too.

"Thank you, Paisley. I appreciate your willingness to help." Tyler set his fork down and took one of her hands in his. "I went to Horizon to the bank. I've had some money saved there from my work away from Horizon over the past four years. It's not much, but it'll go far toward the debt owed on the farm. The way I figure it, we'll seek God's direction on the remaining amount."

"Do you think the bank will allow that?"

"I'm not sure. Waylon said they wouldn't, but it's worth a try. Besides, I've learned after giving my life to the Lord that He's in control and things go a lot smoother when we allow Him to work according to His will."

"I agree." She paused. "There's one other thing I've been meaning to ask you."

"Yes?"

"I noticed a paper in the barn about gold in Caribou Mountain. Were you thinking of moving there?"

"The notion crossed my mind. I thought a lot about it on the way to town and on the way back. It's a rough life and not one I would be particularly fond of you and the children being a part of. Some of those mining towns are full of crime, but if we can make a living that way..."

"You were thinking of moving the entire family to Caribou Mountain?"

"I wouldn't be going alone." Tyler paused. "Did you think I would go alone?"

How could she say the thought had fleetingly crossed her mind? That she hadn't trusted him to keep his vow?

Tyler took her other hand in his. "If we pray about it and decide that God is prompting us to move to Caribou Mountain, then that's what we'll do. It's a lengthy distance away, and it's a decision for us—you and me—to make. Not just a decision for me. I'm ashamed to say that a month ago, I would have said it was only my choice and that what I wanted took precedence. But I've learned so much since then. I've learned to set aside my selfish ways. I made a vow to you that I'd love and honor you all the days of my life. I plan to do that." Tyler cleared his throat. "Our family means more to me—you mean more to me—than anything."

Paisley bit her lip. While the thought that Tyler would do anything to jeopardize their family had only been fleeting, she'd been foolish to even allow it even a second of time in her mind. "Do you want to move to Caribou Mountain?"

"I did at first. I thought it would be beneficial for our family to start over. But then I realized, for reasons I can't fully explain, that I belong here. *We belong here.* This is our farm now. This is our family now. Someday, Lord willing, we'll add to our family, and when we do, I want all of our children raised here in Horizon." He paused. "Do you feel the same?"

"I do."

"I'll never make the same mistake I made before and leave the ones I love. And, Paisley, I love you."

Had she heard him right? Had he said the words she'd longed to hear? The words that expressed how she already felt toward him?

Tyler grinned that handsome grin that had grown on her since the first day she'd met him. He reached forward and gently stroked her cheek. "I love you, Paisley."

"I love you too."

On that day at the dinner table talking over their plans for the future and not knowing what God's plans were pertaining to the farm, Paisley thanked the Lord for the blessing of being Tyler's wife.

Chapter Thirty-Nine

"I HAVE TO GO to Cornwall," Tyler announced the next morning.

Lucy and Albert sat up in their chairs anticipating what Tyler might say next.

"I was wondering if my family members would mind accompanying me."

"Us?" Albert gasped.

"We're your family now, right?" inquired Lucy, her smile showing the beginnings of a new front tooth.

"You are my family, and I thought we'd make the trip to Cornwall an adventure. Of course, I have to spend some time unloading goods and reloading some new items and going to the bank, but I reckon there'll be time for ice cream. What do you say about that, Mae-Mae?"

Mae's face showed a slight hint of a smile, and she nodded.

"Would you want to visit Cornwall again?" Tyler asked Paisley.

To visit Cornwall evoked so many memories within her: memories of hiding in the back of Tyler's wagon, memories of running from Ivan, and memories of the nearby town of Pringle, where she'd lived on the farm with her parents.

"Yes, I would."

"All right then. We'll leave first thing in the morning. We'll stop in Horizon and load up some items, then we'll be on our way."

"I love ice cream!" declared Lucy.

"Have you even ever had ice cream?" asked Albert.

Lucy narrowed her eyes at Albert. "Of course, I have."

"Have you ever had ice cream, Mae-Mae?" Tyler asked.

Mae slowly shook her head.

"You'll love it. It's especially tasty on a hot day," Paisley added. "Tyler, I was wondering if we could also make a brief stop in Pringle."

"That sounds fine." Tyler reached over and placed a hand on Paisley's.

His gesture warmed her heart. "Thank you," Paisley whispered.

"Are you an orphan?" asked Lucy.

Taken aback by Lucy's question, Paisley paused, then nodded. "Yes. It's not easy without our parents, is it?"

"No," muttered Albert.

"But you're our parents now," declared Lucy. "Can I call you Ma and Pa? Or maybe Mama and Papa?"

"We would love that." Paisley felt the sting of tears in her eyes.

Tyler squeezed her hand tighter. "I like the sound of Mama and Papa. What about you, Mrs. Shepherdson?"

"Who's Mrs. Shepherdson?" asked Lucy.

Paisley smiled. "That's my formal name. But you can call me 'Mama'. I'd like that very much."

Lucy stood and wrapped her arms around Paisley's neck. "I'm glad I have a mama again."

Albert scowled and looked from Paisley to Tyler and back to Paisley again, as if trying to understand what had just transpired.

Lucy ran to Tyler and stood in front of him. "And you'll be my papa. Forever, right?"

Tyler put an arm around Lucy's shoulder. "Forever."

Albert folded his arms across his chest and dropped his chin. "Hopefully you won't die like all of our other parents."

Paisley reached for Albert's hand, but he kept it tightly against his chest. "I hope not, Albert. That's why we have to appreciate every day that we're given."

Mae scooted her chair back, stood, and walked to where Paisley sat. She cautiously planted herself in Paisley's lap.

"We're each other's family now," Tyler said, squeezing Paisley's hand.

Lord, I don't know the plans You have for this family, but I pray for your protection, peace, and healing for each and every one of us. And if possible, Lord, could You please save our farm?

After Tyler unloaded the delivery in Cornwall and visited the bank, they continued on the short trek to Pringle. After much coercing, the bank had agreed to wait an additional ten days for the remaining money. Not much time to come up with it, but evidence of God's hand in the matter nonetheless.

Mixed emotions filled Paisley's heart as they passed the familiar scenery.

The same old piece of a steel plow that had been there at least since Paisley and her family moved to Pringle stood abandoned on the side of the road. Likely because of its poor condition and missing parts, no one had bothered to salvage the piece of farm machinery. Weeds grew around it until only a portion of its form showed through the overgrowth of vegetation.

Paisley's heart stuttered. Was that how she would find her parents' farm? Abandoned and forgotten like the piece of the plow?

She thought of how Ivan had attempted to coerce Papa into relinquishing the farm. Ivan would pay for it and Papa would work for him. While Papa hadn't fallen for that particular instance of Ivan's cunning trickery, he *had* agreed to allow his daughter to marry the scheming snake. Paisley was confident that such a lapse in judgment on Papa's part had much to do with the illness that overtook his body and mind in the last days of his life. Oddly enough, Papa had always liked Ivan, even after Paisley disclosed to Papa that she'd discovered Ivan's penchant for lying.

It was as if Papa hadn't even heard her.

How could one man have so much influence over another? Paisley would never know the answer.

"Take a right on the road next to the white house ahead," Paisley said, breaking the silence of the last few miles. Even the children seemed to sense the solemnity of Paisley's return home.

"Are you sure you want to do this?" Tyler transferred the reins to one hand and covered her clammy hand with his calloused one, something he did often. She allowed the warmth of his touch to comfort her.

"I'm sure."

An hour later, Paisley spied the familiar landscape of what had once been her home. A thin strip of the neighboring property, just far enough from the swell of the river and not damaged by the flood, boasted plentiful crops—Ivan's crops—ready in a couple of months for harvest. In the distance, she caught a glimpse of his house, a newly-built extravagant structure standing as a reminder of his wealth in an otherwise humble landscape. The home of the former owners torn down and tossed aside, much as Ivan did with anyone or anything he deemed no longer advantageous.

She shielded her eyes and squinted toward Ivan's house. Had it been completely unscathed by the flood? She couldn't ascertain from this distance, but the amount of land in the area not affected had been minimal.

Paisley returned her gaze again to the road ahead. In a few minutes, they would reach the land her father so proudly attempted to farm. They'd never had much, but Papa valued hard work and did all he could to provide for his wife and daughter.

"It's just ahead on the left," Paisley heard herself say. Her voice in her ears sounded strange, almost foreign.

"Was this your farm?" Lucy asked.

"This is the neighbor's land. Ours is just ahead."

Tears flooded Paisley's eyes. She would never forget the day she lost Mama and Papa.

Whatever she was expecting to see when they decided to go to her parents' farm, she was ill- prepared for the sight before her.

Some water still stood in lower-lying areas. The windmill rested on its side, its one remaining blade spinning in the breeze. Downed trees and splinters of wood rested in thick mud. The barn had been carried downstream with the force of the flood. The quaint two-bedroom whitewashed house with a garden and three rows of Mama's favorite flower—the sunflower—was void of windows and parts of it were missing.

"Paisley, I'll need to stop here so we don't get the wagon stuck." Tyler pulled on the reins. "Whoa," he said, prompting the horses to stop. He climbed down from the wagon and assisted Paisley. Still holding her, his hands firmly on her waist, he whispered tenderly in her ear, "Take your time."

Paisley appreciated Tyler's concern. He knew what it was like to suffer loss. His compassion for her touched her heart. She nodded, thankful she didn't have to rush the painful memories that surged to the forefront of her mind.

She wandered the short distance to the place where her parents were buried, carefully avoiding the mud as best as she could.

Perhaps coming here was a mistake.

Heart violently pounding and mouth dry, Paisley stared at the land that, only weeks earlier, had been covered in surging floodwater.

She had first noticed something amiss that day when dark clouds obscured the horizon. The sweet scent of rain soon followed, but the unexpected hail and violent thunderstorm removed all serenity the rainy scent brought with it.

Hours of rainfall eventually covered the ground, and despite Paisley's and Mama's prayers, the river overflowed its banks.

Rushing straight toward the humble cabin the Abbots called home.

Mama suggested escaping to the roof, but Papa—in his confused state—hadn't recognized the danger. Instead, he called for Lyndon and mumbled about milking the cows as he stumbled out the door, heading for the barn.

A barn the water carried away.

Mama reaching for Papa as he fell was the last time Paisley saw her parents alive.

Just as the water took the barn, so had it stolen her parents.

Paisley had grabbed some food, the deed, and Papa's Bible verse from the shelf in the kitchen. She couldn't remember how she'd made her way to the roof, only that it had been her sanctuary until a couple arrived to rescue her on their raft the following day when the rain ceased and sunshine peered through the clouds. Paisley had never seen the couple again after that day, but she'd made her way slowly to Cornwall, surviving on berries from the higher ground. Due to the intense amount of water, a lake had been formed several miles from Pringle.

Mama and Papa, along with several other townsfolk, were found a few days later. None of them had survived what would become known as the Great Idaho Flood of 1872.

Paisley dropped to her knees, her face buried in her hands. Sobs broke from the depths of her very being. She'd never gotten to tell her parents goodbye. Hadn't been able to tell them how much she loved them.

If only she had locked the door so Papa wouldn't escape through the front door. He'd been found many times wandering alone outside, lost. If she'd barricaded the door somehow, he wouldn't have been able to wander to the porch.

If only she had held on to Mama when Mama reached for Papa. Perhaps then she could have been able to pull her back onto the porch instead of losing her to the dirty rushing water below.

Sobs shook her body. She clutched her stomach and heaved.

So overcome with grief, Paisley almost didn't notice when strong arms wrapped around her and held her. They rocked her back and forth and comforted her.

Tyler.

He held her close and mourned with her. Cocooned in Tyler's embrace, Paisley struggled to experience a sense of peace in her time of grief.

Tyler himself mourned for Paisley's grief. To come back to the place that was once her home and to relive the memory of the disaster that took her parents. Yes, he had lost his parents, which would forever leave a void in his life, but at the very least he still had his home. The realization that Tyler had taken that for granted nearly suffocated him.

"Paisley," Tyler whispered, holding her even tighter.

Lord, please give me the words to comfort her.

Tyler lifted his head above hers and spied the children playing a short distance away. Hopefully they were oblivious to the ongoings around them. He requested they run, play, and stretch their legs from the long trip, but to stay on the far side of the wagon away from any standing water. All three had happily obliged, even Mae. Only Tyler had stayed at the wagon, leaning against it and watching Paisley.

He wanted to be there for her. Always.

"I didn't even get to retrieve my Bible." She pulled from him and her chin trembled. "I found a piece of paper Papa...where Papa had written his favorite Bible verse. I have read it over and over again and have carried it with me since that day. It's from Habakkuk 3:17-19: '*Although the fig tree shall not blossom, neither shall fruit be in the vines; the labour of the olive shall fail, and the fields shall yield no meat; the flock shall be cut off from the fold, and there shall be no herd in the stalls: Yet I will rejoice in the Lord, I will joy in the God of my salvation. The Lord God is my strength, and he will make my feet like hinds' feet, and he will make me to walk upon mine high places.*'"

More than anything, Tyler wanted to take the pain away that tore at her heart.

CHAPTER FORTY

PAISLEY KNELT BESIDE MAMA and Papa's graves on a nearby hill and laid a bouquet of wildflowers she'd picked on each one. She touched the ground above where her parents were buried. She knew they were no longer there, but it gave her comfort. "Mama and Papa, I miss you so much."

She planted herself on the ground. The birds chirped, and in the distance, the children played hide and seek with Tyler.

"You wouldn't believe the life I now live, Mama. I had nowhere to turn after you died, and I did something quite unorthodox. I married a man I didn't even know. He proposed to me and I accepted." Paisley stifled a small hint of a laugh. "I think you and Papa would have liked him. He's a kind, godly man, hardworking and quite dapper. I was beginning to wonder if I'd ever marry, but God's plans and His timing are perfect. I just had to wait on those plans.

"Tyler—that's his name—has a gentle side, one that I've seen especially with Mae, one of my children. Yes, Mama, I have children now—three of them." Paisley paused and glanced over her shoulder at her family. "Tyler lost his parents too and needed someone to care for his brother and sisters. You would have enjoyed meeting Albert, Lucy, and Mae." Paisley paused, realizing for the first time her parents would never have the privilege of being grandparents.

"Tyler is a farmer, and we have a rather good-sized farm in Horizon. It's about a day and a half from here. I'm sorry, Papa, but I just couldn't marry Ivan, even though I know that's what you had in mind for me. I'll not waste time discussing him, but I thank the Lord for His protection and providence in bringing Tyler into my life."

Paisley watched as Mae found Tyler hiding behind a tree. She imagined a tiny smile on Mae's face. "And you know what, Mama, I love Tyler. It's a peculiar thing marrying someone you don't know. But after this time I've spent with him, I've discovered a deeper love, an abiding love I hope remains long after the wedding vows. A real love. Like what you and Papa had."

Her voice caught. Mama and Papa had loved each other so much. The vows they'd made the day they married had carried true. Mama had tended to Papa and stayed by his side in sickness and in health. And at the end of his life, Papa's sickness was almost more than Mama could bear, but she remained his faithful wife.

The sound of a ruckus in the distance caused Paisley to abruptly stand. Sure enough, a man on a horse was exchanging words with Tyler. It didn't appear to be going well, as Mae had plopped on the ground and hid her face in her hands. Lucy cowered behind Tyler, and Albert stood with his hands clenched.

Ivan.

Paisley hiked up her skirt and began running toward them. She should have known Ivan would show up and ruin the day.

"Well, well, look who we have here," Ivan sneered. He'd dismounted and stood glaring at her with his arms crossed. His immoral stare that traveled from the top of her head to the tips of her toes caused her to shiver despite the heat.

"We don't want any trouble, Ivan." Tyler interjected himself between Paisley and Ivan, with a wide stance and straight posture.

"What you want is of no consequence to me." Ivan shoved Tyler roughly on the shoulder, causing Tyler to stumble backward and nearly collide with Paisley.

Tyler started toward Ivan and shoved him hard. "You need to leave, Ivan."

"Tyler, no. Ivan's not worth it." Paisley reached for his arm.

"Listen to your woman, Tyler," mocked Ivan.

Paisley held her breath. The last thing she wanted was to witness a fight. It had already been an emotional day. "Children, please get into the wagon. Lucy, will you please help Mae?"

Ivan fingered the revolver tucked into a holster at his waistband. "I could kill you right now, and I'd get away with it."

A stare down between Tyler and Ivan ensued.

"Are you calling me out for a duel?" Tyler asked.

Ivan's eyes bulged and his face turned red. "Do you doubt that I would win?" he sneered.

"I doubt it very highly," Tyler answered, speaking through gritted teeth.

"Tyler, please..."

"Paisley, get in the wagon with the children," Tyler said, not bothering to remove his eyes from Ivan even for a second.

Tyler glared at Ivan. He didn't want trouble, but there was no way he was going to allow Ivan to win this battle. *Call it pride, call it arrogance, but it's time Ivan learned he can't abuse people the way he's abused Paisley.*

Should he engage in a duel? Tyler recalled a couple of times how he had witnessed such gunfights and shootouts while employed in various towns. It usually occurred after the men had been paid their weekly wages, had spent a majority of their earnings at the saloon, and had allowed their drunkenness to get the better of them. Tyler hadn't been one to visit the saloons or partake in spirits. He had no need for such things. But he had been outside on the boardwalk minding his own business when the men had burst through the swinging doors of the saloon, set on settling a matter through impaired vision and the waving of Colt revolvers.

And yes, Tyler knew he'd win. He had a fast draw and a near-perfect aim. Pa had taught him well when it came to his aim. And the quick draw, well, Tyler had taught that to himself living in areas that corrupt individuals sometimes called home.

Ivan spit to the side. "So what do you say, Shepherdson? Let's make that wife of yours a widow and those young'uns

294

orphans. Paisley and that pathetic piece of land you own in Horizon would be mine. What do you say?"

It hadn't taken Tyler long to realize that Ivan was deranged. How Ivan had managed to acquire so much land was a mystery.

And Ivan's obsession with Paisley caused Tyler more than just a little bit of angst.

Tyler thought of his own revolver ready for use if the need arose. Then he thought of Paisley. What would happen if Tyler lost? Where would that leave her and the children? And if Tyler won, what would that prove? Revenge wasn't his, and the words of Romans 12:19 rang through his mind: *"Dearly beloved, avenge not yourselves, but rather give place unto wrath: for it is written, Vengeance is mine; I will repay, says the Lord."*

The Lord's words.

Competition to see who was the fastest draw tempted Tyler more than he'd been tempted in a long time. Maybe his whole life.

"Well, what do you say?" Ivan repeated.

Tyler took a deep breath. The desire to win against someone like Ivan tempted him. *Lord, make me strong. Help me resist temptation.*

Ivan's mouth curled into a nefarious sneer. "All of a sudden can't speak? Come on, what do you say?"

"I say you're not worth it."

"What?"

"You heard me. You're not worth it."

"Well, what if I say *I* want to have a duel?" Ivan's sour breath smelled of whiskey.

"Then you'll be dueling by yourself," Tyler raised his chin and squared his shoulders. He would fight for Paisley's honor no matter what the cost. But he wouldn't leave her a widow, and he couldn't leave her vulnerable to Ivan once again if Tyler lost.

For the next five minutes, Tyler and Ivan stood facing each other, neither of them speaking.

Lord, forgive me for giving in to my temper.

Finally, Ivan took a step back and spit again. "You're nothing but a yellow-bellied coward, Shepherdson."

Tyler took a deep breath. Words filled his mind that could be used to describe Ivan, words that Tyler would never utter out of respect for his family and for his Lord.

Ivan jabbed Tyler with his finger. "Next time, Shepherdson. And that's a promise." Ivan tucked the revolver back into its holster.

Aware that Ivan could be lying, Tyler backed up slowly toward the wagon. "We'll be leaving now."

"Good riddance," Ivan growled.

Climbing into the wagon, his eyes ever watchful on his opponent, Tyler thanked the Lord for helping him realize that revenge was never his to take.

Paisley watched Ivan ride away, and she worried about their next encounter with him. Would she and her family ever be truly safe?

Paisley leaned closer to Tyler on the buckboard and without giving it a second thought, wrapped her arms around him. "Tyler, you could have been killed. Ivan is so ruthless."

Tyler pulled her to him. "I'll never let him hurt you," he murmured, his lips caressing her hair. "But I couldn't duel him. I couldn't take the chance I'd lose."

Paisley closed her eyes. Tyler had made the right choice, and for that, she was grateful.

Tyler cradled her face in his hands. "Are you all right?"

"Yes." Her voice shook, but she was all right. So much had happened today, and her thoughts spilled over in her mind like boiling water overflowing from a pot on the stove.

"I'm sorry your time with your parents was shortened. Shall we go to Cornwall?"

"Yes."

"For ice cream?" Lucy interjected from the back of the wagon.

"Yes, for ice cream," Tyler agreed. Before he released his tender hold on Paisley, he planted a gentle kiss on her lips.

"Eww! That's disgustin'." Albert covered his eyes with his hands.

CHAPTER FORTY-ONE

THE STOP FOR ICE cream in Cornwall after Tyler loaded the delivery items provided a much-needed diversion from the day's events. It had been years since Paisley herself had partaken in the refreshing dessert with Mama and Papa in Kansas.

Tyler stopped the wagon in front of O'Dell's Soda Fountain and Confectionery. He'd barely placed the brake when Albert and Lucy leapt from the wagon.

"Can we have nuts and figs and raisins on ours?" Albert asked. He pointed to a mammoth wooden sign that detailed all that O'Dell's had to offer.

Tyler removed some coins from his trouser pocket. "You can have whatever you'd like. It's a special day."

"I just can't wait to have some ice cream!" Lucy stood on tiptoe in an attempt to see over the heads of the customers in front of them.

"Me neither!" Albert fidgeted, his eyes wide.

"It's been some time since I've had ice cream as well," Paisley said. "What about you, Mae-Mae? Are you excited about having ice cream too?" She knelt to Mae's height.

A hint of a smile crossed the little girl's face, and she nodded.

"I remember Ma and Pa took me to get ice cream. It's a memory I'll never forget," Tyler added.

When everyone had received their ice cream, they sat at a table near the window.

"Yum!" exclaimed Lucy and Albert in unison.

"What do you think, Mae?" Paisley asked.

"Yum."

Paisley and Tyler's eyes connected. "Did Mae say her first word?" Paisley whispered.

"I reckon she did."

"I wasn't sure if I imagined it."

"It was difficult to hear it, but she spoke." Tyler reached for Paisley's hand. "Our little Mae-Mae is gonna be all right yet."

"Yum," Mae repeated, this time with a soft giggle. She climbed into Paisley's lap with her ice cream.

"Can you say other words too?" Lucy asked, her upper lip covered with ice cream.

Mae slowly nodded. "Ice cweam," she said.

"Oh, Mae!" Paisley wrapped her arms around Mae.

Mae giggled and took another lick of her ice cream.

God was indeed the Author of miracles.

Commotion on the street outside interrupted the joyous occasion of hearing Mae speak for the first time. The sheriff and two deputies rode alongside a handcuffed man on a horse.

Ivan.

"Think I might make a trip to the sheriff's office and see if I can find out some information," said Tyler.

"We'll wait here, but hurry back," Paisley said. If Ivan was truly being apprehended by the sheriff, did that mean her troubles with him were over?

Tyler took long strides down the boardwalk toward the sheriff's office. Inside, the sheriff and his two deputies had remanded Ivan to the jail. "Excuse me, sir," Tyler said, approaching one of the deputies.

"Yes?"

"Can you tell me about this situation?"

"Do you have an interest in this matter?" The deputy tossed Tyler a wary glance.

"I do. This man has made himself a nuisance to our family and has threatened my wife."

"I see. Well, he'll be on trial soon for fraud, assault, and all kinds o' stuff."

Relief overcame him. While he might not have been able to protect Paisley completely from Ivan, God could and this was the method He had chosen.

"Now that Ivan's been apprehended and will likely be sent to prison, we can move to Pringle," Tyler suggested.

Paisley looked into the eyes of the man she'd grown to love. He'd given her so much and now he was offering to

300

give up the life he had in Horizon to move to Pringle. "I think we should stay in Horizon."

"But what about your parents? They're buried on that land."

Paisley squeezed his hand. She knew how much the farm in Horizon meant to her husband. "I've been praying about the situation, and I think we should see about keeping only the area where Mama and Papa are buried. I can visit them whenever we visit Cornwall. I know they've gone on to be with Jesus, but it does give me comfort to visit the place they're buried. I miss them so much. Had Papa been in his right mind, he would have realized the kind of man Ivan was and would have celebrated with us and Mama the justice that will be served against Ivan."

"I understand. I feel the same way about visiting my parents at the cemetery in Horizon. But are you sure you only want to keep that area? We can keep the rest of the farm and lease it out or..."

"Or we could sell the rest of the farm and use that money to pay the bank for what is owed on our land in Horizon. We might even have some funds left to purchase provisions for the winter."

"Paisley, are you sure?"

"I am sure, Tyler. Just the plot where Mama and Papa are buried is all I need. There's nothing left on the rest of the land. Most of it was destroyed by the flood, and if we can use this money, however meager it may be, to save the farm, it will be worth it."

Tyler gave her a crooked grin. "Sounds good to me if that's what you really want."

"It's what I really want."

"And I do want to raise Albert, Lucy, and Mae in Horizon."

"As do I."

"And maybe some other little Shepherdsons in the future, if that's God's plan."

Paisley blushed. "Yes, some other little Shepherdsons too."

Tyler leaned forward and took her into his arms. "Have I ever told you that I love you?"

"Not that I recollect."

"Well, I do."

"Tyler?"

"Yes?"

"I love you too."

And she did.

CHAPTER FORTY-TWO

TODAY WAS DEFINITELY THE day for visits from the townsfolk. Reverend Marshall and Maribel had stopped by earlier, and now a buggy traveled the road toward the farm.

As it edged closer, Paisley recognized Miss Greta. The woman parked near the house and climbed from the buggy with a basket in her hands, heading for the house.

"Hello, Miss Greta. What brings you here on this beautiful sunny day?"

Lucy smirked and finished drying the dishes Paisley had just washed.

"Not sure about a beautiful sunny day. Seems to me it's a mite bit breezy." Miss Greta handed the basket to Paisley. "I found this at the house. Forgot all about havin' it."

Paisley peered into the basket at the pale pink calico. "Thank you, Miss Greta!"

"Yes, well, seein' as how I don't particularly care for that color, I thought you might find it of help for some dresses for you and the girls."

Paisley handed the basket to Lucy and hugged Miss Greta. "You are so thoughtful, and I promise it will be well-used."

Miss Greta stiffened against Paisley's hug. "You don't need to be tellin' anyone I gave you fabric."

Lucy giggled. "We promise not to tell anyone, Miss Greta."

Mae nodded. "We pwomise."

"I do miss havin' you around the place, Paisley. Most of my other boarders are cantankerous sorts. But I am glad you are here at the farm and raisin' these young'uns." She nodded toward Lucy and Mae. "You two behavin'?"

"Yes, ma'am," answered Lucy. "All of us except Albert."

A tiny giggle erupted from Mae. "'Cept Albert."

"I best be on my way."

"Thank you again, Miss Greta. And thank you for allowing me to stay with you before the wedding."

Was Miss Greta attempting to hide a smile beneath her disagreeable demeanor?

Wilhelmina arrived next. When Paisley had prayed for friends, God had answered in a mighty way. Maribel, Tabitha, Wilhelmina, and even Miss Greta had all become dear to her.

The wagon stopped, and Wilhelmina, a small feather hat tilted forward on her head, sashayed toward Paisley. In contrast to Miss Greta's dislike for hugs, Wilhelmina folded Paisley into an embrace. "It's so nice to see you."

Precious Wilhelmina would likely say that even if she and Paisley met each other mere hours before. "It's nice to see you too. What brings you to the Shepherdson farm?"

"I know I could have waited until church on Sunday, but I just had to drive here and tell you how thrilled I am by the curtains you sewed for the restaurant. It has enhanced the place tenfold, and I've received so many compliments."

"You are more than welcome. And thank you for helping me with my most recent recipe. Thus far, I can now make three meals without burning anything."

Wilhelmina laughed. "It's a fine start."

They chatted for a few minutes longer before Wilhelmina left.

Once she ensured no one else would arrive, Paisley tended to the laundry as she reached for one of Tyler's shirts from the metal laundry tub. "Mae, could you please hand me two clothespins?"

Mae grinned and nodded. She pulled open the pocket on her apron and retrieved two clothespins. "Here," she said.

"Thank you." Paisley attempted not to allow emotion to overtake her at the progress Mae had made in the past couple of months. Mae took to saying more and more words, and her demeanor had changed. Yes, Mae regressed on occasion, but overall, her improvement was nothing short of a miracle. Doc had said that the progress would be slow, but Mae was indeed making progress.

An answer to the fervent prayers of Paisley and Tyler.

Paisley clipped the shirt to the clothesline. "Well now, whose little dress is this?" Paisley pulled a purple calico from the laundry tub.

Mae giggled before pointing to herself. "Mine."

"Are you sure?"

Mae's cheerful laughter caused Paisley to laugh too. "I think perhaps you are mistaken, Mae-Mae. I believe this is Papa's. I best hang it so it can dry."

"Not Papa's!" Mae's squinty eyes disappeared with her broad smile. "It's Mae-Mae's!"

"Oh, I see. You are absolutely right. Papa doesn't have any purple shirts. Well, then, if this is Mae-Mae's dress then I wonder if perhaps Mae-Mae would like to help me hang it on the line."

"Yes!" Mae squealed and clapped her hands.

"Do you have a clothespin ready?"

Mae reached into her apron pocket and produced a clothespin. Paisley lifted her and allowed her to clip the dress onto the line. "You did a fine job. Thank you for your help."

Paisley and Mae continued to hang the clothes on the line when a gust of wind interrupted them. "That was actually a welcome breeze on this hot day," Paisley said more to herself than to Mae. She closed her eyes and allowed the breeze to cool her, even if only for a second.

Then she prayed, thanking God for the family He'd blessed her with.

EPILOGUE
ONE YEAR LATER

"CAN I NAME THE baby?" Lucy asked, staring down at the tiny infant cradled in Paisley's arms.

Albert knitted his brows together. "Why would you get to name the baby?"

"I'll name the baby," suggested Mae. She reached down and wrapped the baby's fingers around her own. "I think she likes me."

"You and Lucy just wanted to name the baby because it's a girl. All I ever wanted was a brother." Albert folded his arms across his chest.

"I want to name the baby Dandelion," said Mae.

Tyler chuckled. "I think we already have a name for our baby."

Mae's eyes lit up. "Is it Dandelion?"

"Who would name their baby 'Dandelion'?" scoffed Albert.

"It's not Dandelion," said Paisley, "Although that sounds like a wonderful name for a new dolly sometime, Mae-Mae. Papa and I have decided to name the baby Ruby Caroline after Papa's mother and my mother." Paisley looked down at her precious baby. The name fit her perfectly.

It symbolized the joining in love of two families forever.

"Poor little baby. Where is the rest of her hair?" asked Mae, gently brushing the tuft of Ruby's red hair with her hand.

"I think she's beautiful even though she's almost bald," declared Lucy. "Now I have two younger sisters." She cast a glower in Albert's direction. "And a brother."

Albert puffed out his chest. "A big brother. I'll always be older than you, Lucy."

"And older than me," said Mae, pointing at herself.

Tyler put a hand on Albert's shoulder. "That means you have to take care of your sisters since you're their big brother."

Paisley half expected Albert to argue, but instead his face lit to a broad grin. "I will. I'll make sure no one ever bothers any of you at school or anywhere else."

"Thank you, Albert."

"But, Papa?"

"Yes?"

"I don't think it's fair that I'm the only boy. Can we have a brother next?"

Tyler chuckled. "Maybe so. We'll have to wait and see." He leaned down and placed a kiss on Paisley's cheek. "Have I ever told you I love you?" he asked, his eyes twinkling.

"Not that I recall."

"Well I do. More than anything."

"And I love you too, Tyler Shepherdson."

Paisley took in the view surrounding her and pivoted her gaze from Albert to Lucy, from Mae to Tyler, and then to little Ruby Caroline Shepherdson.

And she knew without a doubt she was the most blessed woman in the world.

Thank You, Lord. For happy endings.

CAN LOVE OVERCOME ALL OBSTACLES?

—— HORIZON SERIES, BOOK TWO ——

Dreams on the Horizon

Sneak Peek

MAE SHEPHERDSON FACED HER pupils and, using sign language, said, "Have a nice evening. See you tomorrow."

The students signed back to her, and Mae thought her heart would explode.

Her charges were learning.

And she was making a difference.

Mae watched as the children gathered their books, waved, and one by one, left the classroom. All except Polly, whom Mae had asked to stay after class.

Polly remained at her desk, drumming her fingers on the worn-out wood. The vibration she felt through her fingertips from the tap-tapping caused a wide grin on Polly's face.

Mae reached inside her own desk, retrieved a wrapped parcel, and walked to Polly's desk. "This is for you," she signed.

Polly's brown eyes lit and she reached for the parcel, opening it with all the enthusiasm a seven-year-old could muster. Pulling the dress from the parcel, Polly stood and held it against herself for size.

The dress Mama made would fit perfectly.

Polly wrapped her thin arms around Mae's neck before taking a step back. Bringing her hand to just below her mouth, she signed, "Thank you."

"You are welcome, Polly. My mother made that dress especially for you. I think you'll look quite lovely in it."

Polly nodded with excitement at Mae's signed words, and Mae knew the little girl would barely reach her room before trying on the dress.

"Yes, Polly, you may be excused, and I will see you tomorrow."

Polly grabbed the dress and her books and ran toward the door, leaving Mae to contemplate.

God had answered Mae's prayers in so many ways. He'd blessed her with a family who loved her; He'd led her to teach at the Horizon School for the Deaf; and He'd allowed her to do something big for the least of these.

Mae turned and erased the chalkboard. She'd been a teacher at the school for two years now, instructing the students in writing, spelling, and reading. If she had more hours afforded to her in a day, Mae would gladly teach history, geography, science, and math as well.

Scooping up her lunch pail and wrap, Mae headed out the door of her classroom and into the hallway. "I'll see you tomorrow, Mrs. Eddington."

"Yes, see you tomorrow, dear. Say, are you going to attend the meeting about the railroad?"

Mae nodded. "Mama and Papa will be there, and I've heard it's an important decision for Horizon. So, yes, I'll go. Will you and Mr. Eddington be in attendance?

"Yes, we'll both be there as well. Gretchen has agreed to supervise the children while we're gone. However, we mightn't stay the entire time as I must serve supper before too long."

"I'll see you there then."

"Yes, dear, and thank you for all your hard work today."

Mae appreciated Mrs. Eddington's gratitude. She and her husband had long dreamed of opening a deaf school after their son had been born deaf. God led them to Horizon four years ago, and they opened the school with the help of donations.

Mae stepped outside and walked along the front yard and out the gate. She turned to look at the school. Not really a school so much as a house. When Mr. and Mrs. Eddington had come upon its abandoned state, it had been nothing more than an enormous run-down shack. With the assistance of Papa, Albert, Timothy, and several of the men in Horizon, the school received a fresh coat of paint, new wood for the porch, and a brand-new fence surrounding the home. Thanks to the women of Horizon, curtains hung in the windows and the school had been cleaned from its attic to the lowest floor.

The school still required many repairs, and volunteers donated their time as often as they could. With the exception of a few, most folks in Horizon had embraced the school. The school existed only because of donations and never turned any child away.

Mae's heart warmed as she thought of The Horizon School for the Deaf and all it represented: A place of acceptance for children who had long been turned aside from society, a place to receive a quality education, and a place to learn how to live and survive in a hearing world.

Mae knew what it was like to be turned away.

To be unloved.

But she also knew the power of God's grace and His miracle in bringing a forever family to her. It was the hope that had flooded her own life that had set her on the path to helping other children.

Especially those whom the world mocked because they were different.

Thank you, Lord, for the school. May it never cease to be a blessing to those who need it most.

Mae took a seat beside her parents in the Horizon Meeting Hall. People crowded into the room, eager to give their opinions.

"If I may have your attention!" Jimmie Traebert, who owned the mercantile with his wife, Tabitha, rapped on the podium.

The room became silent and Jimmie proceeded. "We are here today to discuss and vote on whether we would like to allow Bennick Railways to lay track through our town. If we decide not to allow them to expand the railroad through our town, they'll take a different route from Ingleville to connect the existing lines."

Red, an elderly gent with flaming red hair streaked with gray, voiced his sentiments first. "I don't like change none."

Red's best friend, Whitey, shook his head. "Me neither."

"It would be good for our community," added Miss Greta. "Matter of fact, it would bring more business to my boardin' house, so my vote is 'yes'."

"It's more than just about bringing business to our community," piped up a man from the back of the room. "It'll cause our town to grow. Are we ready for that? With growth can come some problems too. Don't need no hoodlums setting up residence in Horizon."

The livery owner stood. "It's better than the town dryin' up. I heard that any town that doesn't have a railroad should just forget about existin'."

"And Horizon is one of the last towns in Idaho to have a railroad," Papa interjected.

Jimmie cleared his throat. "It appears the railway will go from Cornwall, to Ingleville, to Horizon. Cornwall has had a railroad for some time. It'll just be connecting it to Ingleville and Horizon. Ingleville has already agreed to allow the railroad to build in their town."

"Don't make no difference to me what Ingleville has done. This here is Horizon," muttered a man with a deep voice.

The discussion continued, with the vote resulting in Horizon allowing Bennick Railways to build a spur to their town.

However, a feeling of uncertainty and concern settled within Mae when she heard the verdict.

If you want to be among the first to hear about the next Horizon installment, sign up for Penny's newsletter. You will receive book and writing updates, encouragement, notification of current giveaways, occasional freebies, and special offers.

If you enjoyed this glimpse into the lives of Paisley and Tyler, please consider leaving a review on your social media, Amazon, Goodreads, Barnes and Noble, or BookBub. Reviews are critical to authors, and those stars you give us are such an encouragement.

Author's Note

Dear Reader,

In the 1800s, the setting for *Over the Horizon*, Alzheimer's disease, a type of dementia, had not yet been discovered and wouldn't be until 1906 by a Dr. Alois Alzheimer. From my research, I discovered that prior to that time, dementia and Alzheimer's symptoms, such as those Paisley's father experienced, were seen as some sort of insanity. And since people didn't understand it, there were many times when those with this illness and their families were ostracized. I wanted to show through the pages of *Over the Horizon* the difficulties Paisley and Mama experienced having so little knowledge about the disease that had overtaken Papa's mind.

As I write this book, my sweet grandma, Nanie, is struggling with dementia. The Lord has blessed her with good health her entire life. But now, at ninety-four, culturally, dementia almost seems expected, but it's no less devastating. Nanie is a cute little Swedish woman who is loving, feisty, opinionated, loves painting, and loves her flowers. She has moved in with my aunt and uncle, and they care for her with unparalleled patience and unconditional love.

My grandpa had multiple health issues, including dementia, and Nanie took care of him until he passed away in 2009. She loved her Johnny and he loved his Ruthie in a wonderful love story that has inspired a Christian historical romance I hope to write someday.

Historical romances are my favorite to write, although I have enjoyed venturing into the present day for my contemporaries. Historicals are much more demanding as they require abundant research (wild west duels and Idaho gold, for instance) and constant etymology searches to be sure I'm not using modern vernacular. You would be surprised, much as I have been, by the words that *were* in use in the 1800s and even prior. Words such as "forte" and "trek", for example.

As I neared the end of the book, I wanted the characters to have ice cream in Cornwall. But was ice cream even available in 1872 in the Idaho Territory?

It was. As a matter of fact, a man named J. Easley owned an "Ice Cream Saloon and Confectionery Shop" in Idaho City in 1868. His advertisement provided inspiration for the fictional O'Dell's Soda Fountain and Confectionery.

When Tyler needed to exchange something for Paisley's stay at Miss Greta's, I decided a brand-new outhouse was just what Miss Greta needed for her guests. In my research, I discovered there were some two-story outhouses built, including one in Illinois that was built in 1869 as well as one in Minnesota, built to accommodate a growing family. I also stumbled across a three-story outhouse in Maine.

Caribou Mountain is a real place in southeastern Idaho where gold was found beginning in 1870.

As is always the case, some fictional liberties are taken when writing historicals. The dates were sometimes accelerated for purposes of the story, and Horizon, Cornwall, Ingleville, and Varner City are all fictional towns.

The famous Augusta Terhune is a figment of my imagination as is the *Horizon Herald*. Although, do stay tuned as we will revisit the fictional newspaper for Ruby Caroline's story.

The orphan train arriving in Cornwall with Albert, Lucy, and Mae is fictional.

Idaho has experienced flooding over the years, but the Great Idaho Flood of 1872 is entirely fictional. My idea for a flood was inspired by a recent video I watched of a ranch in my state that underwent damaging floods when the river overflowed due to rapidly-falling rainfall over a short period of time.

I honestly could not write these books without the help of dedicated employees at museums and historical societies. Just as was the case for *Forgotten Memories* (Wyoming)and *Love in Disguise* (Montana), I again found an amazing resource to assist me with my questions. This time, Evie Hergenrather at the Idaho State Archives came to my rescue with answers to my questions about land deeds, land transfer, and whether or not a kettle would be sufficient to sidetrack Ivan during Paisley's escape. Evie also pointed me in the direction of old Idaho newspapers from the 1800s, which I spent *far* too much time perusing, but it was so interesting! For instance, I read a column about a woman who asked her husband what she should do since she was tired of wearing the confining clothes of the era (late 1860s). He suggested she wear something comfortable if she was tired of her regular clothing. Needless to say, the neighbor, a visitor, and even some friends believed her to be a maid when they saw her in her less fancy attire.

And finally, there were some funny things that happened during the writing of this book. As always, there are "bloopers" and goofy words and phrases that end up in the manuscript pre-editing stage. I think we writers get typing so quickly, attempting to get those words on paper, that our fingers can't keep up with what we'd like to write. Again, while not as humorous as John Mark at the salon in *Dreams of the Heart* or Trey squeezing Carleigh's face instead of her hand in *Love in the Headlines,* the bloopers for *Over the Horizon* were rather comical.

For instance, Wilhelmina at one point had two husbands. Well, not *really* two husbands, just one husband with two different names. Yikes! Thankfully, we caught it early and she is married only to Hubert.

It was discovered I had a floating prayer, as in a prayer that was started...but not finished.

And finally, Ivan had *worm* stale breath instead of *warm* stale breath.

As always, I am so grateful to you, my readers, for spending time within the pages of my books.

Blessings,
Penny

Acknowledgments

To my family. I can never thank you enough for your encouragement, support, and patience as I put words to paper. I'm so grateful for you. Thank you for your patient endurance in living with an author who spends her time predominately in the 1800s (and sometimes forgets to come back to the present).

To my Penny's Peeps Street Team and my launch team members. Thank you for spreading the word about my books. I appreciate your encouragement and support.

To my beta readers. You are the ones who see my project at its beginning stages. Thank you for all of your wonderful suggestions.

To Evie Hergenrather of the Idaho State Archives. Thank you for your invaluable help in assisting me in taking a brief journey from the present day to late 1800s Idaho Territory. You provided me with so much great information that I plan to use in future books as well.

To my Facebook followers. I oftentimes ask my Facebook page followers for help in naming secondary and/or minor characters. A huge thank you to Nancy Montegna Ross for suggesting the name "Lottie"; and Cassandra Segovia Samora for suggesting the name "Greta". Your suggestions proved invaluable when it was time for me to create these fun secondary/minor characters.

To my readers. May God bless and guide you as you grow in your walk with Him.

And, most importantly, thank you to my Lord and Savior, Jesus Christ. It is my deepest desire to glorify You with my writing and help bring others to a knowledge of Your saving grace.

Let the words of my mouth and the meditation of my heart be acceptable in your sight, O Lord, my rock and my redeemer.
Psalm 19:14

About the Author

Penny Zeller is known for her heartfelt stories of faith and her passion to impact lives for Christ through fiction. While she has had a love for writing since childhood, she began her adult writing career penning articles for national and regional publications on a wide variety of topics. Today, Penny is the author of nearly two dozen books. She is also a homeschool mom and a fitness instructor.

When Penny is not dreaming up new characters, she enjoys spending time with her husband and two daughters, camping, hiking, canoeing, reading, running, cycling, gardening, and playing volleyball.

She is represented by Tamela Hancock Murray of the Steve Laube Agency and loves to hear from her readers at her website www.pennyzeller.com and her blog, *random thoughts from a day in the life of a wife, mom, and author*, at www.pennyzeller.wordpress.com.

— HORIZON SERIES —

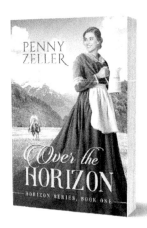

WYOMING SUNRISE SERIES

LOVE LETTERS FROM ELLIS CREEK

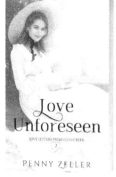

CHRISTIAN CONTEMPORARY ROMANCE

Love in the Headlines

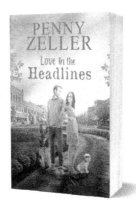

Chokecherry Heights

Printed in Great Britain
by Amazon

40632105R00192